A Well-Earned Death

Also by L. C. Tyler

A Well-Earned Death

L. C. Tyler

CONSTABLE

CONSTABLE

First published in Great Britain in 2023 by Constable

Copyright © L. C. Tyler, 2023

The moral right of the author has been asserted.

A CIP catalogue record for this book is available from the British Library.

ISBN: 978-1-40871-871-1

Typeset in Adobe Caslon Pro by SX Composing DTP, Rayleigh, Essex
Printed and bound in Great Britain by Clays Ltd, Elcograf S.p.A.

Papers used by Constable are from well-managed forests
and other responsible sources.

Constable
An imprint of
Little, Brown Book Group
Carmelite House
50 Victoria Embankment
London EC4Y 0DZ

An Hachette UK Company
www.hachette.co.uk

www.littlebrown.co.uk

For Raya

A Note on Language

I am aware that in writing a story in which slavery plays even a small part, I am in danger of using expressions that may upset some people. I am equally aware that, if I restrict myself to words considered completely acceptable today, then I risk not only historical inaccuracy but the nonsense of presenting a slave trade apparently run by men who are willing to flog, torture and kill people but who are, at the same time, scrupulous in not giving offence in their choice of language. I have therefore tried to minimise use of racial terms that might cause offence today, however common they would have been in the seventeenth century, but not to exclude all of them entirely. To do otherwise would simply make the seventeenth century appear to be an age of racial and religious tolerance. It wasn't.

Some persons in this story

Sir John Grey – that is to say myself. Formerly employed by my Lord Arlington, His Majesty's Secretary of State for the Southern Department and spymaster, but now lord of the manor of Clavershall West in the county of Essex, father of two (almost) perfect children and the fortunate husband of . . .

Aminta, Lady Grey – mother of two (almost) perfect children, renowned playwright and daughter of the amiable but, to be honest with you, somewhat disreputable former cavalier . . .

Sir Felix Clifford – once a close friend of my late mother's (the less said about which the better) and also father of my childhood friend Marius Clifford, sadly killed at the Battle of Worcester many years ago, fighting for . . .

His Majesty King Charles – the second of that illustrious name, in whose service (and Arlington's) I have acquired a number of scars and a wholly unmerited knighthood and whom I continue to serve as a justice of the peace, ably assisted by . . .

Ben Bowman – the village constable, when his more important duties as innkeeper permit, an indispensable help to me in the administration of justice unlike . . .

Mister Josiah Thatcher – the new coroner for this part of north Essex (and kinsman of the Sheriff), who feels that I have until now been overzealous in my work, to the extent of trespassing into his own domain, particularly in respect of the close examination of the bodies of victims of murder, such as that of . . .

Mister Hubert Umfraville – until recently a plantation owner in His Majesty's colony of Barbados, who had, for reasons that do him no credit whatsoever, decided to quit that island under cover of darkness, bringing with him his long-suffering wife . . .

Mistress Elizabeth Umfraville and his children, **George, James, Mary** and (by adoption) **Drusilla**, while leaving behind his slaves, including the very valuable . . .

Nero – a man of many parts and much ability, whose advice is sorely missed by his late master, and who has himself been able to flee Barbados independently, but is being relentlessly pursued by . . .

Mister Daniel Flood – a very respectable slave catcher, a believer in the rights of man (excluding slaves for obvious practical reasons), who apparently knew Umfraville in Barbados and had no love of the said plantation owner, a view shared by . . .

Mister William Robinson – the owner of a property in Essex that Umfraville believed was rightfully his (and might be his again by blackmail or otherwise), and also shared by . . .

Mister Jenks – a carter, whom Umfraville has entertained on the road with tales of his life as a slave owner and subsequently accused of theft, none of which has endeared Umfraville to the carter in question, leading Jenks to conclude that Umfraville's death was most well-earned, something that he points out most firmly to me, that is to say . . .

John Grey, who must soon decide which of the above has killed Hubert Umfraville and indeed who killed another person shortly after. But, if you wish to discover the identity of the second corpse, you will need to read on.

Prologue

Her aunt and uncle had been sold with house. It was, she told herself, probably for the best. They were not unhappy where they were and the long sea journey would have been a trial for them at their age. In any case, the family's departure from Holetown had been both precipitous and shameful. It would have been wrong that these old, thoroughly respectable people should have had to share even a small part of the general humiliation.

Packing had necessarily been done with the greatest secrecy. They had all been instructed to take no more than they required urgently and immediately – a spare dress, a change or two of linen, a favourite book if they possessed such a thing, and any jewellery that had not already been sold. The prohibition against taking lizards had been absolute and inflexible. Their cook had been persuaded not to notice that the silverware and the best china had already been crammed, inexplicably, into the wooden tubs that had appeared early one morning in the kitchen.

Then, shortly after midnight, two ox wagons had arrived at the door. They seemed to have come straight from hell, everything about them rendered either crimson or soot-black by the smoking torches, which flared upwards into the warm, dark, tropical sky. The family were waiting for them outside in the garden, as if to greet an honoured guest. Long before the transport came into sight, the rumble of the approaching wheels could be heard above the insistent, almost deafening whir of the cicadas in the silk cotton trees that surrounded the house.

The trunks and boxes and tubs had been loaded with immense care onto the first of the wagons. The women had been bundled quickly into the second, with the strongbox containing all of the gold they had been able to collect together over the preceding weeks – those final nervous days when their credit still held good in Holetown. The men had walked behind, their pistols loaded, primed and cocked, constantly watching for pursuers, staring with narrowed eyes into every shadowy clump and gully from which an ambush might be launched.

As things turned out, there were no dangers of any sort whatsoever. The carts had rolled, far from soundlessly but completely unmolested, down from the plantation, past the house of the island's only banker, to the squalid little port, where a rising moon revealed the skeletal outline of a three-masted ship, sails neatly furled, nestling with one eye open amongst the ragged palm fronds.

The air clung more closely to the skin here by the harbour. The hot, humid night trapped and distilled the smell of spice and tar and stagnant water that always hovered around the wooden quay. Her father – her adoptive father – had been sweating copiously as the goods were unloaded and transferred to the ship. The beads that ran down his unshaven jowls had to be repeatedly mopped away with a dirty spotted handkerchief. There was a brief, whispered altercation as the owner of the ox carts demanded, and obtained with embarrassing ease, far more money than had originally been agreed. The man's grin flashed briefly in the darkness. They were leaving one person on the island happy at least.

Tomorrow morning, the manager of the bank, who had so foolishly slumbered as they rumbled past, would don his periwig, his best silver-buckled shoes and his embroidered knee-length waistcoat and ascend the hill to discuss in an avuncular way how the family's growing debts might be paid off a little at a time – a question that had been troubling his waking hours. He would find that the answer was that the bank loan sadly would never be repaid – could never be repaid. The estate, which the bank had imagined guaranteed the loan, had already been sold along with its slaves to a neighbouring planter, who in turn would shortly discover to his surprise that the crop of sugar cane ripening in his new fields did not belong to him, having already been purchased by other too-trusting individuals.

The banker would possibly be informed of all this by the abandoned aunt and uncle, huddled together in their quarters at the back of the main house. Or a field slave, if any had elected to remain, might enlighten him on the strange comings and goings they had witnessed. Since these matters still lay in the future, who could possibly say? What was certain was that the unfortunate man would descend the hill, periwig dangling dejectedly from his damp hand, waistcoat over his arm, much less happy than he walked up it.

'You'll set sail at once?' her father – her adoptive father – had asked the captain.

'Within the next hour or two,' came the speculative reply. 'There is no hurry, my good sir. We have a voyage of three or four weeks ahead of us. Why should anyone fret over a trifling delay now? Unless of course . . .' He raised an eyebrow far enough and no more.

Money changed hands. Shortly after, a three-masted ship could have been seen sailing away from Holetown, as quickly as might be, moonlit canvas billowing in a rising wind, heading with a cargo of rum, tobacco and six anxious passengers for the cool, grey waters of the wide Atlantic Ocean. On the far horizon, freedom and safety, things they had briefly lost sight of, beckoned again to the Umfravilles.

They'd been in this new country no more than a fortnight and already it seemed to be dying in front of her. Leaves were falling inexplicably from the trees and lying, unregarded, in golden heaps on the ground. The noise that the carriage wheels made when driving through them was strange but not unpleasant. It reminded her a little of the sound of sugar cane being stacked, which was homely and comforting. But there was none of the rich green of Barbados here. None of the verdant sleekness of its low hills. Even the English birds were dowdy and brown like the trees, though she had noticed a small one with a red breast, which had observed her critically with a bright black eye from a thorn bush. The countryside was full of wonders, to be sure, but it was nothing like her own island. It was nothing like home. The home she increasingly longed for, but would probably never see again.

'Isn't it wonderful to be home, sister?' asked the pinched young woman on the worn leather seat beside her. 'The air is so invigorating, is it not? And the sun is so very cold and civilised. Do you not agree? Drusilla? *Drusilla!* Stop staring out of the window and answer me at once, you stupid girl!'

Drusilla turned from her contemplation of gently undulating Essex in its exotic autumnal glory. 'I'm so sorry, Mary. What did you say?'

'I was asking you, my beloved sister, whether you found your native country pleasant? Now that you are able to view it for the first time.'

Drusilla smiled and gave the only possible reply: 'But of course, sister. I am so pleased that father has brought us here. To England. To Essex.'

'Superior in every respect to Barbados, as you will have noticed. I mean – Holetown scarcely deserves comparison with the meanest port in England. The low stink of spice that hangs about the place! But London ... the shops ... the magnificent public buildings with their stone colonnades ... the grand houses of the gentry ... the fashionable ladies in their finery ... and the *shops* ...'

Indeed, the shops had been wonderful. Drusilla could happily have bought new lace and silk and ribbons all day – if they had been allowed any money to spend. But even wandering through the New Exchange with an empty purse had been glorious enough. It had been more painful visiting St Paul's Churchyard, unable to purchase any of the beautifully bound volumes that were exposed for sale there. She had had no idea there were so many books in the whole world. Or that new leather smelt and shone like that. She had envied the men, glorious in their velvet coats, lace at their necks and wrists, casually leafing through them, ready to exchange their tawdry gold for glittering knowledge. But their father had promised that the time would come when they too would have money again to spare for both amusement and learning. And the two dresses she had been permitted to bring from Barbados, though clearly old-fashioned by London standards, would last a year or two, if she took care of them and patched any tears quickly. She pulled her shabby, second-hand mantle round her shoulders. Hopefully the weather in England got warmer once they were into November.

'Do you think father and the boys will reach the house today?' Drusilla enquired. She was aware that Mary knew no better than she did, but always sought opportunities to defer cravenly to her sister's opinion. That was her job after all. It was her vocation.

'The wagon with our luggage will travel more slowly than this coach,' said Mary, pleased to be explaining something she understood. 'And they will stop more often, I imagine. To water the horses and so on. Which is very necessary for the unfortunate creatures, pulling such a burden. They may not arrive until tomorrow.'

'Indeed,' said their mother – real mother in one case, adoptive mother in the other case – who had been dozing plumply on the seat opposite them, skirts spread proprietorially across the whole width of the carriage. 'They may or they may not. It's all one to me, I assure you. My sole concern is for you poor homeless girls, and to ensure that we take possession of our new house before nightfall. I have no money to waste on an inn nor any love of bed bugs if I did. We need to call first at the manor to collect the keys, then your father will sign the lease whenever he arrives. My signature, by the ancient laws of this country, carries no weight at all. In England, a woman's name is lighter than a mote of dust. But then, I won't have to go to a debtors' prison when your father defaults on the rent. There's that to think of.'

'Is Clavershall West a large town?' asked Drusilla.

Their mother laughed, though her contempt was not aimed at anybody in the coach. 'It's not a town at all. It's scarcely a village. A church, a manor house, an inn, a few cottages with filthy thatch, all joined together by a muddy road or two. That's where your father has decided we shall live.'

Mary frowned. This was not what she expected of glorious England. 'Are there no shops close to the house?'

'There's a weekly market in Saffron Walden, I do know that. Of the place we are to inhabit, the New House, I can tell you nothing, except that it is too expensive by half. But your father's family once lived close by, as he keeps reminding us. Back in the days before the family was cheated out of Brandon Hall. And your father thinks we require a genteel residence for whatever it is he has in mind.'

'So we have come to Essex because ... what? ... father thinks we can somehow recover Brandon Hall and go and live there?' asked Drusilla.

Their mother laughed again. 'When pigs take wing, my girl. He has, I grant you, written threateningly to the current owners, vowing to take action against them for fraud and theft and witchcraft and being secret republicans. But, even if he thinks we can get the house back through the courts, we should be in London, where the case would like as not be heard, not here in the middle of nowhere. And why would somebody who truly thinks one fair house is about to drop into his lap take a three-year lease on another? The truth is, my girl, that some men think the best use for their heads is storing shit.'

Mary had been listening carefully and was not impressed by any part of her father's strategy. 'So why *are* we going to Clavershall West in that case? You say we should be in London where the courts are. And the shops. And rich husbands. There's nothing for us to do in Essex. No dancing. No young gentlemen to come courting me. Nothing to buy even if we had money. It sounds horrid.'

'Ask your father,' said their mother, meaning that her daughter should enquire by all means but not necessarily expect a satisfactory response. 'Why did we go to Barbados? He thought it was a good idea at the time. How can you lose money growing a crop everyone wants with labour that doesn't need paying? Ah well, we've got away from there with a little cash in hand, even if it should legally be in the hands of other people. It will be enough to keep us for a few years if I can prevent your father from drinking it. After that, we'll have to see what turns up. To look on the bright side, somebody in the family may die – I mean somebody in your father's family, not mine – and leave us a little richer than we were. Or one of your father's schemes may come to something. Perhaps he'll breed a flying pig. Hubert the flying pig.'

'Is the New House large?' asked Drusilla.

'Large? I think not. But it is, as I say, very respectable and it is available. Sir Felix Clifford, who owns it, lives at the manor house with his daughter and son-in-law – Sir John and Lady Grey. She writes plays under the name of Aminta Grey and he is a justice of the peace.' She yawned, as if exhausted by this feat of memory. 'And that, for the moment, girls, is all you need to know about anything.'

'They sound very grand,' said Mary. She clearly did not regard grandness as a good thing. At least, not in other people.

'They are no better than us,' said the mother. 'We're Umfravilles. Good Norman stock. We may have no fancy titles and no more money than you can keep in a medium-sized box.

We can probably never set foot in Barbados again without risk of arrest. But we bow to nobody, young lady. You too, Drusilla. Don't forget you're an Umfraville.'

'By adoption,' said Drusilla. 'Norman merely by adoption. That much should be apparent to anyone who looks at me.'

Their mother glanced out of the window. 'The spire in the distance must be Newport,' she said. 'You might call that a real town, I suppose. So, another couple of hours and we'll be at the end of our journey. In the place your father has, in his infinite wisdom, chosen for us to dwell. The New House in Clavershall West in the county of Essex. And may God have mercy on us all.'

Lady Grey was younger than they expected, fair-haired, blue-eyed, with one child clutching her skirt and a baby in her arms. She was slightly built, but with an inner strength that had nothing but amused contempt for physical size.

'We weren't sure when you were arriving, Mistress Umfraville. Otherwise my father or my husband – most certainly one or the other – would have been here to welcome you too. Fortunately I have located the keys to the New House in the place that my father most recently mislaid them. Our steward will accompany you there and see that all is in order. Then Mister Umfraville can sign the lease tomorrow or whenever convenient, and pay us the first quarter's rent in advance – something on which I fear I must insist, even if my father may have inadvertently neglected to inform you of the condition.'

'Of course,' said Mistress Umfraville, as if the payment of a whole year's rent there and then would have been a trifle to a family of undoubted Norman descent. 'I am grateful for your help, Lady Grey. I am more than happy that we leave the men to deal with any legal matters and that we restrict ourselves to the practicalities of running the house.'

'In that respect, I shall help if I can but it's my husband who knows the house best. Though it now belongs to my father, it was once John's mother's and he grew up there. My husband's mother left the house to my father for reasons that are, frankly, too shameful to explain to you now.' She smiled at them, correctly guessing that was already as much family history as they wished to know. 'As I say, you would have met my husband today, but he is away from home – on a social visit, not a judicial one.'

Mistress Umfraville nodded. 'I had of course heard he was a magistrate. But in a setting as peaceful as this one I hope that his duties are pleasant and infrequent.'

'Quite the reverse. There is always work for magistrates. There are few crimes that they have in London that we do not have here, including murder. I should add, however, that my husband's enthusiastic investigations of unlawful killings have been slightly curtailed by the new coroner in Saffron Walden, who prefers to view corpses that are wholly undisturbed. The coroner, a certain Mister Josiah Thatcher, is also related in some way to the Sheriff, who in turn is my husband's judicial superior. You will appreciate that this is an inconvenient state of affairs. I would suggest that you do not mention the dread word "coroner" in my husband's hearing. Or "sheriff". Or "kinsman". Are you familiar with this part of the world, Mistress Umfraville?'

'I do not know it well, but my own husband's people once lived near here.'

'Really? Where?'

'Brandon Hall,' said Mary quickly.

Lady Grey frowned. 'But that was owned by the Lucases before it passed to the Robinsons.'

'My husband's mother was a Lucas,' said Mistress Umfraville.

'Ah,' said Lady Grey. 'Everything is now clear, or as clear as it needs to be. The Hall is no great distance from here anyway. Coincidentally, my father and husband have ridden there today. If Mister Umfravillle's ancestors once owned it, I can understand why he wishes to return to this part of the country.'

'The Hall may be ours again one day...' Mary began eagerly, but a warning glance from her mother silenced her.

A frown passed briefly across Lady Grey's face, then she said brightly: 'The sea journey from Barbados was not too troublesome, I hope?'

'The passage was long and unpleasant, though no more than we expected it to be,' said Mistress Umfraville. 'The six of us, crossing the Atlantic in one cramped cabin, three poor meals a day of salt pork, pickled herring, hard bread, beer and rum, and no diversion other than to stroll on deck, arm in arm, when the weather permitted. I told the captain that it was too bad that we had to put up with such conditions. Well, that's finished and done with now, but I'd forgotten how cold England was, indeed I had.'

Lady Grey turned to Drusilla. 'That dress will hardly keep you warm this winter,' she said. 'I do hope you have another?'

'Two,' laughed Drusilla, 'but sadly they are even thinner than this.'

'I shall let you have one of my old ones,' said Lady Grey. 'My own maid has her eye on it, but I think you need it more – until your mistress can find you something better, I mean.'

'Thank you. That is very kind indeed. But I'm her daughter – not her servant,' said Drusilla.

'How stupid of me,' said Lady Grey. 'I do apologise. But . . .'

'The colour of my skin? I was adopted.'

'But of course. I should have realised. You must think I am very foolish indeed.'

'Please don't let it trouble you, my Lady. I've had to say the same thing at least a dozen times since I arrived in England. People make assumptions. When they see my face. Or my hands. Or any part of me that they decently can, I suppose. And I am not ungrateful for the offer of a warm dress. I'd like it very much. Unless your maid needs it more than I do?'

'Don't worry. She can have the one I had in mind. I have another – newer by a good eighteen months – that I'll look out and bring round to you tomorrow. We're much the same size, you and I. It shouldn't need altering at all. Is there anything else any of you require – until your own things arrive?'

'Nothing, my Lady,' said Mistress Umfraville, very firmly. 'My husband can provide for us perfectly well.'

'Indeed. We'll manage without charity, thank you very much,' said Mary, nevertheless casting an envious glance at Lady Grey's neat costume of glossy, dark-green wool with its lace collar and cuffs.

'Charity? Oh dear, I'm so sorry – I truly did not mean to give offence in that respect either,' said Lady Grey. 'What I offer you, I offer as a neighbour and I hope in due course a friend. We are now well provided with most things here, thank God. But it was not always thus with us. We're in no position to look down on anyone, I can assure you. You would have difficulty being poorer than we once were.'

'Poor and content is rich, and rich enough,' said Drusilla, with a shy smile.

Lady Grey, unused to hearing Shakespeare quoted without embarrassment in north Essex, smiled back and nodded. Mistress Umfraville did not, however, seem content. 'I too have no wish to give offence, Lady Grey, but, however well intended your offer may have been, there's nothing we need from you, my Lady. Only the keys to our house.'

'Excellent,' said Lady Grey. 'Then you are clearly a most fortunate family. It's just a short walk to the New House. I ensured a couple of days ago that the interior was thoroughly dusted and swept and that the beds were made up. You most certainly won't be able to get to Saffron Walden today, so I'll send some food across later.'

'We purchased all we need in Newport.'

'How very resourceful of you. No food then. Just the keys, as you say. Our steward is ready to depart with you. Our footman will come along too – to help carry your bags.'

'We can carry our own bags,' said Mistress Umfraville.

'I never said you couldn't,' said Lady Grey. 'But young Matthew is in danger of getting fat, like a horse who is too much in his stable, and he badly needs a brisk trot. I hope you will not deny him that?'

It was much later when Drusilla woke suddenly to see lemon moonlight flooding through the bedroom windows. She had been dreaming she was back in Barbados, but the sharp air on her face told her that sadly she was not. Her father was cursing something or somebody in the garden below. She edged slowly from between the sheets of her warm bed, shivered and tiptoed a few steps across the well-scrubbed boards. A large cart was standing outside in the lane. Steam was rising up towards her from the broad and shiny backs of the horses that were harnessed to it. One or two boxes remained in the cart, but the garden had become an entrepôt for the rest of their goods, which were making their way by easy stages into the house. She looked down on the balding head of the carter, her father's wide, feathered hat and the cloaked and foreshortened forms of her brothers, moving with laden arms from the garden to the hallway and back again. Though her mother fondly persisted in calling them 'boys', there was no escaping that they were now young men, stronger perhaps, and harder working most certainly, than their father.

Drusilla had been careful to be quiet, but she heard her sister stirring anyway.

'What is it?' asked an irritable heap of blankets in the other bed. 'Why have you stupidly woken me up?'

'Father has arrived with the wagon. They must have been travelling all night, under the moon. George and James are with him, helping to carry the boxes inside.'

'Have they just got here?'

'No, I think they must have arrived and started unloading a while ago. Father seems to have finished blaspheming for the time being and is paying the carter. They all look a little wet. And there are puddles in the road. It rained quite hard . . . I mean, it must have rained earlier. Or that's what I think.'

'Since they are safely here, what you think about the weather matters very little, Drusilla. We shall put on our mantles and our shoes, sister, and go down and welcome them.'

Drusilla hesitated. Her damp mantle was draped over the end of the bed. Her shoes, hidden away underneath it, were even wetter, though they would hopefully no longer obviously be so when anyone next observed them. The heat of her own body had almost dried the thin shift she was wearing. Still, even slightly wet clothing might occasion some questions, as might the omission of a mantle. To go down without some sort of outer garment when Mary was wearing one would be tantamount to criticism of Mary's judgement. Her sister's threats of beatings rarely came to anything, but they were tedious to listen to and better avoided. 'I'm so tired after yesterday's journey,' she said.

'Too tired to welcome your own father and brothers, Drusilla? I cannot believe even you would say such a thing!'

'I'll see them in the morning, dearest one.'

'It must be dawn very soon anyway. Did you not sleep well, sister, here in our delightful English countryside?'

The implication of ingratitude, to both family and country, was too pointed for Drusilla to be able to tell the truth.

'Yes, of course,' she said. Then, after a pause, she added: 'And you, my dearest sister? Were your sweet dreams undisturbed?'

'I have slept soundly since we came up to bed,' said Mary. 'I often tossed and turned for hours in Holetown, with its nasty heat and insects, but I have not lost a moment's blissful slumber since I reached the shores of dear, dear England.'

Drusilla breathed a sigh of relief. All was well then. Unless that cow of a sister was lying.

'So, are you coming down or not?' Mary demanded.

'They'll want to get to bed themselves.'

'They'll want to tell us about their journey and hear about ours.'

'If you tell them about your journey, they'll know all they need to know about mine. Our journeys were much the same, when you think about it. I'm sure they won't mind if they don't see me in person until later.'

'Oh, please yourself then,' Mary snapped. 'You are the most unnatural, thankless creature on God's earth. Why father didn't choose somebody else as my sister, I have no idea.'

Drusilla listened to Mary's shoes thudding, doubtless with much filial love and duty, on the wooden stairs. There were voices below: her sister's ingratiating whine, then a few gruff words in reply from her father. She slipped back between the now cold sheets.

At length she heard the church clock strike one. Dawn was further off than Mary had claimed. The single chime was still dying away in the frosty air when Drusilla heard many footsteps wearily ascending to their respective chambers. She pulled the rough sheet and the blankets over her head and pretended to be asleep. She remained motionless as Mary banged and thumped her way around the room and finally threw herself back into the other bed.

'Are you asleep, my dear Drusilla?' Mary's voice resembled that of a petulant dove.

Drusilla said nothing, scarcely breathing.

'Drusilla! I asked you a question! Are you asleep or not, you silly girl? Answer me!'

Could anyone really slumber through the noise that Mary had been making? Drusilla thought not but, however much Mary might suspect wakefulness, she probably wouldn't bother to get out of an almost-warm bed and come across the room to pinch her.

After a while Drusilla heard the blessed sound of snoring. She reached out and pulled her mantle over the blankets for a little extra warmth, She was pleased to discover in the process that it was now only slightly damp. The shoes might also almost be dry then. She'd definitely got away with her earlier outing. That was all that really mattered.

She rolled over and, with her back to her sister, risked an almost silent fart.

The sun was shining through the window when she awoke again. Even Mary would approve of how well and how gratefully she had passed the last few hours. Across the room, her sister – her adoptive sister – was still slumbering. But the air was like breathable ice. It was colder here, on this autumnal morning, than it had been anywhere ever in Drusilla's life. She shivered, pulled the inadequate mantle round her shoulders and looked forward to the arrival of a warm dress later that day. She hoped her mother would permit her to be friends with the Greys, who seemed to be amiable and to possess books in abundance.

The chamber door opened suddenly. 'Have either of you girls seen your father?' asked Mistress Umfraville. She bit her lip and looked at them uncertainly.

'No,' said Drusilla. 'But he must have been with you . . .'

'He most certainly should have been. But he got up early for some reason. Or perhaps he never came to bed. I was asleep so quickly myself that I don't know. His hat and cloak are hanging in the entrance hall, but he seems to be nowhere in the house, neither in my bed nor in any other proper place, and the front door is strangely unlocked. I begin to fear he may have met with some accident.'

'Have you asked James and George?' asked Mary, sitting up in her bed.

'No. Not yet. I thought I would ask you first.'

'He may have gone out for a morning walk, then,' said Drusilla.

'Don't be an ass,' said Mary. 'He'd hardly go out with a lease that needs signing and a hundred other things to do. Drusilla's wrong, isn't she, mother? She's no idea, has she?'

'Neither of you heard anything at all last night?' asked Mistress Umfraville.

'No,' said Mary.

'I saw him only from the bedroom window when he and the boys arrived,' said Drusilla. 'Then I went straight back to sleep. I was so very tired after the journey from London.'

'You're sure about that?'

'Of course she's sure,' said Mary. 'She just lay there, not troubling herself to greet the men when they arrived after their long and difficult journey. If I saw nothing, I can't see why Drusilla would think she had. I mean, she's only adopted, when all's said and done.'

Drusilla shivered, not through cold but because it was clear that her mother rightly suspected that she had witnessed things that Mary had not. How could she have found out? Who could have told her? Mistress Umfraville seemed to be looking straight at her shoes under the bed.

The expected accusation, however, did not come. Mistress Umfraville made no comment on footwear. Her mind was on higher things. She swallowed hard. 'Then I declare that I simply don't know what's happened to him,' she said. 'I must go and talk to the boys.'

There was a thudding on the stairs. James burst into the room. His shoes and stockings were wet. And there was a smear of blood on his hand. Mistress Umfraville stared at the ominous red streak, suddenly unable to say another word.

The girls too looked at each other aghast. In that instant, all three women knew what had happened. They were merely waiting for James, as the only man in the room, to confirm it for them.

'I've just found father,' he said. 'I went out early to check something and . . . you're not going to believe this, mother. He's lying in the orchard. Lying there on his face with his head smashed in. Father has been murdered in cold blood.'

And, strangely, he did not seem in any way disappointed.

Chapter 1

In which I revisit one of the scenes of my childhood and find a dead body in it

The sun is shining through a crack in the curtains when I wake for the second time. A sharp burst of rain disturbed me briefly during the small hours, but the day has dawned with an autumnal brilliance. I get out of bed and draw back one of the heavy brocade drapes an inch or two. Last night's storm has brought down some of the leaves, but the trees in the park are still magnificent in their dying colours. The deer move in and out of the shadows like dappled ghosts.

'What time did you and my father get back from Brandon?' asks Aminta from our bed.

'I'm sorry – I tried not to disturb you,' I say.

'Well, you have now.'

'At least I didn't wake you when I came to bed. We weren't home until midnight. The church clock was chiming the full twelve as we passed through the park gates. Fortunately there was a moon and no clouds most of the way back.'

'You didn't get wet?'

'It rained before we left the Robinsons and it rained again in the night, but we had a dry journey. Anyway, I'm sorry to have woken you now. I didn't mean to.'

'Little Aphra would have disturbed me soon anyway,' she says, looking towards the cradle. 'She's slept for over six hours. Any more would be miraculous.'

'Both our children are miraculous,' I say.

'You think that because you spend less time with them than I do. They are much like other children, except that we are responsible for feeding them. How were things at Brandon Hall?'

'Well enough. The Robinsons hope to see you next time. They had an excellent harvest this year. They are in good health. But, though they mentioned it only in passing, they seem troubled by another family who believe they have a claim on the Robinsons' property – house, park and farmland.'

'What sort of claim?'

'Oh, you know William. His account was inevitably rather confused and there were points when he paused for a long time because he was wondering whether he'd already told us too much. All I can say is that these people, whoever they are, seem to be threatening legal action in a most aggressive way. Worse still, they are about to arrive in England from Jamaica, where they are sugar planters.'

'Barbados,' says Aminta.

'So it was! How on earth do you know that?'

'I fear the family concerned may be the Umfravilles, my father's new tenants. They arrived yesterday afternoon and the daughter let slip that they hope one day to regain their old family seat at Brandon. The mother hushed her at once but too late not to reveal their design in general terms.'

'Ah ... The Robinsons didn't say what the troublesome family were called – at least, I don't think they did. If your father worked out what was going on, he tactfully said nothing about having provided the Robinsons' sworn enemies with a convenient forward base for their operations. So you've actually met them all? What are they like?'

'I haven't met the litigious father or either of the sons yet – just Mistress Umfraville and the daughters. The mother is in her fifties and prouder than she can afford to be in a threadbare dress that went out of fashion in London five years ago and here in Essex the summer before last. The realisation that she is now poor makes her irritable. She fears that I shall be charitable to them unless she exercises constant vigilance.'

'Did you tell her how poor we have both been? When my mother and I lived at the New House, she could scarcely afford to pay her servants.'

'That, John, is not poverty. So long as you have servants who will continue to work for you free of charge, and occasionally lend you small sums of money, you are not impoverished. When my father and I were exiled to Brussels, in Cromwell's unlamented time, we couldn't afford to buy food, or pay cash for it, anyway. Had my father not flirted outrageously with the grocer's wife – something I regret to say he would probably have done anyway – we might have starved.'

'Perhaps everyone believes they are poor – the King certainly does.'

'His mistresses, on the other hand, are increasingly rich,' says Aminta.

'The two things are not unconnected,' I say. 'Well, my mother's ghost, if it inhabits the New House, will I am sure look upon your father's needy tenants with sympathy, even the prickly Mistress Umfraville. How were the girls? Like the mother?'

'The elder one seemed starved of joy and ideas in equal measure. She was deeply suspicious of any offer of help. The younger one – Drusilla – was charming and seemingly unaware how pretty she is. She quoted Shakespeare at me – "poor and content is rich, and rich enough". I think she meant it.'

'Is that from *The Tempest? Midsummer Night's Dream? Twelfth Night?*'

'*Othello*, strangely enough. You'd have thought it was from a comedy, wouldn't you? I can't imagine Shakespeare really believed it anyway. I am taking the younger daughter some warm clothes this morning. Those she was in were suitable for the tropics but not for Essex in the winter. I might also take a book or two since her interests seem to lie in that direction – she'll find my father left none at the New House, other than an old copy of *The Compleat Justice*. We got off to a bad start unfortunately. I mistook her for a servant.'

'Why?'

'Because of the colour of her skin. She's adopted, apparently.'

'I'm sure I would have assumed the same. There are plenty of African servants in London. Not so many bankers or courtiers. If she's as you describe her, I doubt that she'll worry about it for long.'

'I'm sure you're right. But the Umfravilles are to be our tenants and our neighbours. I'd rather we were friends than otherwise. So, I'll go bearing irreproachably modest gifts.'

'*Timeo Danaos et dona ferentes,*' I observe.

'I'm not offering them a giant wooden horse, John – just good-quality used clothing and the loan of some books. The mother seems willing to countenance charity towards her adoptive daughter even if she rejects it for the rest of the family. I thought perhaps my dark grey dress?'

'That's still quite new, isn't it?'

'It's a serviceable colour and I can spare it. Betterton has agreed to pay me more for my next play, having made himself quite rich with my last one. I can afford to buy another. Maybe two.' She pauses to gauge my reaction to this proposal, then continues: 'Quite possibly three. I should see if I have something for the elder daughter in due course. And Mistress Umfraville, if she'll accept it. There are still one or two of your mother's old dresses in the chest that might fit her. Whatever they say, I don't think they have much money to spare for new clothes and the cold winds of November may change their minds on accepting charity. This isn't Barbados, in almost every possible way, as I think they are discovering.'

'If you are going to be so profligate over your old dresses, and my mother's, let's hope these Umfravilles are more grateful than you suggest. I also hope that your reckless generosity to the Umfravilles doesn't offend our friends the Robinsons, if the two families are sworn enemies.'

'Since we have all spent twenty years being alternately royalist and republican – not an easy trick – I think we can find a way to be both Robinsonian and Umfravilleist. Unless meeting Mister Umfraville sways us irrevocably one way or the other.'

There is a tentative knocking at the chamber door. I open it to find our steward, already dressed for the day ahead but agitated.

'Is there a problem?' I ask.

'Mister Umfraville is waiting for you in the drawing room, Sir John.'

'Eager to sign his lease?' I say. 'Or does he already have a complaint about the drains?'

'Perhaps your mother's ghost has been less obliging than we thought,' says Aminta. 'Perhaps she materialised in the drawing room at midnight and lectured them on ingratitude. That would be worth thirty shillings a quarter off the rent.'

'None of those things,' says our steward, stiffly reproaching our levity. He always had a high regard for my mother. Most of the village did. 'It is young Mister Umfraville who is without, not the leaseholder in person. He says, Sir John, that he wishes you to accompany him to the New House at once. There has been a wholly unexpected death.'

The body has not been moved, more I think because it is large and awkward to shift than out of respect for the forthcoming official investigation. It is clothed in a roomy suit of dark blue broadcloth. No cloak. No hat. No periwig – perhaps they are not yet fashionable in the colonies. Hubert Umfraville lies, face down, on a carpet of damp leaves that are every bit as dead as he is. A few, slightly drier, rest impudently on top of him. The back of his head is a mess of hair and congealed blood. His linen collar has protected his coat from the worst of it, but cleanliness is no longer his biggest problem. He has been struck with something much harder than he was. His head is slightly turned and I think I can also see a bruise above his right eye. Perhaps it is from when he fell – it is certainly a minor wound compared with the other. There is also a slight graze on his large, calloused right hand. I kneel beside Umfraville and am about to question his remains further when I recall the views of the new coroner in Saffron Walden concerning the proper examination of corpses in northwest

Essex. On this subject our Mister Thatcher has been most officiously insistent. That his predecessor raised no objections to my inspecting corpses in situ, that my views on the cause of death were also usually his views, is irrelevant. It is apparently for the coroner to determine how the victim died. Not me. Of course, the figure before us does look very dead indeed and the cause is more than obvious, even to this interfering magistrate.

Still on my knees, I briefly place my hand against Umfraville's cheek. It is icy cold and wet with last night's rain. I run my palm quickly down his equally wet sleeve. Thatcher can scarcely object to my doing that. I stand again, shaking my head at a job that I have left at the best only half done. But the completed half is useful enough. Judging by the dampness of his clothes, Umfraville has been where he is now all night. Around the dead man's head is a modest pool of blood, already darkening and thickening where it hasn't been diluted by the nocturnal precipitation. The thought occurs to me that, next spring, grass will grow long and lush on this spot.

'This is where we found him,' says the young Mister Umfraville who has led us here. He is James Umfraville – as he has informed us on our short journey. His elder brother George, briefly introduced on our arrival, has been waiting patiently with the body, perhaps the more difficult task of the two in a strange grove, with the killer – who knows? – still lurking, only just out of sight. And it is easy to imagine things in the perpetual twilight beneath the trees. Just for a moment I think I see Hubert Umfraville's hand tremble and his chest rise slightly and fall again, but then I realise it is only shadows moving across the orchard floor. The wind drops and the corpse rests easy.

I turn back to James. 'When did you last see him alive?'

'We'd travelled from Harlow yesterday,' says George. 'From sunrise until well into the night. We always seem to be travelling by night, one way or another. By the time we reached here everyone was tired out. We unloaded and took our possessions into the hall. Father disputed the charges for carriage from London, while James and I waited in our wet cloaks, not much caring about an extra shilling or two, just wanting to find our beds. Then, as the cart headed off towards the inn for the night, father decided something was missing – that the carter had improbably contrived to steal part of the load. We suggested that the apparently absent item would probably show up in one place or another in the light of day. But he wouldn't let things be. We left him going through the luggage again, swearing that he'd not let the rascally carter sleep before he had settled the score with him. The rest of us trudged upstairs to bed. I slumbered until James woke me, saying he'd been out and had found father's body. I went down to the orchard with him and mother. There was no doubt that father was dead. We agreed James should report it to you straight away.'

'You examined the body yourselves?'

'As much as we needed to,' says James. 'I did when I first found him, then mother and George later. But it's pretty clear what happened, isn't it?'

For a moment I envy them, untrammelled by the caprices of coroners, free to handle any corpse they choose for as long as they wish.

'The body was clearly out here all night,' I say. 'His clothes are wet through.'

'On the journey from London, his cloak would have protected him from the rain,' says James, 'just as ours did.

He took it off when we arrived and left it in the entrance hall with his hat. So, I suppose you're right.'

I know the rain returned at about three o'clock. It was heavy but didn't last long. Even without a proper examination of the body, I can judge the time of death fairly accurately. After one o'clock but before three.

'It didn't worry you that you didn't hear him come up to his chamber?' I ask.

'We were all sound asleep,' says George. 'And even if we'd been aware he was late coming to bed, we would have assumed that he'd followed the carter back to the inn to continue their argument. Father has become very careful over small things – watching every penny. He was less concerned in Holetown.'

'That may have been the problem, George,' says James.

'And the locusts,' says George. 'And the drought. They may have been the problem too.'

'Other plantations survived them,' says James. 'But their owners consumed less rum and struck better bargains.'

They turn and look at me as if I might be able to adjudicate on the matter – rum or locusts? Locusts or rum? What was Hubert Umfraville's downfall?

'Which chamber did you both occupy?' I ask.

'James and I slept in one of the chambers at the back – overlooking the garden and this orchard. Drusilla and Mary had already taken the smaller chamber at the front and mother and father were to have the largest one, with the curtained bed.'

'So, you would not have heard your father arrive or leave?'

'Not by the front door, which is the only one that was unlocked.'

'But you would have noticed a fight taking place here in the orchard at the back of the house?'

'The casement was closed against the cold. And we had been travelling all day. A pitched battle with muskets, drums and cannons might not have disturbed us.'

I should still very much like to kneel by the body again and examine it more closely, measure the depth of the wound, check the stiffness of the limbs to confirm the time of death . . . Well, let the coroner do that if that's what he wishes. Hubert Umfraville died between one and three o'clock in the morning, killed, as far as I can tell, by a single blow to the back of the head. If Thatcher can do better than that, then good luck to him.

I turn my attention to the scene of the crime. I know it well. Every inch of it. This is the small orchard I played in when I was a boy. This is where I first got to know Aminta, in the days when I regarded her simply as the annoying younger sister of my good friend, Marius. But it has become overgrown since Sir Felix moved out of the New House and into ours. The grass is long and fallen apples litter the ground, too many this year even for the local boys to steal properly. There is no hiding where people have walked. A single, broad path has been trampled from the house to this spot. I try to recall everyone who will have come this way. Hubert Umfraville undoubtedly flattened some grass and so did James, who found him earlier this morning. Unlike his father, James returned the way he had come. Then Mistress Umfraville, George and I added our own footprints. The killer came here too. Came by this clearly marked route and then left exactly the same way, without disturbing the young men in their chamber. There is no small detour branching off right or left – nothing suggesting that the assailant hid behind a tree or shrub and waited for his victim.

Hubert lies facing his new home. It would seem he was discussing something with his murderer then, unwisely, turned towards the house. At which point he was struck on the back of his head – a blow that he clearly did not think he deserved. There was no fight – or none loud enough to wake James and George in their chamber overlooking the garden.

Then I notice, a little way off, a small area of broken stems. I walk towards it and find very much what I expect. There is a rusty axe, a little less bloody no doubt for the rain that has fallen since it was thrown there, but with some red still smearing the blade and the smooth, worn handle. I recall the axe – or one very much like it – being used by our gardener many years ago. It is small and easy to wield. In those far-off days, if it is indeed the same one, it was kept sharp and gleaming. The now-omnipresent rust, and its being left out in the orchard for the convenience of passing murderers, reflects the lax state of horticultural affairs under my father-in-law. In that sad condition, it smashed rather than sliced into the skull. I pick up the axe carefully.

'Do either of you recognise this?' I ask.

James shakes his head.

'We brought nothing like that from Barbados,' says George. 'A useless piece of old iron? It looks as if it has been lying in the orchard for months, if not years. Why would I recognise it . . . you're not suggesting that one of us did this, are you?'

'I've no idea who killed him, except that he didn't kill himself,' I say. 'The lack of evidence for a struggle or an ambush suggests he knew his killer and wasn't expecting to be attacked. That means you might have recognised his attacker too. You're sure you saw nothing from your window?'

They look at me, the same sincerely regretful smile on each of their faces.

Even now, something is telling me to make my usual examination. Would the coroner even know I'd done it? And if he did, what is the worst a minor official like him could do, however closely he is related to the Sheriff? But no – let him ride over from Saffron Walden and get his knees muddy. Anyway, I have a number of things that need to be done urgently. Things that lie undoubtedly in my domain and nobody else's.

'The carter is probably still in the village,' I say. 'I'm sure I noticed the wagon in the yard as we passed the inn earlier. I doubt if he'll have made an early start after your long journey yesterday. I'd better try to speak to him before he decides to leave for London. Please convey to your mother and your sisters my most sincere condolences and say that I'll need to talk with them later. Your father's body must remain here, untouched, until the coroner arrives.'

'Well, I don't think that any of us are planning to go very far today,' says James. He turns to the body. 'Him least of all.'

Chapter 2

In which I am reminded I once committed the sin of being younger than I am now

It's just a short walk from the New House to the inn. To be honest, in this village, nowhere is a long walk to anywhere. I take the road south, using the ancient stepping stones to cross the shallow, sparkling stream that divides the New House (and the village dung heap) from most of the other habitations. Strands of yellowy-green waterweed stream from the half-submerged stones, as if trying to escape to Saffron Walden and beyond. The weather is as gloriously oblivious of Hubert Umfraville as he is of this bright new morning he never lived to see. At the only crossroads we have, I turn left and quickly find myself in front of the inn, which faces the comforting, red park-wall of my own house on the opposite side of the road – the house from which I was summoned less than an hour ago.

I am not too late. I can still see, behind the inn, the polished shaft and iron-bound front wheels of a large cart. Our wagoner, if he is indeed the murderer, has decided not to flee the scene of his crime with suspicious haste.

'Good morning, Sir John,' says the innkeeper cheerfully and almost deferentially, as I duck through the low doorway.

'Morning, Ben,' I say.

'You'll be after a pint of the finest ale in Essex, I assume?'

'Sorry, Ben – I'm here on business,' I say.

'But you'll have one all the same? Shame not to, eh? Since you're here. Best in Essex, that is. Everyone says so.'

I shake my head. Ben is disappointed. There was a time when I could have been easily persuaded to drink a lot more than one, and Ben remembers it well. He respects me as lord of the manor but he once had expectations of me as a regular customer with a purse to empty.

'All well at the Big House, I hope?' he asks, nodding in the direction of my brick wall and the park with my herd of fallow deer.

'Yes, God be praised,' I say.

'Little Aphra is thriving?'

'She is the perfect baby in all respects.'

Ben frowns. 'What made you call her Aphra, then?' he asks.

'She's named after a friend of Aminta's – another playwright.'

Ben nods reluctantly. Children should be called Beth or Jane or Margaret, as his own daughter is. No good can come of giving them fancy names that might cause them to look down on other folk. Ben always claimed to have no preference between King and Parliament – Cromwell or the Stuarts. He was as willing, he so often said, to sell the best ale in the county quite impartially to any royalist or parliamentarian with a thirst. But increasingly I think he disapproves of the current king and his court. He regrets the loss of the decency and orderliness of Cromwell's time. So, whenever I have time to think about it, do I. That doesn't mean that Aphra isn't a very pretty name, of course.

'What's this business we need to discuss, then?' Ben asks cautiously. 'Do you want to talk to me as constable rather than innkeeper?' He hopes not. Only one of those things brings him any profit.

'Unfortunately, yes,' I say. 'There's been a murder in the village, Ben. Hubert Umfraville.'

Ben frowns. Another fancy name. Two, actually. 'Who's he, then?'

'He was about to become the tenant of the New House. Sir Felix has decided there's no point in continuing to pay for the upkeep of his own residence when he spends most of his time at ours. So, he's let it out. Except the tenant has been murdered before he could sign the lease.'

'Ah, so that's who he is. There was a rumour somebody was coming to live there. From the Barbadoes, so I heard.'

'Well, he would have been living here, if he wasn't dead.'

'Where's the body?'

'At the house. In the orchard.'

Ben nods. The orchard. It could be worse, then. 'It's just . . . it's difficult getting away at the moment for constable work. I've a couple of customers here who need looking after. Demanding individuals, both of 'em. I don't mean you, of course, Sir John. You're hardly a customer at all these days.'

Again, there's just a hint of disappointment that I haven't lived up to my early promise as a drinker. He wanted something better for me than that I should become a moderately successful lawyer, lord of the manor and a magistrate. He is, moreover, undecided as to whether my occasional employment on confidential business by the King's Secretary of State, Lord Arlington, is in any way to my credit. But then I'm not sure either. Probably not, on balance.

'You've already been over to the New House, then?' he says.

'Yes,' I say.

'Hope you didn't touch the body.'

I decide to ignore this. It's bad enough taking instructions from the coroner. I'm not having my own constable reminding me of it. 'There's nothing more to be done at the New House for the moment, anyway,' I say. 'But I'd like a word with the owner of the cart in your yard, if he's up and about.'

'Mister Jenks, you mean?'

'If you say so. I mean the man who travelled here with Umfraville's goods. He may have been the last person to see him alive.'

'Except for whoever killed him,' says Ben. Jenks is a customer, after all. And I've heard the name before. I think he stops at the inn quite often on his way to and from Cambridge or Thetford or somewhere. Ben never suspects a regular paying customer of criminal activity. And certainly not murder. Hanging a client would be a ridiculous waste.

'So, is there any chance I could speak to him, Ben?' I say.

'I doubt if Mister Jenks can tell you a lot,' Ben says.

'I'll know better when I've spoken to him,' I say.

Ben sighs. 'I'll call him down,' he says.

I sit at one of the rough oak tables in the low-ceilinged room until I hear footsteps descending the stairs. Jenks pauses for a moment and squints at me, as if the light in here is not as good as in his chamber on the upper floor. I think I do recognise him from his previous visits, though I can't ever remember speaking to him. He seems equally uncertain about me. But then, as I say, I visit the inn less than I used to do.

'Mister Bowman says you want to talk to me?' He is mildly interested why this should be, but no more than that. Ben must have said very little to him, perhaps wishing to distance himself from any awkward accusations that I might choose to make. To be fair, Jenks doesn't look much like a murderer, in his shirtsleeves and brown woollen breeches and shiny leather boots. His remaining hair is short and greying. His face is showing the first few lines of age, but not many. He has a slight bruise on the left-hand side of his face and, I notice, the knuckles on his right hand are red and swollen. I might ask him about that. He is a little below middle height, but his arms are strong, as I suspect they need to be for his work. He has the air of one who is used to ordering people and horses about, and who is used to people and horses not questioning his judgement.

'I'm John Grey,' I say. 'I'm the magistrate here. I need to ask you some questions.'

'Will it take long?'

'Long enough that you may as well sit down,' I say.

'Sorry – I need to get back to London, Mister Grey. Every minute I sit talking to you I'm losing money.'

'The sooner you sit down, the sooner you can stand up again.'

He wonders whether to stare me out for a little longer, then scrapes back the chair on the rush-covered floor and sits. He is not happy, but I wasn't intending to make him happy. That isn't my job.

'You came here with Mister Hubert Umfraville?' I say.

'What exactly is this about? Has Umfraville complained I've stolen his goods? If so, then it's as I told him more than once last night: everything we loaded in London was delivered right here in Essex. If anything's missing, he's mislaid it himself – in his own garden, I shouldn't wonder. I'll swear a Bible oath to it now, if that's what it takes to get me on the road again. I pass this way quite often. Ben Bowman will tell you I'm an honest man who pays his bills. I'm no thief. And you've only to talk to Umfraville for five minutes to know he's a rogue.'

'He may be a rogue, but he's also dead,' I say. 'Murdered last night. He's made no complaints about you before or since. When did you last see Mister Umfraville alive, Mister Jenks?'

'Murdered? Where? How?'

'If you're really so anxious to get back to London, Mister Jenks, just answer my question.'

'When did I last see him? Yesterday – or early this morning, rather. I delivered his goods – all his goods – then went off to find a room here at the inn for myself and stabling for my horses.'

'It doesn't sound as if you liked him much.'

'No, not much. He's a cruel man, Mister Grey, without even an accidental streak of kindness in him – or he was until early this morning. I spent two days travelling from London with Mister Umfraville's goods. His stories about how he treated slaves were enough to put me off tobacco and sugar for life. I've got a strong stomach, but I'd heard enough of brandings and whippings and beatings long before we got to Harlow. Umfraville was a bad lot and that's all there is to it. Perhaps he repented at the last, if he had time and good sense. I hope so for the sake of his soul, may he rest in peace. Can I go now? I've got some valuable sacks of spice back in London that need to be in Kent early next week.'

'As I say, the sooner we finish our business, the sooner you'll be on your way. You tell me you went back to the inn after unloading. At what hour?'

'I can't say precisely. I don't waste my money on watches that will be wrong half the day. Not while there are clocks in church towers. We reached the village a bit after midnight – so, we must have unloaded before one, which would mean I reached the inn just after. Is that good enough for you?'

'Perfectly. And then?'

'Exactly what you would expect. I woke Mister Bowman and enquired if he had a room for me and stabling for my horses. He had, so I went back to the yard and unhitched the wagon, got the horses into the stalls that weren't already taken – there was a fine-looking mare in the stables already, which the stable boy said had arrived while I was with the innkeeper. And that's all there is to tell. I slept well until Bowman woke me early this morning, as I requested he should. And now, if you don't mind, I'd like to be on the road.'

'Whose was the mare in the stable?'

'If you want his name you'll have to ask Bowman. I only caught a glimpse of him. Tall. A gentleman, I'd have said, but looking a bit dishevelled after his ride. He took the other chamber and ordered some ale before he went to bed. Sat there looking thoughtful. I can't say how long he stayed in the parlour and wasn't inclined to sit up with him drinking, even if he'd wanted me to. But he'd vouch for the time I arrived, I'm sure. He can't have missed my cart in the yard or the fact that we were both stabling our horses at about the same time.'

'And that's all that happened?'

'Everything of any importance. So, I can go now?'

'Unfortunately not. You said Umfraville threatened to report you to the magistrate for theft. You haven't told me much about that.'

Jenks is now sorry he blurted that out. He didn't need to.

Only he and Umfraville knew and Umfraville's not in a position to report anything. 'Look, I may have left out a few details to save time, but I've nothing to hide. While we were unloading, Umfraville accused me of losing some box that he couldn't find. I'd told him: if it wasn't there then, it had never been put on the cart in London. I thought that was that. Then, on the way back to the inn, I stopped at the stream for the horses to drink – Umfraville had forbidden me to pause on the way to the house because he'd originally wanted to get there in daylight, and by then the sun had been down for six hours or more. A cruel man with horses as well as with his workers. While I was there, he caught us up again on foot. He said I should pay him for the missing box, or he'd have me up before the magistrates today for theft. Well, I wasn't falling for a trick like that. I told him I wasn't born yesterday. And that really is everything.'

'I don't think so,' I say. 'You've missed the bruise on your face. How did you get that, Mister Jenks? Was it at the same time that you got the marks on your hand there?'

'You get all sorts of knocks and scrapes as a wagoner. Hands, face. You don't tend to remember.'

'Umfraville had a bruise on his face. Does that have any connection with the state of your knuckles? He also had a graze on his hand that might just have something to do with the mark on your cheek.'

Jenks stares at me across the table. I think he's an honest man, but plenty of honest men are capable of murder. 'What exactly are you accusing me of?' he asks.

'You're sure you didn't just go back with Mister Umfraville to the New House, to demonstrate the box was there?' I ask. 'That would be a very reasonable way to prove your point. Then maybe, after an inconclusive search of the entrance hall and the garden in front of the house, you took him to the orchard, telling him you didn't want to disturb the inhabitants of the house arguing with him? There, you finally lost your temper with a man you admit you didn't much like anyway. You struck him. He struck you. You saw the axe lying there. After you'd killed him, you headed back to the river and your horses. Maybe you splashed a bit of water on yourself too, to wash off any blood.'

'I swear to you, Mister Grey, Umfraville was alive when I last saw him. You're right – when we were at the river, Umfraville threw a punch at me and I defended myself. But that was all, because he suddenly heard something and cleared off back to the house.'

'What did he hear?' I ask.

Jenks frowns as if trying to remember. 'Horse's hooves,' he says eventually. 'That was it. Umfraville heard a horse and rider approaching.'

'Did you see them?'

'No. You can't see the house from there.'

'But you've just remembered a mysterious rider, whom Umfraville went to confront. That's very convenient for you.'

'I'm not inventing him, if that's what you mean. I definitely heard the horse's hooves on the wet road. Wait . . . I do actually know who it must have been. It was obviously the owner of the other horse in the stable. The tall gent. He arrived at the inn right behind me. So, if you're trying to find out who killed our slave-owner, you're talking to the wrong person, aren't you, Mister Grey? I wasn't the last person to see him alive.'

'I'll talk to the owner of that horse, I promise you, and maybe he'll have something to tell me. But at the moment it seems to me that you disliked Umfraville a great deal and had every opportunity to kill him.'

'Look, I've admitted I struck Umfraville. Go ahead: fine me for disturbing the peace if you wish. But you can't charge me with killing him on the basis of mere supposition and you can't keep me here.'

'I said nothing about charging you,' I say. 'Not yet. But I can most certainly keep you here – at least until I can ask the gentleman in the other chamber whether he saw Umfraville alive. Even if he confirms your story, you're likely to be needed as a witness at the inquest. You'll need to tell Ben Bowman that you may be staying at the inn another night or two. If you try to go anywhere, Mister Jenks, I'll have you overtaken and arrested long before that cart of yours can get as far as Harlow, let alone to Kent with your load of spices.'

I decide to go and take a look at the stable before I do anything else. Mister Jenks is right. That's a very nice mare. Not cheap. On the way back, I meet Ben in the yard.

'Another quick word with you as constable,' I say. 'Mister Jenks is not to leave for London until I say he can.'

'Yes, I heard you giving him a hard time.'

'No harder than he deserved. You might like to warn your customers that, when questioned by a magistrate, they should tell the whole truth straight away, not let it out in dribs and drabs. Nothing makes a justice of the peace more suspicious than the realisation they've been told only half the story.'

'Look, Jenks has stopped here often, like I say. I'd be happy to vouch for him. He's a decent man.'

'Plenty of murders are committed by decent men.'

'Jenks will have to pay me the usual rates for his room. You're not expecting me to run a prison for free, I trust?'

'He won't like it, but that's what he'll have to do. Tell him it could be worse. I could commit him to the village lock-up if he prefers, though you'll need to clear out any livestock that is currently in it. Apparently, though, Jenks wasn't the only person to arrive late last night. The owner of the mare in the stables did too. You didn't tell me that.'

'Didn't I?'

'No, Ben, you didn't.'

'Yes, but you don't need to talk to him. It's Mister Robinson. From Brandon Hall. A good friend of yours.' Ben pauses as if this were a complete defence to any charge. Because I show no immediate sign of agreeing with him, he feels it necessary to add: 'I know my place well enough, Sir John, not to accuse any friend of yours of murder. Wouldn't be proper, that wouldn't.'

That Robinson is also one of his customers, and has yet to pay him, probably weighs more heavily with Ben than my feelings or the general reputation of the gentry. As for friends of mine committing murder, Robinson would not be the first. I did after all spend some years as a spy.

'Is Mister Robinson still in his chamber?' I ask.

'No, he went over to the Big House to find Sir Felix.'

I consider all of this. So, the mystery rider that Jenks heard was Umfraville's sworn enemy. The man whom Umfraville had threatened to deprive of his home and his livelihood. Has Jenks suddenly become no more than the second most likely murderer in the village?

'I'd better go back to the Big House,' I say. 'I need to talk to my good friend Mister Robinson.'

'And Mister Umfraville's body? What is to become of that?'

'It'll be fine in the orchard for a bit longer,' I say. 'One of the Umfraville sons was watching over it. Could you send your stable boy over to Saffron Walden, though, to inform the coroner and ask if he wants to see the body this morning? Oh, and your boy can say to Thatcher that I have scarcely laid a finger on it, let alone moved it. It's all his, in pristine condition.'

Chapter 3

In which we return Mister William Robinson's hospitality

I arrive at the Big House (as the manor is universally known in the village) to find Sir Felix and Aminta in the drawing room, conversing in a friendly way, over cakes and cups of chocolate, with the man most likely to have killed Hubert Umfraville.

'Ah, John!' says Sir Felix. 'We hoped you would return soon. Breakfast has just been served. What did you discover at the New House?'

'I regret to confirm that your prospective tenant is sadly dead before he could sign the lease,' I say. 'Bludgeoned with an old axe that should not have been left out in the orchard. You might like to have a word with your gardener.'

'How very unfortunate for everyone concerned. I assume you have as usual examined the body with great care and can tell me to the minute when Umfraville died?'

'I have followed the directions of Mister Thatcher,' I say. 'I have hardly touched the body and have very properly sent for the appropriate official to come and tell me what I already know.'

'I am not sure on what basis Thatcher claims the right to examine a body before you do,' he says. 'It is true that in the distant past the office of coroner was held in much higher esteem than it is now, and that the coroner did some of the work that now falls to you. But, from my own time as a magistrate, I can think of no statute that supports his view. Thatcher always seems to me to stand a little too much on his own dignity and to spend too much time reading old law books that would be better used for kindling.'

'Well,' says Aminta, 'I personally have never shared my husband's enthusiasm for corpses. I am pleased rather than otherwise that the coroner is so insistent that John should simply let him do his job as he wishes – Thatcher's wife can wash the mud and blood off his clothes as easily as the servants here can wash John's.'

'But you have identified some witnesses?' Sir Felix asks me. 'That at least is your undoubted right and duty.'

'I have temporarily detained the carter who brought the Umfravilles' goods from London. He had an altercation with Hubert Umfraville. Blows were exchanged – hard enough blows to leave marks on both of them. And Jenks confesses to a strong dislike of the plantation owner. Whether Jenks is actually the murderer remains to be seen, but I need to keep him in the village for the moment.'

I had almost forgotten that Robinson was with us. In spite of his size he has the ability to be almost invisible. I hear an audible sigh of relief as he puts his cup down on the table. Almost immediately he has the decency to look repentant. 'I'm sorry,' he says. 'I wouldn't wish to speak ill of the dead of course.'

'Of course not,' I say.

'But, at the same time, I don't think that the county has lost anything by Hubert Umfraville's murder,' he adds. 'Nothing at all. He was a nasty piece of work. Lying, vindictive and malicious.'

'Well, at least he hadn't signed the lease,' says Sir Felix.

My father-in-law seems remarkably unaffected by our ride from Brandon Hall yesterday evening. He spent his youth in the saddle, riding alongside or very slightly behind Prince Rupert, depending on the qualities of their respective mounts. He fought in some of Rupert's victories and most of his defeats. He has never ceased to ride daily, whenever he could afford to keep or borrow a horse. I, conversely, often nursing unnecessary wounds acquired in Lord Arlington's service, have frequently found even short rides a trial. Sir Felix's moustache and the hair beneath his periwig are now very grey but there is more of a twinkle in his eye than there should be at his age, and there are two widows in the parish who live in hope that he may someday marry again and make one of them Lady Clifford.

He's good friends with the Robinsons, in spite of the fact that William Robinson looks, and indeed was, a natural supporter of Parliament for the duration of the war – whereas Sir Felix was a royalist through thick and thin and lost his only son at the Battle of Worcester, the last over-hopeful throw of the royalists' dice. Marius Clifford died at exactly the moment when there was no longer any point in dying for a cause that was already lost. The aftermath of the battle was a sad and confused affair. Even now, nobody knows exactly where Marius is buried. Royalist bodies were young, plentiful and much alike.

Robinson made the wiser choice and made it early. His black locks are cut just short of his collar, in the style of a pious and resolute Ironside officer of the 1640s. His face, like his body, is long and somewhat mournful. His coat and breeches are good black broadcloth, though still a little muddy from his ride last night. He has somehow scraped his chin quite badly since I saw him at supper, and some of the blood is on his very white linen collar. His hat, which he has placed on a side table, is battered. I do not know exactly what use Cromwell was able to make of him, but there is a good-humoured vagueness in Robinson's eyes that would not induce me to give him more responsibility than necessary.

He coughs, slightly self-consciously. 'As I had started to explain to your father-in-law, Sir John, that was exactly why I rode over. The question of Umfraville's unsuitability as a tenant. Not good. Not good at all, I'm afraid. After you had both departed last night, my wife Harriet and I had wondered whether we should have taken you more into our confidence over the Umfravilles . . . I mean, once we had worked out that they were your new neighbours. You clearly hadn't connected the two things. It wasn't just a matter of any enmity to ourselves . . . it was also that they have a reputation for not paying bills that predates even their departure for the Barbadoes. It seemed possible that you might sign the lease first thing this morning. Harriet therefore urged me to ride after you at once and warn you, but sadly my horse stumbled on the road, just where it passes through the woods, throwing me.' He rubs his chin with a rueful smile. 'By the time I had recovered from the fall and found my hat . . . and the mare of course, which if anything I needed rather more than my hat . . . I knew I was too far behind. But I pressed on anyway.

47

Forti nihil dificile! There was always the hope that you might have met some accident too . . . not that I desired that in any way, of course. I merely meant that I could then . . .' He waves his large, awkward hands in a way that might suggest in equal measure regret for our hypothetical accident and his inability to catch us. 'Well,' he continues, 'since you *most happily* met with no check, I failed to overtake you. Not wishing to trouble your servants so late at night, I resolved to put up at the inn, intending to speak to you as soon as you were awake. And here I am now. I absolutely do not rejoice at Umfraville's death . . . I cannot stress that too strongly . . . but I was pleased to hear that no lease had yet been signed. That is a blessing for which I give my most fervent thanks to God. Could I trouble you for some more of that delicious cake, Lady Grey?'

Sir Felix nods thoughtfully. That God should intervene to save a member of the English gentry a little money is no more than he would have expected. 'I was very slow last night in my understanding,' he says. 'Or perhaps I am getting a little deaf. At all events, I hadn't realised you knew the Umfravilles. You talked of cousin Hubert, of course, William, but you are right: I simply didn't connect the two things.'

I wonder to what extent this is a bare-faced lie and whether Sir Felix simply decided last night not to spoil a perfectly good supper, with excellent wine, by unnecessarily mentioning some awkwardness for which he was personally responsible. On balance, probably that. Any counterargument that it would have been more responsible to have told Robinson at once is now happily negated by Umfraville's death.

'I did understand, of course, but was uncertain what it would be right to tell you,' says Robinson with slightly greater honesty and much greater embarrassment. 'There was no reason to involve you in our family disputes.'

'Very considerate of you,' says Sir Felix magnanimously.

'So, what is the origin of your quarrel with the Umfravilles?' I ask.

Robinson, thinking that the discussion on the Umfravilles was done, has filled his mouth with cake. His answer to my question is therefore delivered with an accompanying shower of crumbs. 'Umfraville may have represented himself to you, Sir Felix, as being an old royalist supporter. And he did indeed volunteer to fight for the King at the very beginning of the war. But the first time he was obliged to engage in an actual battle, at the royalist defeat at Newbury back in '43, he turned on his heels and ran. Facing court martial, and a number of debts that he had no intention of paying, he left for the Barbadoes, where an unsuspecting governor, seeing that he was an English gentleman with some knowledge of Latin and Greek, welcomed him and facilitated his purchase of a large plot of land, where he initially grew tobacco.'

'Nothing so far seems to be a cause for enmity,' I say. 'You could not have been the cause of his running away at Newbury.'

'No, I didn't fight at Newbury . . . though, yes, I do see what you mean. The decision to run was his and his alone. But I really need to explain about Brandon Hall, don't I? Sir Brandon Lucas, who previously owned it, was the very last of a long line, stretching back to the reign of Edward the Third – and further, I suppose, because that ancestor must have come from somewhere. I mean, we're all ultimately descended from Adam and Eve, though some of us must surely be descended from Adam and his first wife, Lilith? I admit that I was never clear exactly where she fitted in with things and our vicar just looked puzzled when I even mentioned her. Anyway, Sir Brandon had previously made it known that his intention, in the absence of any Lucases more closely related to him, was to leave the Hall to Hubert Umfraville, a great nephew and descendant through the female line of past owners. But Hubert's support for the King and his behaviour at Newbury put an end to that. The Hall was left to my father, a cousin in some lesser degree but a solid parliamentarian with two sons – one of whom was me, of course – fighting for Cromwell. My father inherited the Hall in 1655 without challenge, Hubert being absent and wholly ignorant that he was no longer heir. When he eventually discovered his loss, he concluded that only a plot of the most devious nature could explain what had happened. Perhaps ill-wishers had exaggerated the extent of his poltroonery at Newbury, though that would have been difficult. Or perhaps Sir Brandon had changed his will under the influence of witchcraft. These seemed to Hubert to be reasonable explanations for his otherwise inexplicable disinheritance. He determined to get the Hall back at any cost, though his natural idleness delayed his plans for some years.'

'He may have resented that he was disinherited,' I say, 'but there would have been little he could have done about it. Unless the Hall was entailed, which seems not to have been the case, Sir Brandon had every right to leave it to anyone he wished to leave it to. He didn't need to explain himself or have a good reason. There is no suggestion that the will was improperly made or that the testator was not in his right mind?'

'Absolutely not.'

'Then you have nothing to fear.'

Robinson hunches his tall frame over a cup of chocolate and takes a very cautious sip. 'That is not entirely true,' he says. 'I told you that my father had two sons fighting for Cromwell? My brother, Alfred, later worked as one of Cromwell's secretaries.'

'Many of us worked for the Republic,' I say. 'I believe I have been more or less forgiven for my own support for the Lord Protector, though Lord Arlington occasionally reminds me of it when he wants me to do something unusually dangerous or unscrupulous for the King.'

'There are, as you know, many carefully graded degrees of complicity with the former regime. One of Alfred's duties was to assist in drafting the charges levelled at the King when he was tried and executed.'

'Ah,' I say.

'He was therefore, at the King's Restoration, listed amongst the regicides – those whom the King can forgive under no circumstances and who must be found and executed, come what may, in revenge for his father's death.'

'But from what you say, Alfred is still alive?'

'He has been in hiding in the Barbadoes under an assumed name. Indeed, he has prospered there as a trader. Made a new life for himself. Umfraville had discovered his identity. He was threatening to expose him.'

'You mean, expose him to my patron, Lord Arlington?'

'I suppose so . . .' Robinson seems to have realised, a little too late, that he may have made a mistake in confiding his regicide brother's secret hiding place to somebody who is both a magistrate and one of Arlington's creatures, albeit a lapsed creature.

'Let me reassure you that I never accepted any commission from my Lord to hunt down exiled supporters of the Republic,' I say. 'I should find the work distasteful. We have seen more than enough deaths of men who simply tried to serve their country honestly. Moreover, even if Lord Arlington thought your brother's execution would ingratiate him yet further to the King, Barbados is a long way away and the budget for espionage not remotely as large as he would like. But I can see that Umfraville could have destroyed your brother's happy existence by reporting him to the Barbados authorities. What did Umfraville want in return for his silence? That you surrender Brandon Hall to him?'

'No. Though he began by demanding the return of the Hall outright, I got the impression that his real wishes were somewhat different. He desired to conceal himself in Essex, every bit as much as Alfred has concealed himself in the Barbadoes. He wanted to live here comfortably without attracting too much attention. He also wanted to avoid the effort of managing an estate such as Brandon – something which, judging by his lack of success in the West Indies, may have been beyond him anyway. What he was currently demanding was an annuity, funded from the revenues of the estate. He would live in Clavershall West, reasonably close by, to see that the money was paid regularly and that I kept my side of the bargain. Of course, as Harriet pointed out when I suggested that we might try to reach an accommodation with him, the villain could raise his price at any time. He would have been in a perfect position to know when we prospered and when we did not, and what we could afford. All he had to do was ride over occasionally and inspect our fields and our crops. He could have bled us dry without raising a finger, almost.'

I have to admire Umfraville's strategy as being well suited to a relatively lazy but determined blackmailer. That isn't, however, the most interesting part of Robinson's account.

'To conceal himself?' I say. 'Did he expect his enemies in Barbados to pursue him here?'

'Apparently,' says Robinson. 'Though I cannot say who they might have been.'

'He would seem to have defrauded a number of people in Barbados,' says Aminta. 'Mistress Umfraville certainly said he could not go back without risking arrest.'

'Clavershall West would be a long way to come to get revenge,' I say.

'Not if he had behaved to others as he behaved to me,' says Robinson. 'But God be praised! A dark cloud has been lifted from our house and perhaps from others too. Hubert Umfraville is dead. And I, for my part, bless the virtuous hand that slew him!'

A long silence follows this loud, fervent exclamation. Again, Robinson is wondering whether he has made his meaning a little too clear to a magistrate investigating a murder.

'How did you get that cut on your chin?' I ask.

'I said . . . I fell from my horse . . . you're not suggesting that it was in a fight with Umfraville . . .'

'Were you in a fight with him?'

'I give you my word, Sir John – as a gentleman and as a loyal friend and as a neighbour. You surely would not suspect somebody with whom you supped only last night . . .'

'My constable is very much of the same mind as your own – that the local gentry do not commit murders. Especially if they are friends of mine. Sadly the law takes a less charitable view. That you entertained me and Sir Felix very well yesterday – for which I must again thank you and Harriet most kindly – does not mean that you are incapable of killing somebody who was blackmailing you and threatening to destroy your brother.'

'But I didn't kill Umfraville. I didn't even go into the orchard.'

'Are you sure you didn't?'

'Yes, of course.'

'Then how do you know the body was found in the orchard, William? Did Ben tell you?'

Robinson pauses. He knows I can check his answer with Ben.

'It's entirely your choice, William,' I add, 'but my advice would be to tell me the truth now rather than later. The whole truth.'

Robinson puts his head in his hands as if trying to come up with a good story. In the end, he doesn't, or not so that you would notice.

'It's like this,' he says. 'When I reached the New House last night, having given up any hope of seeing you straight away, I thought I should at least check whether the Umfravilles had arrived. I mean, it would be useful to know – reconnaissance is never wasted – and if they weren't there yet, I had more time than I thought. At first, I could see no lights, but then I caught a glimpse of what seemed to be a candle in one of the bedrooms. So, I reined in my horse to check properly. That was a mistake.'

'In what way?'

'Umfraville was coming up the road from the stream and accused me of spying on him. Or rather on his wife, since she was the only one in the bedroom at that moment, as he carefully explained to me. Naturally, I felt very foolish. It was unexpectedly difficult to account for what I was doing. Outside his house like that. I mean, I could have said that I was in the village to tell his landlord that he was a rogue and an unsuitable tenant. But I wasn't sure that was a good idea.

So, I just apologised and went on my way. I didn't tell him who I was, obviously.'

'That's all?"

'Yes.'

'Sorry, but that still doesn't explain how you knew he was murdered in the orchard.'

'No, it doesn't, does it? Well, there is some more, and I'm not very proud of that either. When I finally got to the inn, I decided that I had acted in a most craven manner – apologising to him as if I were at fault rather than he. Not saying who I was. I should have had the whole thing out with him . . . I mean, in spite of the business with the windows, which was an irrelevance, when you think about it. To cut a long story short, I went back, on foot this time, so that I could confront him. Deal with him man to man. As I should have done before.'

'Had you had any of Ben's ale in the meantime?'

'Just one pint. It's quite strong, isn't it? The lights were all off in the house but I thought I heard voices in the orchard. Then I heard a sort of cry, then complete silence, then footsteps, running fast. I didn't see who it was. Maybe more than one person. I could hear their legs brushing against the grass very clearly. I decided it was a bad time to visit. Awkward for everyone. I went back to the road.'

'You had sobered up by then?'

'Yes.'

'And so, with a clear head, you then went straight to the manor to report to the magistrate that you had witnessed a murder and that the murderer – perhaps even more than one – was presumably still in the village?'

'Well, obviously not, because you'd know about it if I

had . . . oh, you mean that's what I should have done. Yes, I see. Well, I wasn't sure what I had witnessed – not at all – or whether anyone would believe me. I mean, it was probably nothing, in which case I'd have been wasting your time. On the other hand, if Umfraville was dead, they'd think I was the killer, wouldn't they? Otherwise, what was I doing there at half past one in the morning? Outside the house of somebody who was blackmailing me. So, I just returned to the inn and my bed. To think things over.'

'You didn't mention the incident to Ben, who happens to be the village constable as well as the innkeeper?'

'He'd gone to bed himself. It was very late.'

Well, I doubt that Ben would have been overjoyed to have to start a hue and cry in the small hours. Ben is not the most enthusiastic of public guardians. I try to recall when he last made an arrest of any sort.

There is a knock on the door and Ben marches in looking very pleased with himself.

'While you've been talking to your friend Mister Robinson,' he says, 'I've made an arrest. I've found the real murderer and detained him at the inn, with the help of two of the Grice brothers, who'd developed a very urgent thirst and happened to be in the parlour.'

'Does your prisoner have a name?'

'Daniel Flood.'

'And how do you know he's the murderer?' I ask.

'First of all,' says Ben, 'I caught him in my hayloft, where he'd been hiding all night, instead of paying for a bed like an honest man.'

'You have only two chambers and they were both occupied,' I say.

'An honest man, assuming he didn't want to share a bed with another traveller, would have asked how much to sleep in the hayloft, wouldn't he? It's comfortable up there. More comfortable than the chambers, actually.'

'Very well,' I say.

'Second of all, he looks like a murderer – rough fellow, unshaven, scar on his face.'

'I have a scar on my face,' I say.

'Ever killed anyone?'

'Only when undertaking work for Arlington.'

Ben nods, his point made.

'It still doesn't mean he killed Umfraville,' I say.

'Third of all,' says Ben, holding up three fingers, 'he was in possession of papers showing that he is from the Barbadoes. That, you will have to admit, is a bit of a coincidence. Not just a foreign place, of which there are apparently several, but actually the Barbadoes. And, fourth of all, when I showed him the proof I had, he admitted that he had business with the Umfraville family, and he won't tell me what, for all that I'm a constable with a right to know such things. I'd say he was our man, wouldn't you?'

We all look at the hand Ben is now holding aloft. As these things go, four fingers of proof isn't bad.

'Is Flood still at the inn?' I ask.

'Unless he's bribed the Grices with ale.'

'Which of the Grices have you left him with?'

'Nathan and Jacob.'

'I'd better come and have a talk with him straight away,' I say.

'So, may I return to Brandon Hall?' asks Robinson meekly. Again, I'd forgotten he was even there in the room with us.

'I'm sorry, William,' I say. 'I'll need to ask you some more questions. At the very least, you seem to have witnessed a murder from a cautious distance. At the worst . . . well, we'll deal with the worst later. You can stay here at the Big House. Think of it as my returning your hospitality. We'll have a footman ride over to Brandon Hall to let your wife know, without worrying her too much, that you will be detained a little longer than you thought on the matter of the Umfravilles. Right, Ben. Let's see how your non-paying customer explains why he is in Clavershall West rather than in His Majesty's colony of Barbados.'

Chapter 4

In which the profession of slave catcher is explained to me and is justified as an honest, necessary and humane form of employment

Young Nathan and Jacob are drinking in a companionable way with the prisoner. They are huddled together at a table in the corner of the inn – the same table at which I formerly drank with their now deceased brother Dickon. Dickon Grice has been buried in the village churchyard since shortly after he decided to shoot me in the back. In those days I was working for the Republic trying to eliminate royalist plotters of the sort that Dickon, slightly to my surprise, turned out to be. I didn't kill him myself, but that's never been a distinction that the Grices have bothered to make. Plenty of other people have since tried to shoot or stab or bludgeon me to death. I lost count some years ago. I mention poor Dickon only to explain why Nathan and Jacob just nod briefly in my direction as I enter the low-ceilinged room. If I was them, I wouldn't feel obliged to raise my hat to their late brother's friend either, even if he is now lord of the manor.

'Good morning, Nathan. Good morning, Jacob,' I say.

'Good day, Sir John,' says Nathan, for both of them it would seem.

'Is your prisoner treating you well?' I ask.

'We've no complaints,' says Nathan.

That's probably about four pints each, then. Flood must have been wondering whether another sixpence or so would secure his escape. The still-full half-pint tankard in front of him suggests that he has been keeping his own head clear. Not that the Grices would care one way or the other if he wanted to take a stroll.

I release them from guard duties and they wander outside, stretching their arms and legs as if after an honest day's work.

'So, Mister Flood,' I ask the Grices' new patron, 'what brings you to Essex and what were you doing hiding in Ben's hayloft?'

'I don't have to tell you that, Mister Magistrate.'

'Then you'll stay where you are until you do.'

'You can't keep me here,' he says.

'You're the third person to say that to me today, and the other two are still in the village. So, I think I probably can keep you here if I want to.'

'Keep me here, then. I don't need to tell you anything. John Lilburne established that in 1638. By law I have a fundamental natural right to be silent.'

'That's the John Lilburne who spent most of his life in prison or in exile?'

'That's the John Lilburne who was a better man than you are, Mister Magistrate. It's the John Lilburne who wrote

An Agreement of the People of England, and the places therewith incorporated, for a secure and present peace, upon grounds of common right, freedom and safety.'

'You are entitled to your views. I would merely remind you that it is the King rather than John Lilburne who is currently detaining you. The King may or may not have the same views on common rights, freedom and safety.'

'I don't need to bow and scrape to a country justice of the peace.'

'That's something we can agree on, at least,' I say. 'But you do need to tell me what you are doing here. There has been a murder.'

'Yes, the constable told me. Hubert Umfraville. Well, it makes no difference to me.'

'It will make a great deal of difference to you if you are hanged for it. Umfraville was from Barbados. Ben says you are too. And that you had business with the family.'

'Your constable discovered that illegally. He seized private papers of mine, without a warrant to authorise the seizure. He had no right to do it. I want them back now. Otherwise I shall obtain a writ of *quo warranto* to oblige him to restore them to me.'

'I'll make sure they are returned in due course to you or to your executors, depending on how things work out. As for the writ, I don't think you know what it is or where you'd get one. So, why are you here, Mister Flood? If it wasn't to kill Umfraville, what on earth brings you from Barbados to Essex?'

'I'm a slave catcher, not that it's any concern of yours. My business here is legal and respectable.'

'Slave catcher? You call that a respectable occupation?'

'More respectable than being a royal lackey as you apparently are. Shame on you as an enemy of the people.' Flood gives me a crooked grin. 'He's named Nero, the one I'm after. He fled the Umfraville estate when they left. But he'd already been sold to another owner along with the rest of the plantation. His new master – that's Mister Greengrass – wants him back. He also wants the thirty-odd slaves Nero caused to escape at the same time, but I'm retained only to find Nero.'

'You've come a long way for one slave.'

'That shows how little you understand these things, Mister Magistrate. Nero's a lettered slave, as you might say. Mulatto – that's half English, half African. Educated to read and write and keep accounts. Used to be the Umfravilles' steward. He knows things that his new owner needs to know. How things work on the estate. What crops can be planted where. Who can be trusted. Who needs to be watched. Greengrass is a good man, but he doesn't know a Mandingo from a Coromantine. So, Nero's worth a deal more to him than you might think. Worth a whole shipload of ordinary slaves.'

'And you believe he's fled here? Why? Surely he would wish to avoid his former master at all costs?'

Flood's grin is a little too wide for somebody with such bad teeth. 'I tried to find Umfraville in London, thinking he might be willing to assist me for a share of the profit. But I missed him. Well, I thought, that was his loss. The one thing I did pick up, though, at some lodgings Umfraville had stayed at, was that he was heading for a place called Clavershall West. Didn't seem worth coming all this way just to talk to Hubert Umfraville, then the following day, asking after the runaway, somebody told me that they'd encountered a Moor who had mentioned the very same place to him. And it sounded as if he was planning to come out that way soon. Well, I thought to myself, that can't be a coincidence. Now, to the untutored eye, like his and indeed your own, a Moor and a mulatto are much of a muchness, so I didn't doubt I'd found my man. Nero had clearly decided to chase after Umfraville to get his revenge. You look surprised? Don't expect to find loyalty or gratitude in a slave, Mister Magistrate. Umfraville fed him, clothed him, housed him, taught him his letters so he could better himself. So, yes, why shouldn't he come over to England and try to kill his kind benefactor?' He shakes his head sorrowfully at the wickedness of the world.

'You expect somebody to be grateful for being enslaved?'

'Nobody enslaved him. To be enslaved you have to be born free. Nero was born a slave. For him, slavery is his natural state. It's what he's used to. It is the station in life to which God has called him. He'd be as unhappy free as we would be if we were slaves. Returning him to his home is a kindness – an act of Christian charity.'

'And if he tells you otherwise?'

'He still has to go back to Barbados. It's the law. It's not in my power or his or yours to change the law, Mister Magistrate. I wish I could do it for him, I really do, but I can't – not for any money. I am the slave of the law every bit as much as Nero is a slave of Mister Greengrass. What you must understand is that Nero is just property – a chattel that can be bought with cash. He's a brief line in the credit column of an accounts book, and when he dies his only epitaph will be a balancing line in the debit column. If Mister Greengrass's watch had been stolen he would be entitled to have it returned. If a customer owed him money, he would have a right to have the debt enforced by the courts. He is entitled to have his slave restored to him. Because, if that wasn't the case – if some property was protected and some not – what use would the law be to any one of us? You should be assisting me – not detaining me here unlawfully. I ought to report you to the Sheriff for dereliction of duty.'

'The Sheriff will tell you, as I am telling you now: English law does not recognise slavery.'

'I think you'll find it doesn't ban it either. Unless you can tell me the name of the statute that does. No? Didn't think so. That's because there isn't one. And the law does recognise the rights of property. All property. I've advertised in London for information about him. A Guinea reward for the man, woman or child who helps me catch him. It's the standard rate – I'm not the sort who would try to cheat anyone of anything. Honest as the day is long – that's me. But Nero has feloniously fled instead of remaining there to be caught as any decent man should. Tell you what I'll do – because, like I say, I'm a fair and reasonable fellow. When I do find him – and I promise you I will – Nero can get himself a lawyer and go to court and prove he's a free man. All right? Or, if he doesn't want to go to the expense and trouble of litigation, he can come along quietly with me. I'll take him somewhere he can have a nice comfortable bed, smart clothes and two square meals a day, all free of charge. I know which I'd do if I were him.'

I know what I'd do too, and it wouldn't be to accompany Flood anywhere, not even for a bowl of corn pone, a lousy straw mattress and a pair of canvas breeches.

'Your problem, Mister Flood,' I say, 'is that if Nero has killed Umfraville, as you claim he was intending to, then you won't be able to take him anywhere.'

Flood shakes his head and laughs at my error. 'I said he

might be trying to. I didn't say he had. Anyway, the Grice brothers tell me you have no idea who the killer is and have already arrested two people for the same crime.'

Well, he has a point there. Perhaps it's time to return to the real subject of our conversation.

'Where were you last night, Mister Flood?' I ask.

'In the hayloft. Hasn't the constable told you?'

'From what hour?'

'I don't know exactly.'

'What a shame that you didn't ask Ben's permission before you snuggled down in the hay. He might have provided your alibi. As it is, you don't have one.'

'Alibi? You can't possibly think I killed Umfraville.'

'You've admitted you knew him, though. You were actually trying to find him in London.'

Flood considers this carefully. 'Of course I knew him. Why should I pretend otherwise? It's a small island. He's lived in Holetown for over twenty years. He grew tobacco when the other planters were growing tobacco. He employed indentured Englishmen and Irishmen in those days. Killed most of them with overwork in the hot sun. He switched to sugar when everyone else switched to sugar and got himself some slaves when everyone else was getting themselves some slaves. Looked after them a bit better because they're not so cheap to replace. But all the smallholders like Umfraville are being bought out now by the big plantation owners. He was a disgrace to the colony and it was surprising he lasted as long as he did. But as for killing him ... it must be clear to you that I gain nothing by his death except maybe more work and more trouble, because Umfraville might have helped me a bit with Nero. But no, he can't even stay alive long enough to do his duty by me. So, I'm the loser here, as I so often have been in my life, Mister Magistrate. I am the poor victim, not the perpetrator. You can't charge me with Umfraville's murder any more than you can charge my Nero.'

'And when did you arrive in Barbados, Mister Flood?'

'When did I *arrive* there? What's that got to do with anything?'

'Just answer the question.'

'Me? I came over in 1660.'

'When the King returned to England?'

'It seemed best. I wasn't expecting to be much in sympathy with the new regime.'

'You feared arrest over here?'

'No honest man is safe when there are kings strutting in their palaces.'

'I assume you're still a republican, then?'

'Unlike you and your constable, I'm nobody's lackey. Look, I still don't see what this has got to do with Umfraville's murder. I had no quarrel with the man's politics, royalist though he claimed to be. And I told you: I'm after an escaped slave, not his former master.'

'So you say. But I still have no good evidence that that is the case. You claim to be a respectable slave catcher – a pillar of Barbadian society. But you seem, on the face of it, to be an extreme republican, an enemy of the State, sleeping uninvited in Ben's hayloft – a common vagrant with no money to pay your way.'

He looks at me. 'Oh, I see. It's like that, is it? A question of money. I should have guessed. How much do you want to release me, Mister Magistrate? Half a crown for you and sixpence for your constable? I might run to that.'

'Is the lock-up empty?' I ask Ben.

'I got the pigs out but I haven't had time to clean it yet.'

'Don't worry about cleaning it. The pigs prefer it as it is.' I go to the door and find that the Grice brothers have not gone far. 'Nathan ... Jacob ... you'll very kindly give Ben a hand in taking Mister Flood to his new quarters.'

Nathan and Jacob look at each other and shrug. Flood's clearly not going to be buying beer for anyone for a while. And there must be a shilling or two in their new assignment. They stroll back into the parlour and place themselves in an easy way on either side of the prisoner.

'You can't do this,' says Flood, but it's pretty obvious to everyone that I can.

'Ben,' I say, 'let me know immediately you hear from the coroner. Yes? In which case, gentlemen, I think that covers everything for the moment. And now I really must return to the New House. They'll be wondering where I am. And I have rather more questions for them than I first thought.'

Chapter 5

In which I learn a little about the home life of the Umfraville
family

Aminta has reached the New House before me, and has
clearly come bearing gifts. I find her in the parlour
with three ladies that I have not met before but who must
be the senior Mistress Umfraville, her elder daughter Mary
and the adopted Drusilla. Aminta has been there long enough
for Drusilla to have accepted and donned a very presentable
grey woollen dress with a white linen collar. It suits her almost
as well as it suited Aminta, though the mother still clearly
regards it with suspicion. Perhaps Mistress Umfraville plans
to have new dresses made for herself and Mary in Saffron
Walden. If so, she will soon realise how much better attired
Drusilla now is.

I offer my condolences to the Umfravilles and my apologies
for having deserted the family earlier.

'My return to the inn was even more urgent than I thought,'
I add. 'In the end I had to detain three possible suspects before

they could leave the village. The carter who brought your goods had come to blows with Mister Umfraville after he left the house. William Robinson, whose name may possibly be familiar to you as the owner of Brandon Hall, also had a late-night encounter with him.'

Mary gives a brief and entirely understandable gasp at this, but is silenced by a glance from her mother.

'And finally,' I say, 'there is Mister Flood, a gentleman from Barbados who seems unreasonably proud of his vocation as a slave catcher and whose recent arrival here is, to say the least, a remarkable coincidence. You may know him too?'

'Ah, Flood ... unfortunately, we do know him a little,' says Mistress Umfraville apologetically. 'Not a pleasant man. No friend of my husband's, but then few people were. I am surprised he has risked coming to England. He fled to Barbados, fearing for his life, when the King came in again. He was an uncompromising republican. Even Cromwell regarded him with suspicion and disgust.'

'He claims to be chasing one of your husband's former slaves – Nero. He had hoped your husband might help him.'

'Flood has actually seen Nero here?'

'No, he merely heard a rumour that he was following you, perhaps seeking revenge against your husband.'

'Seeking revenge? Even by Flood's standards that is nonsense. Nero had no cause to wish Hubert harm. In any case, Nero would know that Essex would be a poor place for a mulatto to hide from those who might seek to recapture him. He'd stand out like a robed and mitred bishop in a country ale house. He would be much better advised to remain in London, if he has reached England at all. It is such a shame that Flood will have had a wasted journey.'

'You think Nero could easily find employment in London?'
'Little about my husband had any value, Sir John, but Nero
is the exception. He had a better head for figures than any of
us, a better understanding of how a plantation should work.
Half English, half African, he was able to live in both worlds.
He was my husband's eyes and ears. Call him a spy if you
like. Of course, you were one yourself and will be aware of the
strange ironies of the spy's existence. You are trusted by your
master, who knows that you do things on his behalf that are
utterly untrustworthy.'

'Yes,' I say.

Trust is indeed a strange thing. I could, if I wished, tell Lord
Arlington that I know where one of the last living regicides is
hiding. But I have no intention of doing so. Of course, I was
only ever an occasional spy, employed as needed, paid when
Arlington could delay payment no longer. But perhaps all
spies believe that they are an exceptional case: a rare honest
man amongst a pack of rogues.

Mistress Umfraville smiles indulgently at my past life. 'So,
I do understand why you in particular might suspect Nero of
duplicity. But you would be wrong. He was utterly devoted to
my husband, who in turn placed his complete confidence in
him. It is not surprising that Greengrass should be demanding
Nero's repatriation and be prepared to pay Flood well for it.
Nero was half the value of the plantation almost. Without
Nero, the plantation was a cannon with no gunpowder,
an oven with no faggots, a well with no bucket. As for his
actually being a slave, however . . . my husband treated Nero
as a free man and had fully intended to sign manumission
papers to make that a legal fact. But Hubert was ever slow to
do something useful.'

Mary wrinkles her nose. 'I never trusted him,' she says. 'I thought him far too familiar for a mere servant. I'm sure Nero stole money from us. He was forever jingling coins in his pocket.'

Drusilla opens her mouth as if to correct her sister, but then thinks better of it. Her loyalties too must be complex.

'There is nothing to be gained,' says Mistress Umfraville, 'by chasing after Nero.'

'Then do you know of anyone else who might have wished your husband dead?' I ask Mistress Umfraville.

'In Barbados, yes, my husband had many enemies. But we had thought him safe in Essex. He thought he would be safe too. He was clearly wrong.'

I nod. After all, Robinson had also implied that Umfraville was hoping for safety by living quietly in England. That much seems agreed by all.

'He was afraid he would be attacked if he remained in Barbados?' I ask.

'Of course,' says Mistress Umfraville. 'And not merely by his fellow plantation owners. You might think, Sir John, that slaves fear their masters — and rightly. The masters can have their estate workers whipped. They can put them in spiked collars and chains. They can imprison them in dungeons dug into the red earth. They can kill them for any reason at all, if they are willing to pay a trifling fine. The law of the sugar plantations is that the slaves should be made to cower. But the owners also tremble before the slaves. You must not forget that. When my husband first arrived in Barbados there were twenty thousand stout English and Irish and no more than a few hundred African slaves. Twenty-five years later, there are as many slaves as there are English. Soon we shall be outnumbered, if we are not already. Every time a new slave ship arrives, our people's eyes light up with greed, but at the same time an ice-cold shiver runs down their spines. How many more can they bring in before the enslaved decide they are strong enough to rise up against their enslavers and throw us back into the salt waves from which we came? You cannot load a slave with chains when he works in the fields, Sir John. He cannot cut cane without a stout knife that will also cut throats. All you can do is watch him in the cane fields and listen outside his door at nights. But every evening at the supper table the whole company would stare wide eyed at the window when they heard uninvited footsteps approach in the dark. Hard bare feet slapping on the dirt path.'

'Surely if you merely treated your people with kindness . . .' says Aminta.

'There is no tradition of kindness on the plantations, Lady Grey. Those who came out as indentured labour, as soon as they were freed and in possession of land themselves, treated their workers as they had been treated when they were unfree. That tiny mustard seed of cruelty, once sown, could not be weeded out. The planters determined that, if they could not be kind, they would be strong, and if they could not be strong and good, they would be strong and bad.'

'We treated our slaves well enough,' says Mary. 'Better than on any other plantation in Barbados, I should say.'

'Other plantations lacked a Nero,' says Mistress Umfraville. 'He quietly forgot to carry out many a flogging that your father ordered. Well, I must not keep you from your work, Sir John. Might my husband's body at least now be carried somewhere more suitable? George has been watching over it but it would be better inside the house. I do not like the thought of it on the worm-filled ground, amongst those ghostly shadows.'

'I'm afraid it can't be moved anywhere until the coroner arrives,' I say. 'But I shall go to the orchard next and see George before I return to the inn. I need to speak to him again.'

'I have told Drusilla that she may visit our library and borrow whatever books she would like to read,' Aminta says to me. 'Mistress Umfraville has kindly raised no objection to this plan, even though it takes Drusilla away from her chores here. So, if you will all excuse us, we shall walk back to the Big House together. There is a chill in the air, but fortunately I think the two of us are now both well enough dressed for it, are we not, Drusilla?'

Hubert Umfraville's body has been covered over with an old linen sheet. It has become an obscure object, off-white, the length and the width of a man. The axe still lies close by, since the coroner will doubtless wish to examine it. If it is judged to be the murder weapon, then, by law, it will become the property of the King – a deodand. I'm sure His Majesty will find a good use for it.

A late, unseasonal fly is buzzing around the sheeting, but if the new coroner wants to view a sweet-smelling corpse then he must ride quickly. As Mistress Umfraville foresaw, the shadows still play around the orchard floor, rippling across the sheeting. Again, just for a moment, I think I see his arm move, but the breeze drops and Hubert Umfraville is quietly dead again, as he should be.

George is standing guard in this strange twilight world – or rather he is sitting with his back against a tree, reading a book. Butler's *Hudibras*, as it happens. He looks up when he hears my footsteps, and tips his hat back to observe me better. I explain who I have so far detained and why his father will have to wait where he is a little longer.

'So Flood is here?' George replies, rising to his feet and closing the small leatherbound volume. 'And he tells you Nero is too?'

'Yes, I have only his word for it that your father's slave may be in Essex. Your mother doubted it, for what seemed to me to be very good reasons. As an escaped slave, he would be safer in London. But she said that your father intended formally to free Nero?'

'It is Nero's misfortune that he did not do so before we were obliged to sell everything we owned. While we were in Barbados and still had credit, the matter did not seem urgent. Everyone understood the position. Nobody would have thought it in any way odd to see Nero, in an old and roomy suit of clothes of my father's, riding down the hill to the harbour to buy supplies. Nobody would have raised an eyebrow if they found him on the quay, inspecting the latest consignment of slaves, conversing with them in their own languages in a way that neither the ship's captain nor the plantation owners ever could. Perhaps even up to last night my father could have gone to a lawyer – to you, indeed – and made a declaration that Nero was a free man. But his death, on top of the forced sale of the estate and its contents, confuses things a great deal. Nothing I could sign as my father's heir could prove that Nero was a free man before the plantation was transferred to Greengrass. That is a stroke of luck for Flood, when you think about it.'

'Your mother said that Nero could not possibly be suspected of killing your father?'

'I would suspect you, Sir John, before I suspected Nero.

He was a member of the family. Had we kept the plantation, rather than drunk it away, Nero and I would have worked hand in hand to improve it. And we'd have succeeded. There were locusts in '63, the great hurricane of '67, drought in '68 and ruinous rains in '69. But the bank was amiable and the prospects were good. We could and should have survived. Others did. Yet my father still found a way to throw away the effort that James and Nero and I had put in. Eventually even Nero had to concede that we could not go on.'

'I can see you might resent that. Does James also feel aggrieved?'

'More than any of us. Didn't anyone explain that?'

'Because of the loss of his inheritance?'

'Because of the loss of the woman he wished to marry. Lucy. We left her behind with everything else.'

'I can see that James may find it difficult to return to Barbados. But could Lucy not travel to England? If James's prospects here prove good enough and she still wishes to marry, then her parents' consent might be obtained.'

George laughs. 'She's the daughter of one of the neighbouring planters. She is also his sole heir. My father sold our sugar crop to him – and simultaneously to other people. Lucy's father would scarcely wish to form an alliance with the family that defrauded him and left him looking so foolish – let alone offer the dowry that he can probably no longer afford. He'll be planning to have Lucy married to somebody else, as quickly as may be. And there will be no shortage of suitors. There's a rich old tobacco grower up on the lonely north side of the island. Now his third wife is dead, of fever or more likely of her husband's drunken rages, he'll be looking for another. No dowry required.'

'Is there no hope at all?'

'I didn't say that,' says George. 'No, I think there is hope. I wouldn't have said so yesterday, but I would today.'

We look down at the sheet-covered person on the ground. Had he lived, who would have benefited? Who would have lost? Contrary to what he would have had me believe, Flood has undoubtedly gained, in the sense that Nero was never freed as intended. Flood could not have returned a free man to Barbados. Nero's position is, by the same logic, made more precarious. As for Robinson, he has been relieved of an awkward adversary by Umfraville's death. Of that there is no doubt at all. But what about James? Is George implying that Umfraville's death may soften the resolve of Lucy's defrauded father?

'Last night,' I say, 'did James get up? Did he leave the chamber you were both in?'

'I slept too soundly to know the answer to that question, Sir John. But he didn't kill our father. He had no reason to do so.'

'Where is James now?' I ask.

'He went into the village,' says George. 'I think he was going to the inn.'

'Did he say why?'

'To get drunk, I think.'

'I'd better talk to him before he succeeds, then.'

As I leave the orchard I turn back briefly. The white shroud seems to be waving me farewell. Is the late Hubert Umfraville wishing me good luck or is he merely saying 'good riddance'? I have no idea. After all, I know him less well than I have known other murdered men that I have met. I have Thatcher to thank for that.

Chapter 6

In which James Umfraville is less than honest with me

Today the seasons hang in the balance. Fewer leaves cling to the damson tree in front of the inn than were there yesterday, but Ben has left the front door ajar and opened a couple of windows to acknowledge that winter is not yet quite upon us.

James sits at a table close to the tree, enjoying the slanting autumn sun. At this season, you never know when pleasant days will be put back in their box for another year. A battered tankard stands on the table in front of him. Ben's pint tankards come in various sizes, some notably more generous than others. This one is middling, which suggests that Ben has not made up his mind one way or the other about the youngest of the Umfraville men.

'Do you mind if I join you, Mister Umfraville?'

'Why?'

'To ask you a few questions.'

'Do I have any choice in the matter?'

'No, not really.'

'In that case I'd be truly honoured if you would sit with me, Sir John. I look forward to being both entertained and informed.'

'You have only to answer my questions in a plain manner, Mister Umfraville. If I need sarcasm there are plenty of other places I can find it, even in a village this size.'

Umfraville is still smirking at his own cleverness. I detect something of his sister Mary in him – at least when Ben's ale causes the mask of politeness to slip. I think I like him less than I like George. 'What do you want to know, then?' he demands. 'I told you, when we were walking back to the house, that I had no idea who could have killed my father.'

'You didn't tell me that your father had effectively prevented your marriage to Lucy.'

'Who told you that? George?'

'Yes.'

'It's none of his business. I had a plan to get Lucy out with our own family. George could have helped me. He chose not to.'

'Why?'

Umfraville laughs. 'Because he is the wise and prudent member of the family. He said that Lucy's disappearance, even for an hour, might have alerted a number of people to what my father was doing. He said that, if that happened, we'd probably have been ambushed on the way down to the harbour and charged with the abduction of an heiress. He was probably right. He is about most things, so he always tells me. But it would still have been worth trying.'

'You must have resented your father's actions.'

'You mean enough to kill him? I thought we'd discussed

that already. Anyway, all's not lost yet. There is certainly more cause to be hopeful now than there was yesterday.'

So, it's not only George who thinks that.

'You seem very confident,' I say.

He smiles, like a sphinx who has drunk a little too much strong ale.

'Would you like to explain why you think that?' I say.

James Umfraville looks into the distance. He has had enough of this conversation. He'd like a different one. And preferably not with me.

'Are we done with this?' he asks. 'It's just that I have a lot more beer to drink this morning. It's rather important that I get on with it. I want to do it properly.'

'We're a long way from being done,' I say. 'But I'll leave you to drown your sorrows, if that's what you think is best.'

'I'm not drowning my sorrows,' he says. 'I'm celebrating my good fortune.'

Ben stops me as I am leaving for the Big House.

'Is Mister James under arrest too, then?'

'No,' I say.

'It's just that everyone you speak to today seems to end up under lock and key. So, I thought I'd better ask.'

'I haven't finished with him yet, but I don't think he's planning to run away. Just let him get drunk, if that's what he wants to do and he has the money to pay.'

'I'm pleased to hear that, anyway. You've already got Jenks detained here and Flood in the pigsty – I mean village lock-up. And Mister Robinson at the Big House. You're running out of places to keep all your prisoners. Have you made up your mind which one you're going to commit to the assizes?'

'Not yet. Is there any sign of the coroner?'

'No. The stable boy went to fetch him but they haven't arrived yet. Hopefully they'll be here soon and Mister Thatcher will tell us what's what. In the meantime, I'd say you've got at least two innocent men under lock and key there.'

'Umfraville has been dead less than half a day, Ben. I'd rather take my time and commit the right one.'

'I suppose you're right.'

'Trust me. I'm a lawyer. You can't undo a hanging.'

'Flood's not best pleased, I'll tell you that much for nothing.'

I nod. Ben's evident unhappiness seems to arise mainly from having to deal with the slave catcher.

'How annoyed is he?' I ask.

'Have you ever trapped an adder underneath a pail, then wondered how you were going to get your pail back without being bitten?'

'No, I can't say I have.'

'Well, go down to the lock-up and you'll find out what that feels like. I should warn you, Sir John – Flood's talking habeas corpus. And, unlike that other thing he was threatening us with, I think he actually knows what it is. He says you can't keep him there without proper charges. He's probably right that I can't keep him in the lock-up. I hadn't looked at it for a while. The door's rotten and the hinges could give way at any moment.'

'Can you give him a secure room at the inn?' I ask.

'At his expense, like Jenks?'

'Of course.'

'Good. I don't do free rooms. Not even for you and the King. I'll go and collect him after dinner.'

'I'd go before dinner, or you'll miss selling him a perfectly good meal.'

'You're right as ever, Sir John. That's what a legal education does for you, I suppose. I'll need some help, though, if Flood's not to make a run for it. Like I say, the stable boy's still not back from Saffron Walden and I don't know where the Grice brothers are. They took Flood to the lock-up and then vanished off somewhere.'

'They'll be helping their mother with work on the farm.'

'Work? Them? Don't make me laugh.'

'I'll come down to the lock-up with you,' I say. 'I made you put him there, after all. I'll help you get him out.'

'That's good of you. I'm not looking forward to this.'

'Nor am I, Ben. How did you get your pail back, by the way? Just out of interest.'

'I got the Grice brothers to do it. A pint of ale apiece. They can give you a nasty bite, adders can.'

Flood is smug.

'Well, you came running pretty quickly, once your constable explained the law to you,' he says.

'I know the law, Mister Flood,' I say. 'What I needed to have explained to me was the state of these hinges. You're still going to be held securely, until we're in a position to know whether we can charge you.'

'I didn't kill Umfraville,' he says, 'and there's no way you're going to be able to convince a judge that I did. As for keeping me here, I'm not leaving without Nero anyway.'

'I said: you'll get no help from me on that.'

'I won't need you. I had a word with the Grice brothers as we walked down here. It looks as if they'll assist me for a very reasonable price, once I'm free, as I should be soon. They're good lads, the Grices. Shame about what happened to their brother, Dickon. They told me all about him. He sounded like a good lad too.'

'Most of his life I also thought that,' I say.

We reach the inn without mishap. I accompany Ben to the room in which Flood is to be detained and watch as, with a great flourish, he locks the door. We nod to each other, our duty to the King's majesty discharged. As I leave the inn again, I notice that James has finished celebrating his good fortune. His seat is now empty.

The long case-clock in the hall is striking twelve as I enter the house, but the noise from the dining room reminds me we are keeping country hours rather than London ones.

'We decided not to wait,' says Aminta. 'There were apparently one or two people in the village that you had not yet detained and, fearing you might wish to do the job properly, we started dinner without you.'

I nod at Robinson, the only suspect present, who is currently better fed than I am. Drusilla is also at the table. She must somehow have obtained permission from her mother for a longer visit – at least, she has received no orders to return. Sir Felix has inevitably invited her to sit next to him, but is on his best behaviour in his daughter's presence.

'Well, I'm here now,' I say.

'I wondered if you were bringing the coroner,' Aminta adds. 'He must need feeding.'

'If he's arrived, maybe he's gone straight to the New House. Ben sent for him, but hasn't seen him yet – at least not when we spoke at the inn. I went there to talk to James. He had planned to marry a woman called Lucy before the family left Barbados. Hubert Umfraville defrauded her father, which has caused a rift. But it would seem that James has not entirely given up hope that the marriage would be possible.'

'I am sure that James will continue to hope, because that is in his nature,' says Drusilla.

'Both he and George were more hopeful today than yesterday. Do you know what they meant? James declined to explain.'

Drusilla shakes her head apologetically. 'My father's death changes nothing, if that's what you mean.'

'It would not remove the enmity between your families?'

'Lucy's father will still resent the money he has lost. And we have no way of repaying it.'

That remains a mystery then, as do many other things. I console myself that the broad facts of the case are beyond dispute. Umfraville arrived last night and died suddenly in the orchard shortly afterwards, almost certainly at the hands of somebody who knew him.

It is at this point that I realise that an altercation is taking place in the hallway. Our steward is assuring somebody that I am at dinner but will be with them shortly. Somebody is telling our steward that he will see me at once and to stand out of his way or face the consequences. It isn't Flood's voice, but on reflection I do recognise it.

The door bursts open and a small, neatly dressed man strides into the dining room, broad-brimmed hat firmly placed on his bewigged head. It is the coroner from Saffron Walden, a kinsman of the Sheriff. He sneers briefly and economically at the various diners at my table, raises a very straight arm and aims his finger at me alone.

'Is this some sort of joke, Sir John?' he demands.

'Is what a joke, Mister Thatcher?' I enquire politely.

'I have, at the request of your constable, come all the way from Saffron Walden, where I had much to occupy me. I was told that there had been a murder. So, naturally, I abandoned everything and saddled my horse. I did not expect the basic courtesy of the local magistrate being there to greet me at the place the crime was committed. Why should I? I am used to the disrespect of magistrates in this part of the world for the ancient and once highly esteemed office of coroner. I did not expect to be offered refreshment after a long journey. I am, as I say, merely a hard-working officer of the King's trying to oblige my social superiors, not a wealthy gentleman with a grand house and deer park and time on my hands. I expected none of the things I mentioned, which is as well, for none was offered. But I did expect a corpse.'

'It's in the orchard,' I say. 'Under the sheet. I promise you I have not laid a hand on it. Or not very much. Everything is as I found it.'

'It most certainly is not in the orchard, nor yet is it under any sheet.'

'I'll come with you and show you,' I say.

'Do you take me for a fool, Grey? I obviously asked the lady of the house to lead me to her husband's body.'

'And . . . ?'

'We went to the orchard. She expressed some surprise at the absence of Mister Umfraville. It puzzled her. She regretted she was unable to help me further in the matter.'

'But you saw the blood on the ground?'

'I cannot be expected to hold an inquest for a pool of blood.'

'So the victim . . .'

'Has apparently walked off. Leaving behind his sheet and a rusty axe. You did check that he was actually dead?'

'Of course I did,' I say.

I review my reasons for thinking Umfraville was dead. Various Umfravilles had assured me of the fact. I inspected the wound – one that certainly ought to have killed him. I touched his ice-cold face. I confirmed that his clothes were damp from lying out overnight. I stood up and inspected the ground where he was lying. I drew my conclusions from the trampled grass. I found the axe. I hurried away to interview my witnesses. Less, admittedly, than I would usually do, but surely enough? Hubert Umfraville could not possibly have walked away from the orchard. And yet there is no body.

'So, where is he, then?' asks Thatcher.

'Somebody has clearly removed the corpse,' I say. 'You have instructed me, Mister Thatcher, that you wished to inspect the body yourself. I therefore did not make extensive examination of the body that I would normally make. I cannot give you as precise a time of death as I would like, nor have I measured the depth of the wound. But there is no possible doubt that Hubert Umfraville was dead.'

'Did you check if he was breathing?'

I am about to say that I always check for breathing, then I remember that I didn't do what I always do. This morning, against all my instincts, I did something else. I close my eyes and picture the scene. The body was completely still. Surely I, who have seen so many corpses, would have noticed at once if he was breathing? Yes, it is true that just for a moment I thought I saw his chest and his hand move, but that was no more than a trick of the light. I could not possibly have been mistaken on something so fundamental. Umfraville was dead.

'Had you not said, Mister Thatcher, that you didn't want corpses to be in any way disturbed, I would have examined him exactly as I have in the past.'

'What I said applied to corpses. Mister Umfraville clearly wasn't one. So, the defence of your conduct falls at the first hurdle, doesn't it? And you have detained how many suspects for this non-murder?'

'Three,' I say. 'All with good motives and the opportunity to have killed him.'

'Well, if I were you, I'd release them. Because there has clearly been no murder, except in your imagination.'

'Right,' I say. 'Enough of this nonsense, Mister Thatcher. We're going to the New House now to find out what has really happened. Bodies don't just vanish – at least, they don't vanish without leaving some evidence as to how they did it.'

Chapter 7

In which I (and others) doubt my sanity

The orchard is much as it was before, but Hubert Umfraville is gone.

There is certainly no shortage of blood. Now the body no longer conceals some of it, there is more than enough on view to keep any reasonable coroner happy. The cloth that was covering the corpse has, as if in some strange autumnal parody of the Resurrection, been cast to one side. I can still make out the indentation where the body lay from about one o'clock in the morning until dinner time the same day. But, where before there was a single neat track of flattened grass running through the orchard, now there is a maze of paths in all directions. The area has been searched thoroughly by a number of people.

'He was still there when I went to dinner,' says George. 'But now he's gone.'

'Did you see anyone near the house?' I ask. 'Anyone who could have removed the body?'

'Not while I was in the orchard. Later we were in the dining room, of course. You can't see the orchard from there, as you will know.'

'He must have just come to and walked away,' says Mistress Umfraville. There is nothing in her voice to show whether she thinks this is a good or a bad thing.

'He cannot possibly have walked anywhere,' I say. 'He was dead.'

'But was he?' asks Josiah Thatcher. He gives us all a smug little smile. 'Did any of you people check properly for signs of life? Or did you just assume, for whatever reason, that he must be beyond help and that it was now merely a question of finding his killer? The family might be excused for their mistake. But I would have hoped for something better from a magistrate. You are a fool, Sir John. My predecessor spoke well of you, but he would appear to have been a fool too.'

'Hubert Umfraville,' I say, 'had received a single but most grievous blow to the back of the head with an axe.'

'Which would not necessarily kill him.'

'You can see how much blood there is,' I say. But even as I say it, I know that quite minor wounds can produce a great deal of blood. And men can survive blows that ought to kill them twice over.

The coroner, who also knows these things, raises an amused eyebrow.

'We all jumped too quickly to the wrong conclusion,' says Mistress Umfraville helpfully. 'I see that now. I came here in the early morning and saw my husband lying there amid so much blood. So very much blood, gentlemen. I knelt down beside Hubert and touched his stone-cold cheek. What else was I to think but that he had perished? I can only apologise to you, Mister Thatcher, and to you, Sir John, for my foolish error. The blame is entirely mine. Could I perhaps offer you both some refreshment in the house? A glass of Canary to warm you? There is, as you can see, no longer anything to detain us in this damp, gloomy orchard.'

'Someone has clearly been here and taken the body,' I say.

'And why would they do that?' asks Thatcher. He gives a snort of contempt.

Of course he's right. It's a very good point, actually. Why would the murderer leave the body here for all to see and then, some hours later, return and remove it? It makes no sense at all. If you're going to go to the trouble of hiding a corpse, it's best done straight away. Or you can leave it where it is and then brazen it out. Say, if questioned, that you know nothing about it. Say that the murder must have been perpetrated by some unknown footpad, who has since fled. What you definitely don't do is to let a magistrate view the body and then make it vanish, proving, beyond much doubt, that the killer is still in the village.

'Lawks, gentlemen! There really is no mystery here,' says Mistress Umfraville. 'My husband was attacked by somebody last night and laid low. But while George was away, he opened his eyes and simply wandered off. As to where he is now . . . well, you said, Sir John, that the wound we saw was a grievous one. It's difficult to believe that he would have been thinking rationally after a blow like that. He might be anywhere.'

'Very well,' I say. 'Whether he is alive or dead, we have to find him. If he is alive, which I strongly doubt, he will be dazed and covered in blood. It is unlikely that anyone seeing him will have forgotten it quickly. If, conversely, he is dead and his body has been taken away, anyone walking through the village with a bloody corpse over their shoulder would also be very visible. You seem to have searched the garden already? And the house?'

'The house? Of course we've looked there. And the out-buildings. And the garden,' says George. A sweep of his hand takes in the much-trampled grass. 'Check for yourself if you wish, but we'll be wasting valuable time. If, as my mother believes, he is alive, then we need to find my father urgently.'

I nod. 'Where we search will be much the same whatever we think we're looking for. We must check roads, grass verges, woods, streams, outbuildings. And we must question both travellers and residents of the village who might have seen him. I agree that speed is essential, so it would be best if we divide up the task. Mister Thatcher, would you care to take the road north from here? George – perhaps you could ask if anyone has seen anything out in the direction of Saffron Walden? Where's James? He'd left the inn when I last checked.'

'I don't know exactly,' says George. 'But I'll get him to help when I find him.'

I nod. 'I'll head back to the inn and alert the constable, and organise a search of the other roads. If we all act quickly we should at least be able to find somebody who saw the body being taken away – or Mister Umfraville alive and walking, if you prefer.'

'I beg you to excuse me,' says Thatcher. 'I don't think I need to take part in this children's game of hide and seek. My role in this case, my only role, is to establish the cause of death. When you can show that there has actually been such a thing, and you are certain you will not be wasting my time again, then kindly send one of your servants to me and I shall do my best to assist you. Until then, unlike you apparently, I have other work to do.'

'So, he's gone then?' says Ben. 'Umfraville's really vanished?'

'Yes,' I say. 'The killer must have returned and taken the body. We have to find it, Ben.'

'That'll be a lot of work for somebody,' says Ben, meaning himself in the first instance. He seems to think I've been careless. Most magistrates don't let corpses escape.

'I suppose so,' I say. 'We have a lot of ground to cover.'

Ben looks at me for a moment and then pulls the face he pulls when he sees an easy way out of something. He's done it too many times for me to think it's any other sort of face. 'Unless Mistress Umfraville is right,' he says. 'I mean, it wouldn't be the first time a mistake like that had been made – thinking somebody was dead when he wasn't. Harry Hardy once told me he could remember a family who'd actually ordered a coffin for their grandfather when he suddenly sat up in his bed. They'd already wrapped him up in his winding sheet, which must have given him cause for thought. Another day and he'd have been six foot under and a good woollen shroud wasted. That was back in King James's time, apparently, and he died the following year of the Plague, so they had to bury him anyway. Still, maybe we should wait a bit, just in case. See if he just turns up.'

'Nobody could just walk away after the blow Umfraville received,' I say.

'Maybe somebody helped him walk?'

'If somebody had found him, and they wished to help him, they'd have just taken him to his own house, a few yards away.'

'What if he was worried his attacker would come back if he stayed round here?'

'We have all of the suspects under lock and key, one way or another.'

'He wouldn't know that, though, would he? Not lying there in the orchard under the sheet. Anyway, there's one suspect we don't have.'

'Which one?'

'This slave, Nero.'

'We've only Flood's word for it that Nero is in Essex, and that's just based on a rumour he'd heard in London. Nobody's actually claiming to have seen Nero anywhere.'

'Yes, they have. I was going to tell you. Kit Mansell, the charcoal burner, was at the inn half an hour ago. I told him about Umfraville and he said he saw something odd in the woods a couple of evenings ago. A Moor creeping around. Kit reckoned, since he was a foreigner, he must be up to no good, so he followed him for a bit, but the light was fading and he lost him. Kit went back that way this morning and found a little shelter the man had made to sleep in, and a pile of horseshit beside it. No sign of the Moor, though. So Kit reckoned he'd like as not ridden here, done whatever he came to do, then ridden off again afterwards. It's probably like Flood told you – the slave came here to get his revenge, it's just Flood was a bit too late to catch him. Noted for their cunning, the Moors are. And, as is well known, they always speak in rhyming couplets.'

'Do they?'

'They do in that thing they act in the yard every Christmas.'

But of course. Ben's knowledge of Moors is almost certainly limited to the black-faced characters in our local mummers' play. And the occasional inn sign. Neither can be entirely trusted as an accurate representation of the people of North Africa. Anyway, Nero is from Barbados, not Morocco.

'Nero isn't strictly speaking a Moor,' I say. 'He's ... well, he's not a Moor. Can you get some of the villagers together, Ben, and arrange for a search of all the more likely places a dead body might have been taken? Especially along the road north to Cambridge – that's the only route that doesn't take you through the middle of the village, so that's the most likely. George Umfraville is already searching along the Saffron Walden road, but he may need some help. I'll go down to the charcoal burners' encampment and talk to them about this stranger.'

'So you still want a search, then?' says Ben.

'Yes.'

'In spite of what I said?'

'Yes.'

'Even though Umfraville could be alive?'

'He's dead,' I say. 'He's as dead this afternoon as he was this morning. It's just that I don't know where he is any more.'

'That's where he was camping, Sir John,' says Kit.

Kit Mansell is still the leader of the charcoal burners, as he has been for at least a dozen years. In a former life, before the war, he was Sir Felix's steward and did his best to prevent my stealing apples from the orchard of the house that is now mine. He called me by less respectful names than 'Sir John' then.

The light scarcely penetrates the canopy of golden leaves above us, but in front of us I can make out a bivouac of broken branches, skilfully put together, the work of somebody who has had to conceal himself before. On the ground, not too far away, there is indeed evidence that a horse has been here at some point in the not too distant past.

'It was you who saw him?' I ask.

'I was on my way back to our huts. I noticed just a shadow moving ahead of me. Then he turned and I saw his face. Not a Negro exactly – lighter skinned.'

'Could he have been a mulatto?'

'What's that exactly?'

'Somebody who is half Negro. He might look a bit like a North African.'

Kit scratches his head. My explanation hasn't helped him greatly. 'Ah . . . possibly,' he says.

'Can you tell me anything else about him?' I ask.

'Not really. I only saw him for a moment.'

'Did you see what he was wearing?'

He frowns then says: 'Yes I did. Oddly enough, he seemed to be dressed as a sailor – blue canvas suit. Blue shirt.'

Well, that would explain exactly how Nero has got over to England from Barbados. There would have been plenty of ships that would have taken him on as a member of the crew, asking no more questions than they had to, glad to get somebody with his knowledge and ability.

'When was that?' I ask.

'The day before yesterday. Just as the light was fading. Maybe six o'clock or a little earlier. So, do you think he killed Sir Felix's new tenant last night?'

'He's come a long way to do something,' I say. 'I don't know what, but I wouldn't have travelled all the way from Barbados just for a night or two in the woods.'

'The body's still in the orchard, I take it, waiting for the coroner?'

'No, the coroner's already been here. As for the body, it has vanished.'

'Vanished? How's that?'

'It looks as if the murderer has belatedly decided to conceal the remains, though the family seem to think he wasn't dead and has just walked away. The coroner thinks so too.'

'Could they be right?'

'No, Kit, they couldn't. We've got people out searching.'

'We could check the woods for you. If the body has just been concealed in the bushes rather than properly buried, it's only decent we try to find it before the foxes do.'

'Good afternoon, Sir John.'

I am on my way back to the inn. Harry Hardy is sitting outside his cottage, as he has on and off all my life. He's probably the oldest person in Clavershall West, well able to tell stories about King James's time and perhaps even Queen Elizabeth's. His true age is a matter of conjecture but nobody can remember the village without him. In spite of the coldness that has followed hard on the heels of the setting sun, Harry has a pipe of tobacco to finish before he goes in. Though a widower for many years, he keeps to his late wife's rule of not smoking in the parlour.

'Good afternoon, Harry,' I say.

'There's been a lot of commotion today. I've lost count of the number of people who've asked me if I've seen a dead man walking about the place.'

'And have you?'

'Not me. Did see one strange thing yesterday evening, though. A Moor, almost as close to me as I am to you now. You don't see them very often. Not round here, though I'm sure they're common enough in Guinny and Binny and places like that. I was just coming out of the house as he was passing. I bid him good day but he just looked confused, as if he maybe didn't speak English. I asked him, very slowly and clearly, who he was and he just said "Nemo".'

'Could that have been "Nero"?'

'I thought it was "Nemo" but I suppose you could be right. I've been getting a little deaf of late, so others tell me. Anyway, he carried on along the Cambridge road – up towards the New House. Didn't see him come back.'

'What time?' I ask.

'Evening. A little after the church clock had struck six. It was almost dark. Darker than it is now and the clouds gathering for rain, as they do at this season of the year.'

'How was he dressed?'

'Blue canvas. Like a sailor. Funny little beard.'

'Was he armed?'

'Not that I could see,' says Harry. 'But he might have had a knife tucked into his belt. A bit curved no doubt, as infidels' daggers so often are.'

I nod. So Nero was indeed in the village. A couple of days ago he found himself a safe place to conceal himself in the woods. Then, just before six o'clock yesterday, he spoke briefly to Harry, though not apparently in rhyming couplets. He was last seen heading off towards the New House. A few hours later, Hubert Umfraville was struck down. A blow to the back of his head rather than the thrust of a purely speculative curved dagger, of course. Still, it's useful to know he may be armed.

'Thanks, Harry,' I say. 'That's very helpful.'

'Hope you catch the murderer,' he says. 'If Umfraville was murdered, of course.'

'He was murdered,' I say. 'Don't believe anyone who tells you something different.'

'Didn't like that new coroner,' he says.

'You saw him?'

'He almost rode me down on that horse of his. Heading back to Saffron Walden he was, as fast as he could. Cursed me as he went by. Said everyone in this village was a fool.'

'You suffered no hurt, I hope?'

'I'm not too old to jump out of the way of those who consider themselves my betters.'

'He's just doing his job,' I say.

'Doesn't mean I have to like him.'

'Did you manage to find people to search for Umfraville?' I ask.

'Every route out of the village,' says Ben. His tone implies that it will be a fourfold waste of time.

'The charcoal burners are searching the woods,' I say.

Ben nods. That's a fivefold waste of time, then.

'Flood's got wind of the rumour that Umfraville has walked off,' he says. 'No idea how, but the Grice brothers were in earlier. Flood says you can't keep him here, now there's no body. He says you have to have a body to charge him. Is that part of this habeas corpus he was talking about?'

'Not exactly, Ben. But the lack of a body is certainly going to be a problem in charging him with murder.'

'We could charge him with assault. Somebody certainly attacked Umfraville.'

'I've no evidence now to charge anyone with anything. Not even a coroner's verdict that it was an unlawful killing. No, you'd better release Flood but tell him we haven't finished questioning him yet.'

'And Mister Jenks?'

'We'll need to release the carter too.'

'He'll want to go back to London.'

'At least we can find him again if we need him. He comes this way quite often, doesn't he?'

'Every two or three weeks. Good customer, Jenks is.'

'I'll go and talk to him and warn him he remains a suspect. Then I'll let Robinson know he can also go home. I can find him easily enough too if we need him.'

'But you think this Nero person could have killed the plantation owner?'

'Well, Kit and Harry both saw somebody who seems to have been Nero. If that's who it was, I can't see why he was here unless it was to kill Umfraville. It's true that he might have had some business with the family, but none of them has said they saw him, which is strange if he was in Essex for any honest reason. I've wondered how the killer later removed the body – they'd have needed help – but this man apparently had a horse. The family scoff at the idea of Nero killing Umfraville, but would they know how he really felt about being enslaved? So, we can't rule out the possibility that he did kill him.'

'If he was planning to kill Umfraville,' says Ben, 'why did he give his name to Harry?'

'I agree that's odd, but I'm not sure he did. Harry said at first that the man called himself "Nemo". I thought it was just that Harry's getting deaf, but maybe that's what he actually said.'

'Is "Nemo" a real name, then?'

'It's Latin for "nobody". Flood did say that Nero was well educated.'

'Over-confident, I'd have called it. I wouldn't be joking if I was about to commit a murder.'

'If he did commit murder. I've said we can't rule it out. The problem is, however much he hated Umfraville, why would he risk sacrificing his newly won freedom so rashly? Much better to live quietly and avoid attracting attention.'

'Maybe he didn't think that way, not being English and reasonable like you and me.'

'It would be good to talk to Nero and form a view on that. But I'm not sure we'll get the chance. With a horse at his disposal, I don't doubt that he is already on his way back to London. Why would he stay here?'

Ben shakes his head. There's no predicting what a Moor might choose to do to vex an honest Christian.

'I'd better go back and check how our searchers are doing and whether they've found Umfraville yet or anyone who saw the body being taken away. A man in a sailor's suit leading a horse with a bloody corpse on it – you'd have thought that would have been quite memorable, wouldn't you?'

'Has the search for Umfraville's body been called off?' asks Sir Felix.

A long day is finally coming to an end. When I arrive back at the Big House, the candles have already been lit.

'Only for tonight,' I say. 'No sign of any corpse so far. No witnesses to anything, except that Kit and Harry may have seen Nero. I've told Ben and Kit to stand everyone else down until the morning, though there's still some of the woods to check. Tomorrow, we'll visit the streams, the rest of the woods and any outbuildings that we might have missed today.'

'William Robinson was very grateful that you told him that he could go home,' says Sir Felix.

'I've released the others,' I say. 'It would have been cruel to keep him here. Has Drusilla returned to her family?'

'Yes,' says Aminta. 'She spent almost the entire day here, with her mother's permission, but she's gone now.'

'I suppose the family will stay in Clavershall West no longer than it takes to establish what happened to Hubert,' I say. 'Whatever his plans were to blackmail Robinson, they will presumably abandon them, now he's dead. On the whole they seem decent people.'

'I'm not sure what their intentions are as to the Robinsons and Brandon Hall,' says Sir Felix. 'But George came over during the afternoon to sign the lease and pay the rent until Lady Day next year. They propose to stay that long at least. And George was very confident that his father was still alive. Or that's what he told me.'

'Did he say why he thought that?' I ask.

'Not really. But families cling on to hope for a long time, however unlikely it is.'

I nod. It was years before Sir Felix finally accepted that his son, Marius, was dead. It's natural to hope for the best until the worst is confirmed. Perhaps the Umfravilles' contention that Hubert survived is really no more than that.

'So, if the family believe he will return, what will they do in the meantime?' I ask.

'It seems they intend to live off the land. They asked if I knew who owned the field next to the house and whether it might be rented. You own the field by the way, so that would be your decision. They have ordered two-dozen chickens from William Taylor and a pig and a couple of geese from the Grices. They'll put cows in the field if they can get it.'

'All without consulting the missing Hubert?'

'So it would seem.'

'Maybe they believe he's alive but hope that he's not coming back,' says Aminta. 'That's what Drusilla thinks. They're secretly relieved he's gone. But she says she'll miss him.'

'He was her father, after all,' I say.

'Her adoptive father,' says Aminta.

Chapter 8

In which a number of people are thoughtful enough to teach me my business

Flood is breaking his fast greedily on beer and cold mutton. He sits in the parlour of the inn, a greasy wooden trencher and a pewter mug in front of him. The morning sun slants across the floor in a window-shaped oblong. A log is smouldering damply on the fire. The smell of smoke, mutton fat and last night's ale hangs in the air.

'I assume you will be returning to London soon,' I say, 'since I cannot oblige you to remain here. However, I should be grateful if you would let the constable know where you can be found, because sooner or later we'll have a body and there will be an inquest, whatever the coroner thinks, and you will be required to attend it.'

'If you're worried I might make a run for it, then I've some very good news for you,' says Flood. 'I'm going nowhere. Not till I get my hands on Nero.'

'I'd like to talk to Nero as well,' I say, 'but the last sighting of him was the day before yesterday. Whatever he came here for, there's nothing I know of that would keep him. Slave catching is your business, not mine, Mister Flood, but you'd be wise to assume he's already gone.'

Flood nods approvingly. 'You and I think alike in many ways, Mister Magistrate, because that's what I'd decided too. I admit I was ready to pack my bag and get out of Essex. But a traveller stopped by here earlier. He said he'd just seen a Turk, clear as daylight, up near the New House. That's this very morning. Dressed in blue sailor clothes, he was – just like the charcoal burners reported. Bit of a beard, which he didn't have in Barbados, but must have grown since then in an attempt to disguise himself. The skulking Turk, as my informant was ignorantly pleased to call him, vanished almost as soon as he was spotted, but he's somewhere around here all right. While good sense tells us Nero should've run for it, maybe he's just not as clever as you or I. Or maybe he still has business in Clavershall West. Whatever his reasons, I'm going to discover where he's hiding and take him. What's more, you're going to help me. You want him. I want him. We're both in this together. When we find him, you get to question him. If you can't prove he's the murderer, I get to ship him to Barbados. That's more than fair, when you think about it.'

'I fear you are mistaken in every possible respect,' I say.

'Not a bit of it. Actually, you don't have any choice in the matter. I have a right to regain possession of my slave. You are responsible for enforcing the law. If you choose not to seek him as a suspect then I demand that you instruct your constable to assist me in tracking him down as an escaped slave.'

'If what you've heard is true and Nero is indeed still in the village, I'll hold him for as long as I need to in order to question him. Afterwards he may be released or put before a jury. What I can assure you is that he won't be handed over to you.'

'You arrested me without cause. You detained me for murder when nobody had even been killed. That's malfeasance in public office, that is. If you don't give me the help I need, I'll report you to the Sheriff.'

'Do by all means. He'll tell you the same as I am telling you. It isn't my job to help you find slaves. If the Sheriff feels that I have done anything amiss, I think it will be that I have released you too quickly, before the inquest could be held.'

'Inquest? No body, no murder. Everyone knows that.'

'That maxim has no legal foundation of any sort.'

'You'll find most juries believe it, though. You've no evidence Umfraville is even dead.'

'But I shall, Mister Flood. Make no mistake about that. And now, if you'll excuse me, I must resume the search for his remains.'

'The Grice brothers will help me, then.'

'That is between you and the Grice brothers. My only advice is that you should not pay them until the job is complete. And, if you are going to pay them in advance, do not pay them in ale.'

'The Grice brothers don't like you very much.'

'Well, at least I don't make my living catching slaves, Mister Flood. I'll leave you to finish your breakfast.'

'Any news, Kit?'

The charcoal burner shakes his head. 'We haven't found Umfraville's body, if that's what you mean. None of us here has seen the Moor again, either. He hasn't been back to his shelter.'

'Nero is apparently still in the village, though. A traveller saw him.'

'Perhaps he doesn't like to stay twice in the same place. Or perhaps he's just good at not leaving too many traces.'

'He's an escaped slave,' I say. 'He probably knows Flood's after him. And he has no idea how people in this country will treat him – whether they'll help him or just hand him over for the reward of one guinea. So he's right to be wary. By all accounts, the Umfravilles would have hidden and protected him, but for some reason he apparently chose not to make himself known to the family.'

Kit shakes his head. 'He'd have hardly made his presence known if he planned to kill Hubert Umfraville.'

That was very much Ben's point too. It's the strongest argument, when you think about it, for Nero being the murderer.

'I suppose not,' I say.

'I couldn't keep the men searching any longer,' says Ben. 'They say they've looked everywhere they reasonably can. There's no sign of Umfraville. Or the Moor, for that matter. No disloyalty to you, Sir John – they'd do more if they could – but they need to get back to their work or starve.'

'I'm grateful to them for doing as much as they did,' I say.

'Looks like he did just wander off, then?'

'Dead men don't wander off, Ben. Somebody moves them or they stay where they are. Umfraville was a big man, I grant you – bigger than you or I or his sons for that matter – but that's what must have happened.'

Ben frowns. He clearly disagrees with me, but in the end he decides it's easier not to say so.

'Must be Nero who killed him, then. He had the horse to move the body.'

'Jenks has four horses,' I say.

'What of it?' asks Ben.

'You kept Jenks under close guard at this inn all yesterday – didn't you?'

'As close as any man reasonably could.'

'You'd have seen him leaving the yard? With one horse or the wagon and the whole team?'

Ben nods. However tied up my constable was with his other duties, I think he would have at least heard the rumble of the wagon wheels. Even the sound of a single iron-shod carthorse being led carefully towards the New House would not have escaped his attention. Probably.

'And Mister Robinson?' asks Ben.

I should congratulate Ben on this neat counter-thrust. How well did I attend to my own prisoner's security while I was searching the countryside? Can I be certain that my father-in-law didn't take his eye off Robinson for long enough for him to visit the orchard with his own very fine horse?

'I'm sure that he could not have left the Big House without somebody remarking on it,' I say. 'Especially if he visited the stables first to collect his mare. There's always somebody working around there. And he could not have moved the body far unaided.'

'Which rules out Mister Flood too,' says Ben. 'No horse at all. Anyway, when the body was being moved, he was confined to the pigsty – I mean lock-up,' says Ben. 'Not that there's much we can do about any of them without a corpse – no body, no murder.'

There seem to be a lot of people round here who believe that.

'Bad law, Ben. No statute says anything of the sort. It's just that, after the Chipping Campden case a few years ago, juries are reluctant to convict without a body.'

'Was that the case where Mister Harris disappeared?'

'Harrison. He vanished without trace. On fairly doubtful evidence, his servant, together with the servant's brother and mother, were hanged for his murder. Two years later the murdered man showed up, very much alive, claiming to have been kidnapped by Turks, enslaved and later rescued. His story was unlikely in almost every respect, but what was undoubtedly true was that nobody had murdered him. And his servant's family were undoubtedly dead and buried. Since then, juries have been more cautious and convictions more difficult to obtain unless you can show them a corpse.'

'There you are, then. No body, no murder. Just like I said. It's what other people in the village are saying too.'

I shake my head. Legally I'm right. In every other respect the rest of the village is. If I want to have somebody convicted, it would be better all round if I had a body.

'I'm sure they are, Ben,' I say. 'And saying a lot of other things, no doubt. I'll let the Umfraville family know that we've called off the search for the moment.'

'I'm very pleased to hear it,' says Mistress Umfraville, 'if others were being inconvenienced the way we were. Your constable insisted that his men searched this house and grounds. As if we would not have noticed my husband's presence and told you at once! Their time would have been better spent in more likely places.'

Ben hadn't mentioned that. Of course, it was wise to include the house in the search, even though the family had assured us Hubert was not there. Ben was just doing his job properly.

But it would have been better if he had asked me to accompany him, knowing the property as I do.

'I'm sorry you were troubled,' I say. 'I assume they found nothing?'

'Of course not. What on earth could they have found? I am aware, Sir John, that you are reluctant to admit that you were wrong. But if Hubert is dead, surely you would have found the body by now? If he'd been carried away, surely somebody would have witnessed it? On the other hand, he could have vanished into the countryside, on his own two legs, quite easily by one obscure footpath or another. I ask you, Sir John, putting your own stubbornness to one side, which is more likely?'

'If he was alive, he would have been badly injured and unable to travel very far or very fast on his own.'

'Perhaps his wounds were a lot less serious than they appeared to be. Like most men, Hubert habitually exaggerated every little difficulty.'

'My examination suggested the blow was more than enough to kill him.'

'Your examination was somewhat superficial – at least in the view of the coroner. I say that with the greatest respect, but you cannot deny that is what Mister Thatcher said.'

'That Mister Thatcher said it does not make it true. You know that a man resembling Nero has been seen in the village?'

'A Moor in a blue sailor suit, with a beard? Everyone in the village seems to have heard that.'

'You know Nero and the rest of the village doesn't. Could it be him?'

'I can see why Nero would be mistaken for a North African. I cannot say what clothes he might be wearing now or whether he has grown a beard.'

'But, clothes apart, you think it is Nero?'

She shakes her head. 'Purely from the description, yes, of course. But you would have to form your own judgement on whether Nero would risk coming here, Sir John. I would have said that would be both dangerous and foolish.'

I nod. I cannot disagree with that assessment. 'I am told that you intend to stay and farm what land you have?' I ask. 'Indeed, that you might be interested in renting an additional field from us?'

'If it can be had at a reasonable price. These are the rocks on which my husband chose to wreck his ship and I have no way of going elsewhere until a better ship arrives. My husband, Sir John, made his living from human misery and he did not even do that competently. That he should have departed suddenly and without any thought for the rest of us is less of a surprise to me than you might imagine. But I am still relatively young. Should my husband choose not to return, then so much the worse for him. I believe I have a number of opportunities that I might pursue. Agriculture on modest scale is one of them.'

'You understand animal husbandry?'

'Every bit as much as my husband understood growing sugar cane, Sir John. But I intend to learn.'

As I approach the stream I see that a small party of men is already in the process of crossing. Flood is in the lead, a newly cut staff in his hand. Two of the Grice brothers are following. Nathan is about to launch himself uncertainly on to the first of the stepping stones. The autumn rains have swollen the stream. In my younger days, I often made the same crossing myself after an evening at the inn, and I found the steps inconveniently irregular and slippery when the water was this high. Nathan's frown suggests that, contrary to my advice, Flood has had to treat the brothers to a few tankards of ale to persuade them to set out on their quest. I have never regarded the Grice brothers as particularly principled people, but today's work, as assistant slave catchers, represents a new low point in their moral trajectory.

I pause on the road, my way across for the moment impeded by the search party, unless I wish to get my shoes and stockings soaked. Flood smiles. Blocking the crossing is only a small inconvenience to me, but it is nevertheless one that he can savour.

He stands on the second stone from the near bank, steadied by the staff planted in the stream, the bright water rushing noisily just below his shoes. 'So, have you found Umfraville?' he demands.

'Not yet,' I say.

He smirks. 'No body, no murder,' he says.

Behind him, Nathan, whose progress is also impeded by his employer, wobbles uncertainly in mid-passage. This may or may not end well for him.

'He's gone, Grey,' Flood continues. 'It wouldn't surprise me if he'd faked his own death to avoid his creditors.'

'The family seem convinced he's alive,' I say.

'The best way to get somebody like you – somebody who thinks more than is good for him – to believe a man is dead is to tell you over and over again that he's alive. It's the oldest trick in the book. Didn't Lord Arlington teach you anything about espionage? Is the family upset in any way over his death?'

'No,' I say. 'Except maybe Drusilla.'

'There you are, then. They're all in it together. Except maybe, as you say, that girl they've adopted. No point in grieving over somebody who is alive and well.'

'Are you saying Umfraville was merely feigning death in the orchard and the family knows that?'

'You can do a lot with a bit of pig's blood. Of course, if you'd inspected the body properly, they'd never have got away with it. But they knew you were under the coroner's thumb and would do no such thing. They had to get Umfraville out of the way, of course, before the coroner arrived. There would have been no pulling the wool over his eyes. Yours maybe, but not Thatcher. Do you understand now?'

'Are you going to stand there all day, Mister Flood?' I ask. 'I'd like to cross the stream.'

Flood smiles. 'You should stop wasting your time trying to find a corpse that isn't there and help me find Nero. You haven't done anything useful today like looking for my slave, I suppose?'

'He's not your slave, Mister Flood. Now he is in England, he is arguably nobody's slave, and he's certainly not yours.'

'He's been in the woods sure enough,' says Flood. 'We sought out his nasty little den. Too good for the likes of him. So, we destroyed it, didn't we, boys? Beat it down and smashed every stick. Pissed on it for good measure. He'll not be sleeping there again.'

Nathan, still trying to find firm footing on his sloping rock, nods cautiously. Jacob is now sitting on the far bank – the one I wish to reach – staring downstream. The water hasn't been this high since last winter.

'Well, I suppose you wouldn't want an escaped slave to enjoy a good night's rest,' I say.

'Exactly,' says Flood. 'You have to wear your quarry down.

Make them fear stopping for food or drink or even a moment's sleep. I always think hunting a lettered slave is much better sport than hunting an illiterate one. It's like a good game of chess, though one in which you've hidden most of your opponent's pieces. Wouldn't you agree, Mister Magistrate?'

There is a splash behind him. Nathan is on his hands and knees in the stream, up to his elbows in crystal-clear water.

'I'll have to go home and change,' he says.

'No you won't,' says Flood. 'I've paid for your ale, now you'll work as contracted, wet or dry. Hopefully that's sobered you up enough to be useful, damn you. So, stop that stupid shivering and follow me.'

Flood shoulders his staff and skips nimbly over the final stone and on to the bank. He strides off confidently without a backward glance. I don't think he's interested in my views on slave catching after all. Jacob crosses, step by careful step, not wishing to repeat his brother's error. Nathan stands and squeezes some of the water out of his woollen breeches, then out of his sleeves. He still seems pretty wet and very cold. He scowls at me and the world in general.

I cross the stream myself and head back at a leisurely pace into the village. Behind me, above the gentle trill of the water lapping against the stones, I can hear the squelching of Nathan's wet and resentful footsteps. I glance back just as Nathan does the same thing. There's no doubt. He blames me for everything bad that has ever happened to him. His look tells me he'd like to get even for as much of it as possible. But, as Ben would doubtless point out if he were here, Nathan and Jacob don't like me much anyway.

Chapter 9

In which I see a ghost in broad daylight

I arrive home to find my wife, father-in-law and one of our gardeners about to set off somewhere. The three of them seem to be expecting trouble. Sir Felix is wearing his sword on a dark blue, fringed sash. Amos is carrying a pitchfork in a menacing manner. Aminta is unarmed but has a look on her face that may be worth more than the sword and pitchfork put together.

'Amos saw a man acting suspiciously in our orchard,' says Aminta. 'He watched him climb in over the wall.'

'A Moor,' says Amos. 'In sailor's clothes. Might be after our apples. Might be after the children. You can't tell with Moors. I wasn't armed so I came straight back to the Big House to report it. Now we're going to see him off, right back to Africa, where he belongs.'

'I'll come with you,' I say.

'Do you want to collect your sword first, John?' asks Sir Felix.

'I don't want to delay you,' I say. 'Anyway, if it's Nero, as I suspect, I'd like a word with him and too much shining steel may frighten him off. Once he's made a run for London I'll never find him again. The sooner I can sit down with him and ask him some questions, the better.'

We work our way round the outbuildings and then along the orchard wall. When we reach the entrance to the enclosure, I peer round cautiously. I'd rather he didn't make a run for either London or Africa, whatever Amos's wishes in the matter may be. At first I see nobody, then on the far side I make out, in the shadows, a man crouching, dressed, as Amos has described, in the blue canvas of a seaman. He is filling his pockets with the last of the year's windfalls. He has to fling a lot of rotten ones aside, so his progress is slower than he might like. We proceed carefully and he doesn't even notice us until we are twenty yards or so from him. Then he looks up suddenly, like a startled deer.

I'm not sure what I expected. I have, after all, met a few mulattos, especially on my visits to London. I can see why those who saw him described him as a Moor. He is very much like the inhabitants of Morocco and Algiers. At first sight, an Arab, not a Negro at all – almost as I might look myself if I had spent my life under the African sun. But he is somehow older-looking than I expected. Talking to the Umfraville brothers, I had assumed he was much the same age as they were, but perhaps life in Barbados has just been harder for Nero than for George or James. He stares in puzzlement at the strange party that has come to greet him – an aged cavalier brandishing a well-polished sword, a soberly dressed and wholly unarmed magistrate, a lady fashionably attired albeit that the hem of her skirt is distinctly damp from the wet grass, and, very much at the rear of the group, a serving man apologetically carrying a large piece of agricultural equipment. Slowly the intruder gets to his feet, stuffing a final red apple into his coat pocket.

'If you are Nero,' I say, 'you have nothing to fear from us, if you've broken no laws. We're not here to recapture you and send you back to Barbados. And you can keep the apples – we already have more in store than we can use. But I need to talk to you about the death of Hubert Umfraville. I want you to come back to the Big House with us. I have to ask you some questions. After that, if you've done nothing wrong, you'll be free to go wherever you wish.'

The so-called Moor isn't paying much attention to me. He's looking at Sir Felix and frowning. My father-in-law does, after all, present the most immediate danger. It would be ironic to escape from slavery in the West Indies only to be run through with a cavalry sword for no reason at all in a quiet Essex village. The man's puzzled gaze turns back to me and then to Aminta. He is almost as wary of us as he is of Sir Felix.

'Why don't you begin by telling us who you are?' I suggest. 'Is your name Nero? Or maybe it's Nemo?'

At the mention of this alias, he gives me a very thin smile and starts to back away. Strangely he seems more embarrassed than scared. It is almost as if he finds himself in an awkward social situation from which he'd like to extract himself as soon as ordinary politeness will allow.

'Where are you from?' I ask.

This too is a matter on which our intruder feels he would rather not express an opinion.

'He don't talk proper English, do he?' says Amos, behind me. 'Like as not, he talks some heathen tongue, just to confuse us.'

But we are not to discover what languages he speaks. He has quickly turned on his heels and flung himself at the wall of the orchard – the one that runs along the side of the road. It's a wall I climbed myself in my youth, when I too stole apples, and I have to admire the way he uses first the buttress and then a handhold in the brickwork to hoist himself up and over. He may not be as old as his lined face suggests.

I run at the wall to try to grab at his ankles, but he is too fast. We hear his feet hit the ground on the far side and the sound of running on the road. It takes me longer than it once did to pull myself up by the same route and to view the King's highway beyond. I rest my elbows on the smooth top, slightly out of breath. The man has long gone – off into the woods, probably. That's what Dickon and I used to do when Kit was after us. I let myself back down to the ground in carefully judged stages and brush a little red brick-dust off my black coat and breeches.

'So,' I say, 'what do you think? Was that our man? Was that Nero?'

Amos, who is now bravely menacing the wall with his pitchfork, turns and shrugs. How is he supposed to know who it was?

I turn to Sir Felix, who, strangely, appears at least as disconcerted as the intruder was.

'You look as if you've seen a ghost,' I say.

But before he can reply, there are footsteps behind us. We turn. It's Ben and he's red-faced and puffing.

'Something urgent, Ben?' I ask.

His reply comes as a series of gasps. 'The mulatto . . . Nero . . . ten minutes ago . . . over by the church.'

'That's not possible,' I say. 'He was here in the orchard only a moment since and had been here for some time before that.'

'Sounds like we do have a ghost, then,' says Amos. 'Either our one or the one in the churchyard. Or both. It's not natural. And our one just floated over the wall.'

'He didn't float,' I say. 'He climbed very nimbly, but he didn't float.'

'Didn't make a sound, that one. Unnatural. That's what it is,' says Amos.

'We heard his footsteps very clearly,' I say.

'I didn't,' says Amos.

He's made up his mind. There was something unearthly about what we've just witnessed.

'Who saw the man in the churchyard?' I ask.

Ben has recovered his breath a little. 'Harry Hardy,' he says. 'He tried to give chase but he's not that fast any more, Harry. So he came back to the inn and reported it to me.'

I nod. I'm beginning to understand how this very explicable event happened. Ben's ten minutes is not to be taken literally. Allowing the time it would take Harry to get from the church to the inn and the time it would take for Ben to finish whatever he was doing and come over to the Big House and then locate us in the orchard . . . yes, the man would have been able to run down here, climb the wall and seem to be in two places at once. No need for anyone to have supernatural powers. All we've really learned from the last few minutes is that Nero is a fast runner and he may have been hiding in the church.

I look at Amos. He's not going to be robbed of his ghost-in-the-orchard story. By tonight half of the village will believe it. By tomorrow night it will be an established fact. For the next hundred years, the village will be telling the story of how the squire met a Moor in the orchard, how the squire asked him his name and the Moor in response just floated off over the wall, leaving no trace. Obviously it would be good if, having seen this ill omen, I perished in some dreadful way over the next day or so. That would, from a literary point of view, round the tale off nicely. I look at Aminta and Sir Felix, hoping to share the joke, but I think they are both very much of Amos's mind. We've just seen some supernatural being and it bodes no good at all.

'Well,' I say, 'if that wasn't Nero in the flesh, I don't know who it was. We've lost him for the moment, but I'm curious to know why he was at the church. I'll come back with you now, Ben, and we can search the churchyard and maybe the church itself.'

A number of straw-stuffed hassocks have been piled in one corner to make a passable bed.

'Church is never locked,' says Ben. 'If you come in after dark, nobody much would trouble you until the next morning. Not that I'd want to sleep here amongst so many old tombs.'

'You might if the alternative was capture and a fast return to Barbados,' I say. 'You might risk it then.'

'Easy for you to say that, Sir John. Most of the tombs are your dead ancestors anyway. I dare say they'd let you have an easy night.'

'My mother's dead ancestors,' I say. 'They're all Wests, not Greys.'

'Well, none of mine are here, on either side of the family. They're all outside in the churchyard, sun, rain or snow.'

'Equality is not to be expected, Ben – not in this life or the next. We may be equal in the sight of God, but not in the sight of the Church of England. Some get their own pews on a Sunday, some sit behind them, wherever they can. Some get to be buried in the vaults, some have to make do with a few feet of rough turf. There used to be a painting on one of these walls showing Judgement Day. The Wests, dressed in very superior shrouds, are shown introducing the villagers to Saint Peter, with whom the family already seem to be on the best of terms.'

'What happened to it?' asks Ben.

'It was white-washed over some time in the reign of Edward VI. No great loss. But there is a drawing of it in the archives – or there was a few years back.'

'Flood thinks there should be equality for everyone. Except slaves. I'll keep an eye open for Nero, then, since he's obviously still around. And I'll let you know before I tell Flood anything, paying customer though he now is. I assume we've given up looking for Umfraville for the moment?'

'We've covered all of the obvious places, and I can't really expect the village men to do more. Mistress Umfraville tells me you have even searched the New House, which I appreciate, even though she is still complaining about our officiousness. I agree it was important we didn't just accept their word he wasn't there.'

'Complaint? She suggested I search.'

'Did she?'

'Of course. I wouldn't have searched a house belonging to your family without informing you, except that your tenant more or less made me do it. We'd agreed the priority was to search the roads and woods.'

'I wonder why she did that, then?'

'Couldn't say. Maybe to clear her name quickly. She must reckon we'd suspect her a bit, even though she pays rent to Sir Felix.'

'We've accused her of nothing. They're a strange family, Ben. Always looking to read the worst into everything we do for them. But I suppose we'll get used to them in time.'

'They're staying, then?'

'Apparently,' I say. 'They've bought livestock from the Grices, which is unlikely to have been cheap. I doubt Mistress Umfraville will have needed to accuse that family of unlooked-for charity as she did us.'

'Are you planning to toss and turn all night,' asks Aminta, 'or just until little Aphra wakes me up for a feed?'

'I'm sorry,' I say. 'I didn't mean to disturb you.'

'Don't worry. I can't sleep either. Are you still cross with Thatcher? Is that what is keeping you awake?'

'No, it's not that. I'm cross with myself, of course. I should have checked the body properly whatever Thatcher wanted me to do. Thatcher's quite right that it's the coroner's job, not mine, to hold an inquest and determine the cause of death. And maybe in the past coroners were entitled to view the bodies where they lay – I've no idea. There's nothing in any of the books in the library that can tell me. But I should still have examined the body more carefully than I did.'

'So you admit you're annoyed enough about Thatcher to have consulted your law books?'

'Yes, I'm annoyed enough to have consulted my law books. But that's not the point. I should have persuaded him we could work together. We're on the same side. His predecessor was more pragmatic. He didn't mind if I did much of his work for him before the inquest took place.'

'That's because you are better at establishing the cause of death than any coroner.'

'Possibly.'

'No, you are. You've spent your life studying corpses. They are to you what game birds and trout are to other country magistrates. You gather your facts and then apply logic and science to determining how a death occurred. That's why the old coroner was happy for you to do whatever you wanted to do. I'm not surprised that you resent Thatcher's rather narrow approach.'

'It's true I have seen a lot of bodies,' I say. 'A few on Arlington's behalf. Dozens – hundreds – on the battlefields when I was a boy. Unlike your brother Marius, I was too young to have fought. But my mother was constantly searching for my father in one place or another.'

'She had only to look in my mother's bed. That's where he was whenever my father was away. Oh dear – could our parents have really been so badly behaved? In former times this village was morally very lax indeed.'

'I'm surprised, with the parents that we have had, that we are the people we are.'

'I think it was predictable, under the circumstances, that you would turn into the very worst sort of puritan. So, if you're not seething with anger over Thatcher, what is stopping you sleeping?'

'The thing that puzzles me most,' I say, 'apart from the fact that you still think I am a puritan, is why the killer left the body there in the orchard at first, but then felt obliged to move it later. When I was discussing things with Thatcher I couldn't explain why anyone should do that, and it still makes no sense to me now. There's no point in coming back for a body that everyone has seen.'

'But there is a very simple explanation, John. Umfraville

was alive, exactly as both Thatcher and Flood claim. The killer didn't return and remove the corpse. The corpse just got up and left.'

'Flood said the family helped him. He said the death was faked so that Umfraville could escape his debts.'

'Is that possible?'

'There's certainly something the family aren't telling me. That business of there being renewed hope that James could marry Lucy, for example. Flood implied there were things they hadn't told Drusilla too.'

'That could be true. They were surprisingly keen that Drusilla stayed here with me. Perhaps it was important that she shouldn't know what was happening.'

'I was certain he was dead,' I say, 'but ...'

There's a strange stillness to a corpse – a complete stillness. And yet, as Harry Hardy reminded me, it is not unknown for somebody to be pronounced dead by those who ought to know their business, and then prove to be very much alive. I close my eyes and picture the scene again.

'But what?' says Aminta.

'I thought I saw a slight movement of Umfraville's hand,' I say. 'And his chest. But that was just a trick of the light. The moving shadows under the apple trees.'

'You're sure it was just the shadows?'

I sigh. 'No, I'm not. Maybe his hand really did move. Flood's right about one thing – the family are certainly not grieving for him, except maybe Drusilla. And asking Ben to search the New House could be part of the deception – proving, when they really had no need to, that they were not concealing Hubert, dead or alive. Flood said they were telling me he was alive to convince me he was dead.'

Aminta laughs. 'How well Flood knows you!' she says. 'I think you've worked for Arlington too long. You prefer labyrinthine deceit and trickery to the simple and straightforward. Anyway, why was Flood so willing to enlighten you on Umfraville's plan? It's not as if you're giving him any help in return. Flood may just want to spread confusion for the sake of spreading confusion. He seems the sort of man who would enjoy that.'

'If Umfraville is still alive and hiding in the house, it would explain why we haven't found a body. It explains why nobody has seen him. What if he's still there, waiting to escape early one morning when we've all stopped looking?'

'But you've said: Ben checked the house.'

'Not as well as somebody who once lived there himself could have done. That's exactly why they encouraged Ben to do it. So that I wouldn't. The safest place to hide something is a place which has already been searched. I'm going back to do the job properly first thing tomorrow.'

Down in the hallway the clock strikes midnight.

'You mean later today,' says Aminta.

'I mean later today,' I say. 'Why were you still awake, by the way? What's troubling you?'

Aminta pauses for a long time. 'Nothing,' she says. 'Or nothing important. The man in the orchard . . .'

So, it was not only Sir Felix who found the intruder more disconcerting than I did.

'He's gone,' I say. 'I've still no idea if he was Nero, but he was never any danger to any of us. And I doubt he'll be coming back.'

'I'm sure you're right. I said it wasn't important. Let's try to get some sleep. You have a house to search and, if you're right, they may not give you as easy a time as Ben had.'

But a noise from the nearby crib tells us that sleep may be further off than we wish. Slowly I get out of bed and light a candle.

Chapter 10

In which I see a ghost by candlelight

'I told you: your constable has already rummaged the entire house,' says Mistress Umfraville. Perhaps Aminta was right, as she so often is. The Umfravilles were very happy to have Ben search when it suited them, but they are not at all amenable to my repeating the process.

'I know the house better than Ben does,' I say.

'My lease, Sir John, entitles me to the quiet enjoyment of the property. If this continues, I shall have to ask for a reduction in the rent.'

'My father-in-law is your landlord. Any matters relating to the lease must be referred to him. Matters relating to the disappearance of your husband are conversely my concern.'

'This is most irregular. I made no official protest over yesterday's search. Today's is one too many. You appear determined to disturb us all. You may rest assured I shall complain to the Sheriff.' She is red-faced and her voice is raised.

'I shall let you have the Sheriff's name and address if that will assist you,' I say. 'And now, I'll start on the upper floor, if that's all the same to you? Then I shall search the ground floor, the outbuildings, the garden and the orchard.'

'The whole house, the gardens and the orchard!' she exclaims. 'Whatever next?'

'I intend to look everywhere so as not to have to trouble you again,' I say.

I await another loud condemnation of my conduct or Ben's, but fortunately Mistress Umfraville has finally run out of objections. For a moment we stand there looking at each other with no sound other than the ticking of the clock in the hall and the birdsong outside in the garden. Then, somewhere in the house, a door slams and the brief, fragile silence is broken. As if released by some evil spirit from a spell, Mistress Umfraville's face relaxes and she actually smiles.

'Well, I should at least steer clear of the orchard, if I were you. The pig is now installed there. As you know, we bought him from the Grices. Like all of that family, he is of uncertain temper. We have named him Hubert.'

I work my way from room to room, frequently glancing out of the windows in case the family decide to move anything or anyone around in the garden, stopping and listening for any suspicious movement in the house, which, as Mistress Umfraville has repeatedly pointed out, is not large. But the only footsteps are mine.

Revisiting my old home releases a host of memories. My father. My old friend Dickon. Sir Felix's frequent and apparently inexplicable visits to my mother. The ghost of Marius, Aminta's long-dead elder brother, another frequent visitor, also hovers about the place. My mother's presence here is a more substantial thing. I can tell she does not entirely approve of my wasting my time in this frivolous manner. Don't I have better things to do than search for the killer of Hubert Umfraville?

There is a priest hole, almost certainly unknown to Ben, that I locate and check. I don't think any of the Wests were ever Catholics, but it would have been like them to make suitable provision, just in case they wished to turn traitor at some future date. It is however empty. The Umfravilles have not discovered it any more than Ben did. Generations of industrious spiders have lived and died here since it was last cleaned. I climb up to the attic, where there are some cupboards under the sloping eaves, but again there is no evidence of recent human habitation.

I move on to the garden, checking mechanically everywhere a dead (or living) former slave owner might be concealed. I check for any sign of recent occupation of some obscure spot that would not normally be occupied – a mattress in an unlikely place, an untidy heap of blankets, a dirty plate, a half-full wine bottle. The outhouses contain only what outhouses should contain. The pig has indeed made himself at home amongst the apple trees. I recall that Mistress Umfraville warned me against entering the orchard because of the animal's uncertain temper. I therefore open the gate and proceed to examine the ground. The pig does no more than glance up at me briefly as if I have no business there. I probably don't – it is not a good hiding place for the living or the dead. The undergrowth is excessive but not enough to conceal a habitation for a living man for very long. Porcine exploration has begun in order to establish what is edible beneath the surface but there is no excavation big enough to be the grave of somebody of Umfraville's considerable size. Were Mistress Umfraville's warnings about the pig simply intended to dupe me into thinking that something must be afoot in the orchard? To waste time that might more profitably be spent elsewhere? Again, I wonder if I am seeing plots where there is none. Perhaps she just wisely believed that any pig supplied by the Grices would be ill disposed towards mankind generally and me in particular.

'My mother asked me to present her compliments and enquire if you were done with us.'

I turn to see George standing by the gate. I think Mistress Umfraville may have sent him to search for me and check that all is well.

'Yes, pretty much,' I say.

'Are you any closer to deciding what happened to my father?'

'I admit I can find nothing in the house or garden to suggest he is here. No more than I have found any sign of him in the village or in the woods.'

'In that case, Sir John, don't you think you must concede he's fled?'

'From whom or what?' I ask.

'Flood, surely? Nobody knows when he arrived in the village – only that he chose to find a place in Ben's hayloft some time after my father was attacked. He could easily have come here that evening and confronted my father. Perhaps Flood had a commission not only from Greengrass but also from my father's creditors to track him down and recover what he'd stolen from them. Perhaps my father threatened to ensure Flood never reported back to them. Perhaps Flood then hit him over the head. Who knows? When my father finally came round twelve hours later, he decided it would be safest if he left the village.'

It's certainly true that things are pointing more and more to Flood's involvement, one way or another. His evident dislike of Umfraville. His attempt to get me to believe that Umfraville's disappearance was a family plot. His attempt to distract me from my investigation of the murder by insisting I help him recover Nero. The main objection to Flood as the assailant, that he had no way of subsequently transporting the body, vanishes if there really was no body to transport. There's one other objection, though.

'Your father clearly had some very specific plan in coming here,' I say. 'Would he simply abandon it like that?'

'He's already abandoned the King's army, Barbados and his plantation when it suited him to do so. Why not his family too?'

It's a good point. I think I'll talk to Flood again.

'There was no need to search the New House yourself,' says Ben. 'I'd already searched it. I made a good job of it. You didn't find anything I'd missed, did you?'

'No.'

'You should have trusted me then, shouldn't you?'

'It wasn't that I didn't trust you.'

'What was it then?'

Actually, thinking about it, it was that I didn't trust him. Ben's right that I should have ensured he knew what was going on, of course, but that's an apology for another day. It can at least wait until I've spoken to the slave catcher.

'Is Mister Flood in his chamber?' I ask.

Ben looks at me cautiously. He's done more than enough constable work over the past few days.

'He went out early this morning.'

'He's employed the Grice brothers again, then?'

'No. They refused to work for him after yesterday. They say he treats them like dirt and they're not having any more of it. They say they're free Englishmen. Nobody's going to make slaves of them.'

'Do you know which way he went?'

'I asked him that very question, simply hoping to be of service to a customer, as he now is, but he wouldn't tell me.'

'In that case, would you very kindly send word to me when he returns?'

'Is that all you need me for?'

'Yes,' I say.

Ben breathes a sigh of relief.

'The moment he's back, Sir John, I'll let you know. You can count on me for that. Always at your service and His Majesty's.'

The shadows are growing long, and I am thinking of calling for candles, when a familiar face appears at the door of our library.

'Good afternoon, Sir John,' says Robinson. 'One of your footmen admitted me. I told him I could find my own way to the library. Which, as you will see, I have in fact done. I was trying to find Flood.'

'Well, he's certainly not here,' I say. 'Ben told me he'd gone out and wasn't back yet. But that was hours ago. He should have returned to the inn by now. It's getting too dark for him to search much longer for missing slaves, especially in the woods.'

Robinson shakes his head wearily. 'I've just come from the inn – it was the second time I'd been there. Flood's still not back.'

'I suppose he might have gone out to the Grices' farm to see if he could persuade them to carry on working for him after all.'

'No, I saw Jacob Grice at the inn. They haven't seen him all day.'

'Then he might be out in the fields,' I say. 'Or perhaps he stopped to talk to the charcoal burners.'

'No, I asked the charcoal burners. They hadn't seen him either. Nobody has seen him anywhere.'

'You've been very thorough then, William. When I meet with him again, I can tell him you had ridden over and were asking for him. Is it urgent?'

'I've no idea. He wrote me a letter saying that he needed to speak to me.'

'Did he say what about?'

'In a roundabout way. But he is wholly mistaken. I can assure you of that. There is no truth in it whatsoever.'

I wait to see if Robinson plans to tell me more, but it transpires that he doesn't.

'I hope you find him,' I say. 'Will you stay for a glass of wine before you return home?'

'I won't, thank you,' he says. 'As you say, the sun will be setting soon. I've had a long and wasted day. Not your fault in any way. But completely wasted for all that.'

'You're late coming to bed,' says Aminta.

'I had to do the accounts for the estate. They were getting behind.'

'I'm not surprised, your having frittered away so much time looking for Umfraville.'

'It's my job. It's what the King expects me to do on his behalf. More or less. Amos and I searched further along the Cambridge road this afternoon but drew a blank. I think we've done all we can for the moment. Ben made it clear this morning that he thinks he's done all he can too.'

'I'm sure other magistrates are much less conscientious on the King's behalf. I take it Flood has had equally little success tracking his missing slave?'

'He's still looking, so he hasn't given up hope. Robinson rode over to find Flood, but wouldn't tell me why, other than that the slave catcher had written to him and that, whatever Flood had said, it was untrue.'

'How strange. I hadn't seen Flood as a great letter writer. Does Flood know Robinson, then?'

'I don't think they've ever met. Perhaps, like Umfraville, Flood has discovered the regicide brother's hiding place and hopes to profit from the fact. Whatever it was, Robinson certainly didn't want to tell me. Maybe we'll find out when Flood gets back. I need to talk to him again as soon as he returns anyway. Ben was supposed to let me know, but he didn't.'

'That's because Ben is giving due priority to his business, as you are finally doing to yours.'

'Ben's normally very reliable. I'll have to go over tomorrow and find out what's happened.'

'Well, you're certainly not going now.'

'Of course I'm not. Aphra appears to be sleeping soundly. We might just get an unbroken night's rest if we're lucky.'

*

Then, suddenly, I am awake. Aphra is still dreaming of whatever babies dream of. But I can tell that Aminta is lying tensely at my side, alert to something.

'Did you hear the noise?' she whispers.

'What noise?' I say, trying to work out what time it is. There is bright moonlight outside, but I think we are still a long way from sunrise.

'Shh! Keep your voice down!'

'Sorry,' I say more quietly. 'What noise?'

'The one that had just woken us both up.'

'I don't know what woke me up.'

'It was a sort of scraping noise. As if somebody was raising a sash window.'

We listen in the silvery silence of our bedchamber. Outside an owl hoots. A gust of wind stirs the trees. Aphra wakes, says something in a language known only to herself and goes back to sleep. Then nothing. Nothing at all. We must have imagined it. Time to roll over and go back to sleep.

'You're not going to ignore it, are you?' asks Aminta.

That had seemed a good plan to me. Probably better than the one Aminta is about to suggest.

'I'd take your sword if I were you,' says Aminta.

I get out of bed as silently as I can. I collect my sword from where it is leaning, in its scabbard, against the chest. I turn the door handle in tiny, carefully judged stages and a moment later I am tiptoeing down the wide, curving wooden staircase. I pause in the entrance hall. The moon, shining through the tall, diamond-paned windows, means that I require no candle, but I can see a long needle of flickering orange light under the door of the library and another down the side. It is not fully closed. I can therefore push it open very slowly and almost completely silently on its heavy steel hinges. The air in the room is colder than the hall, in spite of the smouldering remains of a fire in the hearth. That, I realise, is because a window is wide open. On a side table close to the fireplace a candle flame waves to and fro. There is a faint, and wholly inexplicable, scent of tar. At first I think there is nobody in the room except myself – that somebody has come in, lit a candle and gone out again through the window. But then I see the outline of a shoulder. A man is sitting in one of the wing-backed chairs, completely concealed except for one angular elbow. I remain where I am, looking for any other sign of a human presence. One of the lessons that I learned while working for Arlington is that a surprising number of things can prove to be traps. That you can see only one man doesn't mean there aren't two. Or ten. And the stillness of the intruder is suspicious. He must realise by now that I am there.

'You may as well come in,' he says. He turns and peers round the wing of the chair. His face is dark, as is his hair. He has a short, reasonably well-kept beard on his chin, though no moustache on his upper lip. His coat appears to be the canvas one of a sailor. It is without any doubt at all the man we all saw in the orchard. It would seem that the much-sought-after Nero has finally come to visit me.

'You've made yourself at home,' I say. 'This time, would you like to tell me who you are?'

He gives a snort of contempt. 'I'm obviously at home,' he says. 'Who, however, are you?' He has certainly gained in confidence since I last saw him. You might have thought it was his house, not mine, that we were in. He stands and puts a book down on the table. One of his reasons for breaking in was clearly to consult my library. Perhaps to read Livy or

Virgil if he knows Latin as well as he seems to. The light's not good enough to make out the words on the spine, but I think it's the *Aeneid* he has there. 'I assume you must be the steward or something of the sort?' he adds. 'You were in the orchard with Sir Felix and the others.'

His English is perfect, but then I suppose that everyone on Barbados must speak it – masters and slaves alike. It's odd that he knows who Sir Felix is, while not having the first idea who I am. But I decide not to hold it against him.

'I'm the owner of this house,' I say.

He frowns. 'You can't be. That isn't possible.'

'I've owned it since I inherited it from my mother,' I say. 'And she'd owned it, for all practical purposes, since she married Colonel Payne some years ago. Not that it's any business of yours.'

'I would have said, sir, it was very much my business. Instead of giving me your family history, could you please simply answer my question. Who exactly are you?'

I pause because I am sure that I have heard this voice before somewhere. But where?

'My name is Sir John Grey,' I say to him. 'I'm a magistrate and I'm about to arrest you for breaking and entering. Now, who are you – *exactly*?'

The intruder picks up the candle and thrusts it forward at head height. I cannot now see his own face, behind the bright flame, but I can tell he is studying me carefully.

'John?' he says. 'By God, it really is you! And you are now a knight? But what are you doing here? I looked for you at the New House, but other people seemed to have moved in. I assumed that you and your family had gone away. So, of course, I came here. It was the obvious place to come. The servants are all abed, so I climbed in through a window, as I'd often done before.'

Then I finally recognise the voice. It is one that I have not heard for twenty years. He lowers the candle again and I can study his face. Yes, of course. No wonder he looks older than I was expecting.

'I don't believe it!' I say. 'Unless you are about to claim to be a ghost, in which case I don't believe that either.'

I hear footsteps behind me and turn to see Aminta.

'You seem to be on very good terms with the man who has come to murder us,' she says. Then she stops suddenly and puts her hand over her mouth. I don't think it's because she has also smelt the tar and is worried about her furniture.

'Oh my God! It's the thief from the orchard. It's ...'

'Yes,' I say. 'It's your brother, Aminta. Marius has finally come home.'

Chapter 11

In which we are told a story and the world becomes a darker place

Sir Felix has been summoned from his own chamber and now sits on one side of the fireplace. He blows his nose on a fairly clean linen handkerchief. There is a strict limit to the number of tears one of Prince Rupert's cavalry officers is permitted to shed. He had thought that the man in the orchard looked remarkably like his long-lost son, but doubted his own eyes. It couldn't be true. Now he knows it is.

Marius has received a slightly confused account from us all of the forced sale, not long after the Battle of Worcester, of his childhood home to Colonel Payne; my mother's adroit marriage to the same prosperous roundhead; Aminta's and Sir Felix's exile to Brussels with the King; my mother's death and my own marriage to Aminta; my wholly undeserved acquisition of a knighthood – a complex series of events, sad and joyous by turns, which has led to various people that Marius knew very well in 1650 now living in the Big House, though none of us in quite the role that he had expected. His assumption that I might be the steward was not entirely unreasonable. By the end of our tale we are all happy and laughing except Marius, who attempts to smile without quite succeeding.

'I congratulate you, John,' he says, looking into the dying embers in the fireplace. 'When I tried to imagine what might be happening here in my absence, one of my dearest wishes was that you and my sister might have married. It was such an obvious thing to have happened.'

'Not obvious to John unfortunately,' says Aminta. 'It took some years for him to see sense, but we got there eventually.' She gives my hand a squeeze to show that she almost forgives me for my slowness.

'And you now have two children?' he says.

'Charles and Aphra,' I say. 'Your nephew and niece.'

'Aphra?'

'Named after the playwright.'

He shakes his head. 'I have no idea who you mean, but I have been away a long time. When I left, Cromwell had closed all of the theatres in London. There were no playwrights.'

'So, what did happen to you?' I ask. 'Your family are assembled before you. We have told you our story. We are anxious to hear yours. Unless you need some refreshment first? We have cold ham. And good Canary wine. Or beer if you prefer. The servants may still be in their beds, but will scarcely object to being summoned in the middle of the night on an occasion like this one. Those old enough to remember you – and some were not even born when you left – will be as overjoyed as we are.'

He shakes his head again. 'Thank you, but no,' he says. 'Please don't disturb them. I couldn't . . . Anyway, I don't eat or drink the things I used to. None of the things you mentioned anyway.'

'Just tell us what you would like then,' says Aminta. 'We have a larder full to bursting with this year's harvest. There must be something.'

'I suppose what I would really like is couscous,' he says. 'But I doubt you have any.'

'Couscous? I don't even know what that is, Marius. Is it what they eat wherever you've been for the past twenty years?'

'Yes. They eat it quite a lot there, just as we eat bread here.'

'So, where were you?' she asks.

'Morocco,' he says.

'What on earth were you doing there all that time?'

He sighs. 'All sorts of things. It's difficult to sum up in a few words.'

'Then just tell us the whole story. None of us is planning to go back to bed. Not with you here. We have the whole night before us, if need be.'

'I shall tell you my story,' he says, 'but you will soon understand why, if I could, I would rather say nothing at all about the past twenty years and just slip back into my old life, as if it were 1651 and I had been away only a few weeks. But that isn't possible for so many reasons.'

'Marius,' says Aminta, wagging a sisterly finger at him, 'just get on with your tale. It is possible to try the patience even of the longest-lost of families. Forget the prologue. Just start at the beginning and keep going to the end.'

Sir Felix coughs uneasily. 'I think,' he says, 'that we should let Marius tell us whatever he wants to tell us in his own time. We don't need to know everything all at once. Not if he doesn't want us to.'

'On the contrary,' says Aminta. 'I've waited twenty years for this. Start now, Marius, or I'll make sure the servants never serve you . . . what was it?'

'Couscous.'

'Exactly. You'll never eat couscous again. Not in this village.'

'The Battle of Worcester was a confused affair,' Marius begins, 'but which battles are not? I can tell you little about what happened to the south of the town, where Cromwell's troops routed Pitscottie, and where General Keith's men, outflanked and a long way from home, turned and ran. I was with the King in the attack he led on Red Hill, and we might have won the day, but Cromwell crossed the river again, over a bridge of boats, and drove us back into the town. We barricaded the gates and tried to assess our position—'

'Marius,' says Aminta, holding up a palm. 'Our father may be interested to know how Cromwell crossed the river. John may be curious to hear if anyone died in a particularly unusual or interesting way. But what I want to know is why you ended up in Morocco and what you did there. Could you go a little faster please? If there was any further fighting all you need to say is that there was another battle, then move on quickly.'

'I need to tell this in my own way.'

'No you don't, Marius. You're doing this just to annoy me. You really haven't changed a bit.'

'It's your brother's story, Aminta,' says Sir Felix. 'Carry on, Marius, exactly as you wish. And stop if telling it becomes too hard.'

At first, I think Marius hasn't heard his father, but then he nods. 'In the end, as you must know already, most of the royalist army at Worcester were killed or captured. I was in a small party that got clear of the town and made our way down to Bristol, travelling as much as possible by night. Cromwell was searching for fleeing royalists and it wasn't easy to avoid detection. But there was word that some of the colonies in the West Indies were holding out for the King and that, if we could only get a ship sailing for the Americas, we might join them and keep the fight going. The accursed roundheads reached Bristol before we did and posted notices offering a reward for our capture – and indeed for the King's – but we eventually found a passage on the *Golden Gain*, Thomas Champion master, bound for Barbados. Champion was well aware who and what we were, but he was anxious to sign up anyone as a crew member who was willing to sail with him. We found out why when the *Golden Gain* headed not on a direct course for the West Indies but southwards, bound for a trading station on the Guinea coast to take on a shipment of African slaves. It transpired that I and my companions, not being seasoned sailors, were there to oversee the living, breathing cargo and maintain order, with cudgels and whips as required.'

Marius pauses and rubs his eyes, as if trying to see back through so many years has tired them. In spite of Aminta's very clear warning about the pacing of the story, something which to be fair she knows a lot about, we wait patiently. We can see that this may be a more difficult tale to tell than we thought. Perhaps a difficult tale to listen to, as well. Finally, Marius takes up his narrative again. 'But we never got to Guinea, any more than we reached Barbados. As we approached the shores of Morocco, we sighted a couple of heavily armed frigates. These, we were told, were some of the Sallee Rovers, a species of Barbary privateers who preyed on English ships that dared to venture close to their base on the African coast. Many of our crew looked fearfully upon them, but Champion assured us that we were well enough gunned ourselves to see them off, unless they attacked in numbers. That was some comfort, but I didn't like the way they hung around us all day, just out of the range of our cannons, as if waiting for us to make a mistake. All might have been well, but we ran into a storm that night and were driven on to a sandbank within a hundred yards of the beach. At first light, some of the pirates came over to us in rowing boats. There was no question of our fighting them. Our ship was a broken heap of timber, our cannons were useless at close quarters, even if we could have found a level surface to mount one on, and most of our powder barrels had split in the wreck.

'They looked like brigands of the worst sort, but spoke fair and assured us that we would be well treated and found ships that would take us back to England or wherever we wished to go, because the brotherhood of the sea applied in Africa every bit as well as in England or France, and no advantage could or would be taken of a distressed mariner. So we surrendered our swords to them, on the promise of honourable treatment, and were taken ashore without protest. We soon discovered our mistake. No sooner had we set foot on the hot sand than the local children started to pelt us with stones. Our new owners, for such they were, did nothing to discourage them. As our little procession pressed on through the miserable town we were jeered and spat at even by the beggars. We were dying of thirst. No drink was on offer, nor any bread. But that first day was nothing compared with what was to come.

'We were all lowered by rope into an underground prison,' he continues, looking into the smouldering remains of the fire.

'An iron grille was placed over the entrance and we were left to fend for ourselves until the evening, when we were given brackish water and a few handfuls of dates. Then the grille was put in place again. It would be tedious to describe the following days one by one. In any case, after a while, one day merged into the next. We were marched across the desert in the full heat of the sun. Whole days were spent ascending into the barren hills, others on equally long descents into green and pleasant groves. But we were never allowed an hour's more rest than was essential to keep us alive. Those who could not keep up were knocked on the head and left by the side of the road. And not for a moment was the irony lost on us that we were there because we had embarked on a slave ship.'

'Perhaps,' says Sir Felix, 'we should let you stop there and continue tomorrow morning. After you have rested.'

But Marius shakes his head. There is, for him, no stopping now any more than there was then.

'At times,' Marius continues, 'we thought the journey would never end. But, even if we did not know where we were going, we knew what we were going to. We were heading for one or other of the slave markets to be sold. In the end, many of our crew had nothing to fear, because they were dead long before we reached our destination. Only once there, were we finally allowed some rest and were we fed enough to fatten us up again. This last was not done out of kindness. Our owners wanted to ensure that they got the best possible return on their investment and that meant having us in the best condition for sale. We were consigned once more to a damp underground prison, this time with hundreds of others – men, women and children – until the time came to exhibit us in the market. Then we were hauled back up into the blinding sunlight to be inspected and prodded like so many cattle. More times than I could remember a potential buyer wrenched my mouth open to inspect my teeth. None of us protested. We knew that it had to be borne if we wished to stay alive. Our price depended on our fitness for work and our experience. Ship's captains were considered worth having. So were gunners and carpenters. So were masons, though we had none in our party. I do not know what lies my captors told about my abilities, but I was selected as part of the consignment that was allocated to the Sultan himself and set to work building the Sultan's new palace in Marrakech. That was where I was to spend the next two years, hauling stones into place under the unrelenting sun.

'In some ways they were happy times for me. None of us had yet given up hope that we might be rescued. Those who had been sailors knew that ships were often taken by the Sallee Rovers and that, infrequently it must be admitted, attempts were made by the English government to ransom the crews. Families petitioned the King and eventually the King would send somebody who was willing to take the risk of being ambassador to Morocco or Algiers or Tunis to see what might be done at a reasonable price. Every evening we told ourselves that perhaps tomorrow an envoy would arrive from England with money to buy some of us back. My problem was, of course, that nobody knew I was there – I had aimed to leave England as quietly as I could. But I never lost all hope that word might somehow have reached Essex and my friends might attempt to find me.'

Out in the hall the long-case clock has been ticking the minutes away. Now we listen as it chimes three o'clock. Then the silence is broken again only by the steady beat of the pendulum.

'But I digress,' Marius continues. 'No such rescue came. Not for any of us. For two years, as I say, I worked as a slave for the Sultan of Morocco. We saw him relatively little, which was as well. We were scarcely supposed to look at him at all. When he came on his inspection tours we all had to throw ourselves at once to the ground and not glance up until he had gone. He had men executed for the slightest thing – often we had no idea what the cause of his anger might be. One day one of his household slaves – an African from somewhere to the south – dutifully held the Sultan's stirrup while he mounted his horse. No sooner was the Sultan in his saddle than he drew his sword and sliced off the poor man's head with a single stroke – or so somebody who had viewed the scene through his fingers told us. I just heard the head hitting the sand. Nobody knew in what way the slave had offended him and most certainly nobody dared to ask. The man's body and head remained where they fell. As soon as the Sultan had ridden away, we masons all resumed our work, treading on the dry and the blood-soaked ground impartially, as if nothing had happened. We simply pretended the body wasn't there.'

In the silence that follows, I ask: 'But you say you remained there for only two of the twenty years that you were away. What happened next?'

Marius sighs. 'The Moors were constantly urging us to convert to their religion – both by impressing on us the many advantages, in this world and the next, of doing so and by threatening to beat us when we rejected their offer. To begin with, we saw it as a sort of trial, such as the early Christians had undergone, and refused to give in to temptation. But as the months passed, one or two of my companions turned Turk, as the saying was. They were not freed, but some were given more pleasant duties. We saw them and envied them but there was, our great and abiding love of the Church of England apart, one reason why we held back. We knew that the English government would not ransom any of us who became Muslims, because we would then have been what they called "renegades". That small, dwindling hope of freedom was worth the privations we endured.'

'But you did nevertheless at least pretend to convert?' I say. 'You made life easier for yourself?'

He looks away from the fire and straight at me. 'There was no pretence,' he says. 'I became a Muslim. I am a Muslim.'

'Very well, you are still a Muslim. For the moment at least. And that made your captivity more bearable?' I ask.

'The day after it was known that I had converted, the Sultan visited the building works. Somebody had told him that one of the Christians had seen reason. He asked that I should be pointed out to him amongst the crouching workmen. He ordered me to stand and asked what work I should like to do, now I was no longer an infidel dog. I feared it could be a trick, for such things were rumoured to be common, so I replied cautiously that my desire was to perform whatever duties would most please him for as long as he wished. He asked what I had done before and I told him of my service in the royalist army. Without further discussion, purely on a whim, he made me a captain in his own forces. I could have no more protested my unfitness for the post than I could have corrected him on any other matter. Nor, I knew, could any of his generals have refused to admit me or criticised his judgement. I was now indisputably a captain in a regiment of Moroccan foot guards. That evening, the last I would spend in chains, magnificent new clothes were brought to me.

A gleaming sword was tied to my waist. I was led away to my new quarters in the palace barracks. And, whatever my former companions may have felt privately about my turning Turk, none dared even to glance in my direction, lest in my new role I ordered their execution on the spot. I was still a slave, but I was suddenly a person of consequence in Morocco. For the next eighteen years, I served the Sultan, and his successors, in various parts of his dominions. Then I was posted to the sea coast. I was able to get myself rowed out to an English man-of-war, anchored not far away. The captain showed some reluctance to take me at first, not wishing to be the cause of some new dispute with the Sultan, but he eventually agreed to disguise me as one of his crew in these blue canvas clothes. I sailed back to England and travelled by stages to Essex, still in my sailor's canvas suit, for I had no other. At first I was unwilling – ashamed almost – to make myself known to people here. I saw Harry Hardy and spoke to him, but he clearly had no idea who I was and I could not bring myself to tell him. When he asked me direct, I told him I was nobody. "Nemo". Because that's who I felt I was.

'I knew then that I had changed beyond all recognition. For some days I hid in the woods and observed you all coming and going. But I needed food and decided that the one place I could lawfully steal from was the orchard of my own home. You surprised me in the act and I fled in shame and confusion. Tonight I decided I would try again. You would find me in the morning, not a thief in the orchard but in my rightful place, in my father's library. I discovered a window unlatched and climbed in, waiting to see you all when you came down in the morning. But I was too clumsy. John and Aminta heard me entering. And so, here we all are. I have, as Aminta requested, reached the conclusion of the story, with everyone here in their rightful place. The cycle of the drama is complete. I am back where I began. And everyone lived in happiness and great contentment ever after. The end.' Even by the light of the candles, I can see very clearly how false his smile is.

The long, long silence is eventually broken by Sir Felix.

'A strange and wonderful tale,' he says. 'But we must now let you have some rest, Marius. Aminta will find you a chamber and a clean nightshirt. You can't sleep in these coarse clothes, smelling of ships and the sea. We shall talk again in the morning, when we shall also find you a coat and breeches and make you look like a proper English gentleman again rather than a Mohammedan renegade. Goodnight, Marius. And welcome home.'

The door closes behind the two of them. Sir Felix slumps back into his chair and gives a long sigh.

'As you have said, Marius's is a strange and wonderful tale,' I say.

'I wonder, John, which parts are true?'

'I suspect that all we have been told is true enough. But he covered eighteen years of military service very economically.'

'Yes,' says Sir Felix, 'I thought so too. We military men like to bore people a little with descriptions of our marches and manoeuvres. I may have mentioned one or two of my own.'

'Occasionally,' I say.

'He was not reluctant to tell us about the relatively brief Battle of Worcester – how the two sides conducted themselves – by what scurvy trick Cromwell defeated us. On the other hand, he chose to say very little about his years of service in Morocco. Perhaps nothing happened between his being presented with a gleaming sword and finding a rowing boat eighteen years later.'

'That is what we are invited to assume.'

'Well, at least he spent most of his time in Morocco as a soldier and not as a common slave.'

'Is that any sort of consolation?'

'Oh yes, I think so. Don't you?'

'It wasn't his fault he became a slave,' I say. 'Nobody deserves to become a slave.'

'You think so? Even Marius drew our attention to the irony of his capture.'

'I must speak to the vicar,' I say. 'Being a Muslim will have helped Marius in Africa, but it won't here. Whatever he regards himself as now, we need to find out what the process is for readmitting him to the Church of England as quickly as we can.'

'Do Mohammedans really not eat pork or drink wine?'

'So I understand. They are like the Jews – at least in respect of pork.'

'Then it would be inconvenient for the servants if he did not become a Christian again, and quickly, as you say. For that reason if nothing else we must put a stop to his delusion that he is a Mohammedan. On the other hand, if none of us says anything in the village about his ever being a worshipper of Mohammed, perhaps we don't need to trouble the vicar. We could simply deal with the matter quietly amongst ourselves . . .'

'I don't think it's going to be that easy,' I say.

For a long time I lie there, looking up at the canopy above the bed.

'Are you awake?' Aminta asks.

'I still can't sleep. Too much excitement,' I say. 'And it will soon be dawn. Did Marius like his new quarters?'

'He didn't say. He didn't say much at all to me, as it happens. I'd expected him to be so pleased that he was back here.'

'But he's not?'

'Not as far as I could tell.'

'Is it because I am now the owner of the house that might have been his? I mean, if Marius had been here and not in Morocco, your father might not have sold up to Colonel Payne. Marius would be the heir to this property.'

'I don't think so. In the first place, my father's financial position was dire. He'd lent the King every penny he had, with no hope he'd ever get anything back. Then he had to pay fines to Cromwell for having lent the money to the King. He'd have had to sell to Colonel Payne whether Marius was here or not. Marius would have been the heir to nothing. And second, I don't think Marius cares much about it one way or the other. I'm not sure that he cares about anything. I honestly think he'd rather be back in Morocco with his regiment than here in England with his family.'

'I wonder what he was doing for those eighteen years as a soldier in Africa.'

'I wonder what he was doing during his time in the woods here.'

'Yes, that worries me too,' I say. 'It worries me a lot.'

Chapter 12

In which we deal with certain matters of religion

'No,' says Ben. 'Flood never came back last night. I said I would let you know when he did, but there was nothing to report.'

'Could he have returned to London?'

'His bag is still in his chamber, along with his wooden staff.'

'Well, I'm sure he'll turn up, then.'

'It's funny, though – he's been hunting all this time for this African slave and it turns out that people had just seen Mister Marius – not Nero at all. I can't wait to see Flood's face when he finds out.'

Some of the servants from the Big House must have been to the inn this morning. Ben is reasonably well informed anyway. I wonder what else he's heard.

'Yes,' I say. 'The African sun has tanned Marius's skin so much that he looks as if he was born there. Doubtless he'll resemble a member of the Essex gentry again by the end of the winter. My father has found him a decent suit of clothes and ordered that the blue canvas ones should be consigned to the fire. The tar will make them burn well at least.'

Ben picks up a tankard and starts to polish it – a sure sign that he wishes to put something off for a minute or so.

'Sir Felix must be delighted to have Mister Marius back,' he says eventually. 'As you must, I assume.'

'Of course,' I say. 'We all are.'

'And so am I. So is the whole village.'

'That's good to hear.'

'He's been in Africa then, Mister Marius?'

'Yes. That's what I said.'

'Captured by the corsairs?'

'Yes,' I say. 'The Sallee Rovers.'

Ben pauses his polishing and looks at me. He may be about to come to the point. 'I'd just heard Mister Marius was . . . well, not quite as he was before he went away. Can that be true?'

'Twenty years is a long time, Ben. We've all changed in the past twenty years.'

'So we have. It's not to be expected that he would come back exactly as he used to be. Mister Marius will have a few tales to tell, I shouldn't wonder. About the desert and so forth. Very different from Essex. Lions. Camels. Elephants. Cannibals with tails and two heads, no doubt. We look forward to welcoming him here. Tell him his ale will be on the house when he comes.'

'He doesn't drink ale any more.'

'How's that then?'

'He became a Muslim.'

'Muslim? What's a Muslim?'

'A Mohammedan. A Turk.'

'Oh, a Turk,' says Ben. He's heard of them. 'And Turks don't drink ale?'

'No.'

'Are you sure? The ones in the play do. Or at the least, afterwards, the men playing the Turks drink as much free ale as the ones who were playing Christians. More, if anything.'

'I'm certain.'

'Well, I've heard some strange things in my time but none as strange as that. Still, now he's back in England he's a Christian again, surely? Stands to reason, doesn't it? The moment he sets foot on English soil, he's a member of the Church of England. That's the law.'

'I'm off to see the vicar now for advice on exactly that point.'

'It is certainly a very interesting problem,' says the vicar. 'I have not had to deal with a similar case myself, but I recall that there is a ceremony prescribed for the readmittance of a lapsed member of the Church. The person concerned has, I think, to acknowledge their sin and ask humbly to be accepted again into the Church of England, which of course is very happy to oblige them. I think it is in one of these books on this shelf...let me check...ah yes, it's here. *The Laudian Rite for Returned Renegades.* "Let the offender be appointed to stand in the porch of the church in a penitent fashion in a white sheet and with a white wand in his hand, his head uncovered, his countenance dejected. Let him, in a humble and devout manner, kiss the bottom stone of the font, strike his breast, and presently depart into the church porch as before." Then ... some other things. Well, that's all perfectly straightforward. Nothing to get worried about in any way. I should need to check whether there is any fee to be collected, but I would be more or less happy to forgo it in view of the fact that it is a member of your family.'

'Thank you, vicar,' I say. 'And what if the person concerned feels that they have not committed any sin by converting?'

'Is that how Marius feels about the matter?'

'I think so. He seems to have a deep and abiding respect for his new faith.'

'Well, the Laudian Rite is only a form of words, when all's said and done. He doesn't need to believe any of it, any more than he needs to believe a great deal else we all say every Sunday. He just has to read out what it says in the book. As you are aware, it is the appearance of conformity that matters to the present government. So long as there are no ripples on the surface, the Church offers a great deal of latitude down below. I mean, Marius can't bring a prayer mat to church with him, but much of the Mohammedan faith is not incompatible with what you and I believe. I've read the Reverend Alexander Ross's translation of the Alcoran and most of it is surprisingly unobjectionable. I'd actually say we could learn a great deal from it, though I wouldn't say that in front of the Bishop.'

'It wouldn't be possible for Marius simply to attend services occasionally, as if nothing had happened?'

'You're worried from a legal viewpoint? I mean that you are obliged to enforce church attendance, including that of your own family?'

'It's more that I think prayer with his neighbours around him might help. He seems quite troubled.'

'There is no doubt that ritual, within the legally permitted limits, is very soothing.'

'So that might be possible then?'

The vicar considers this carefully. 'We must consider the danger the Bishop might find out,' he says. 'An avowed and completely unrepentant Mohammedan attending communion services. Some officious parishioner might decide to write and tell him. You know the sort? It could be awkward for both of us if that happened. More awkward for me than for you, but there's no point in inviting trouble when we don't have to. That's what I always think. Better to stick to the rules, even if you don't agree with them entirely. This time, at least.'

'I wouldn't wish to inconvenience you,' I say.

'Thank you,' he says. 'I appreciate that more than I can say. But if you'll take my advice, Sir John, I'd tread carefully. There's the question of his immortal soul to consider, obviously, but, more important, if your brother-in-law insists on being a Mohammedan, here in the heart of Essex, people may not take kindly to it. Of course, we're all different – it's just not a good idea to be too different. Not in Essex. There's a great deal to be said for sensible conformity.'

I think of Ben's objection to the use of Aphra as a Christian name. You don't have to do much to raise eyebrows.

'Well,' says the vicar, 'I'm sure you will find a prudent middle way. That is what we are all trying to do, after all.'

I wish him good day and I step out into the mild, prudent, autumnal sunshine.

Harry Hardy is in his garden. He too has heard the rumours.

'I'm so pleased, Sir John, that Mister Marius is back amongst us,' he says. 'We thought he had gone for ever. Please convey my best wishes to him and say we all hope to see him soon. I'm sorry I didn't recognise him when I saw him the other day, but it has been a long time and he had disguised himself as a stranger.'

'I'm sure he will be out and about in the village before too long,' I say. 'And I know that he doesn't hold it against you that you didn't know who he was. He could have introduced himself after all.'

'Calling himself "Nemo" was a joke then?'

'I think he just didn't know what to say. The word just means "nobody" in Latin. It will all be different next time. You'll see.'

'That's good to hear, Sir John. It's kind of you to spend the time explaining it to me. I thought we'd all see him this morning, though – that he'd want to come and see us, now he's back officially as it were. Is he unwell?'

'Merely tired after his travels, I think.'

'And he's been a slave for twenty years?'

'So it would seem.'

'He was how old when he was taken . . . twenty?'

'A little younger, I think.'

'That's a time when a young man thinks of taking a wife. Having children. Making a career. A whole generation has been born and grown up in Clavershall West since Mister Marius left. A lot of those who were scarcely more than babies then have children of their own now. Children who are already walking and talking. He must think of that a lot.'

'Yes, I suppose he does.'

'Ah well, he's free at last. Nobody's a slave in England, are they? He must put the past behind him. Regrets weigh you down worse than a sack of wet barley.'

From out of nowhere, a sharp gust of wind causes an untidy heap of leaves by the road to whirl upwards. The words uttered years ago in the Cartwright case come to my mind: 'this air is too pure for a slave to breathe in'. Perhaps if he takes a few more breaths of good Essex air Marius really will be wholly free again.

*

I meet him as I walk back across the park to the Big House. His eyes are cast downwards and I think he is not going to acknowledge me at all, then he looks up and gives me a half-smile.

'I am sorry, John. I was distracted. I did not mean to walk straight past you.'

'Are you going into the village?' I ask. 'Everyone wants to see you and welcome you home.'

'Not today, I think. I still can't bear . . . well, I'd rather not, anyway. I had planned to walk out on the Saffron Walden road, away from things. To be by myself for a while. For a long time I had little chance to do that or any choice as to who my companions were.'

'They'll welcome you at the inn when you are ready.'

'You know that it is against my religion to touch alcohol of any sort.'

'The vicar is of the opinion that it would be easy for you to be readmitted to the Church and, by logical extension, to the village inn. There is an unnecessarily humiliating ceremony you will have to go through for the Church – it just has to be done – but I doubt Ben will ask you to do any form of penance for your having lapsed as an ale drinker.'

'I do not wish to be readmitted to anything. I am a Muslim. I am a Muslim by choice, not by compulsion.'

'But surely . . .'

He shakes his head. 'What do you think my first duties were in the Sultan's army, John?'

'I have no idea. Probably rather unexciting guard duty somewhere.'

'I was responsible for maintaining order amongst the workers who were formerly my friends.'

'That would have been difficult. Did they condemn you for changing sides?'

'They would not have dared.'

'I suppose not.'

'In the first month I had two of them whipped, for failing to complete their daily quota. One was beaten almost senseless in front of me. It was for me to order the beating to cease, but I knew if it was stopped too soon the Sultan might simply command that the man should be executed instead. So, I had him beaten half to death to save his life. And to save mine, I suppose. If I showed too much leniency, his punishment might easily have become my own.'

'It sounds as if you had no choice, then.'

'Perhaps not then, but other times,' he says. 'Sometimes, it really can be as simple as your beating or theirs. Your life or theirs. It can be quite evenly balanced. My former friends all knew that, as they waited patiently for me to order that the man's beating should stop.'

I think of decisions I have had to make in Arlington's service. Yes, some meant that I lived and somebody else died. That's why I'm still here.

'I became a Muslim,' Marius continues. 'But I hadn't realised how others might have to pay for it. I could have no respect for myself if, now all danger was past, I chose to slip back into my old ways. Drinking ale. Eating pork. Rejecting the teaching I have received. I will not heap betrayal on betrayal.'

'You were coerced,' I say. 'You cannot say that your decision to become a Muslim was really of your own free will – that you would have done it even if you had remained here in England. And whatever you had to do in the Sultan's service – whatever wrongs you may feel you have committed – you bear no blame for it.'

'No blame at all? That's good English law, is it?'

'Very well, not legally. But morally, certainly. I refuse to hold you responsible for things that you had no choice but to do.'

'Then you are a fool,' says Marius. 'Because you have no idea what I have done.'

I turn and see Ben hurrying towards me from the direction of the inn.

'Good day, Sir John. Good day, Mister Marius. It's good to have you back, sir.' He swallows hard. 'I need you to come with me, Sir John. They've found Flood. His body is in the woods, just north of the New House. And it's not a pretty sight.'

I turn to see what Marius's reaction is to this news, but he is staring into the distance, as if he had forgotten that Ben and I were there.

Chapter 13

In which I do not make the same mistake twice

Flood's body lies in a small area of woodland, just off the road leading to Cambridge. The killer's attempt to conceal it has been good enough to delay its discovery by a few hours, but not much more. The first moderately observant traveller passing the woods this morning – Jim Ruggles, as it happens – spotted it and reported it to the constable, delaying the start of ploughing by thirty minutes.

'Mister Thatcher won't like you doing that,' says Ben over my shoulder.

'Just making sure he's dead, Ben. I wouldn't want to trouble the coroner unnecessarily. Not after last time.'

'He's as stiff as a board. Even Jim, who found him, didn't have any doubts.'

'Perhaps Flood, like Mister Umfraville, will nevertheless miraculously recover.'

'You really think so?'

'No, Ben, I don't. But, this time, we're going to do things properly. Do you see the livor mortis?'

'I might if I knew what it was.'

'It's the bruising where the blood has settled after death.'

'So the blood flows upwards then?'

'No, it flows downwards.'

'So, why is it . . . oh, I see. You reckon the body has been moved.'

'I'm certain of it. And look at the ground around him. When Umfraville was hit on the back of the head there was blood everywhere. There's almost none here. And Flood must have been struck . . . how many times?'

'Four? Five? It's difficult to say. Enough to kill him and then some.'

I examine the head more carefully. There are certainly two deep wounds at the back, slicing through the bone. There is a third that seems to have missed the head and struck the shoulder, half severing the arm. A fourth has struck just below the left eye. He probably turned as the weapon descended on him. Then there seems to be another at the back, at a slightly different angle to the first two. A half-hearted valedictory blow that made very little difference to anything much, except to show that the killer had few regrets about the other four. Flood's position looks quite natural. He was moved before rigor mortis set in and he has stiffened in his new position. I'd say he was probably killed twelve to eighteen hours ago. So, that's yesterday afternoon or evening, with the body moved before midnight.

I walk a few yards down the road, but the ground has no plans to help me. Then I notice an almost imperceptible track leading into the woods. It is the sort of thing wild deer might make, but there is something glinting in the grass. It is a small steel clasp knife – still shining, without a speck of rust. Somebody has most certainly been this way recently. I pick up the knife and drop it into my pocket. Then I press on through the narrow gap in the bushes, where I find myself in a clearing.

I hear Ben struggling to get his rotund form through the gap after me and a brief curse as some part of his clothing snags on a thorn. Then he is standing beside me, viewing what I am viewing.

'Who do you think made that, then?' asks Ben.

We survey the rough structure in front of us. It would once have given a man protection for a night's sleep, but has now been thoroughly trashed.

'Difficult to tell,' I say.

'Looks like it was the same person who made the one in the woods that the charcoal burners use,' says Ben. 'And I reckon it was kicked in by the same people who destroyed the other one.'

I nod. Before Flood and his minions dealt with them, the two shelters would have been very similar. Rough and ready but good for a few nights.

'So, the builder was disturbed at his previous place and moved up here?' says Ben. 'Or maybe he was disturbed here and moved to the woods?'

'One or the other,' I say.

'And we all thought the other one was built by that slave, Nero?'

'Yes.'

'Except we now think it was Mister Marius all along? Because Nero was never in the village?' says Ben.

I nod again. This wasn't what I wanted to find. Not at all.

My hand closes for a moment on the clasp knife in my pocket and then releases it again.

'So, this shelter Mister Marius may have built is right by where we found the body?' says Ben helpfully, just in case I haven't made the connection myself.

Ben is reluctant to tell me to my face that my newly returned brother-in-law could be a murderer, but his meaning is as clear as it needs to be.

'The body had been moved,' I say. 'We know that. Its position relative to the shelter may not be significant.'

'Maybe it wasn't moved so very far,' says Ben. 'Flood's a bit lighter than Umfraville, I'll grant you that, but you still wouldn't want to drag it a long way.'

'There's no sign of it being dragged. It's more likely it was carried. And there's no blood by the camp. Nothing, in short, to connect the murder with this mess of branches, whoever built it. We've done as much as we can for the moment. Could you please send my compliments to Mister Thatcher and say that it won't be a complete waste of his time if he comes over to Clavershall West later today?'

'So,' says Thatcher. 'This is the slave catcher you suspected of killing Umfraville.'

'Daniel Flood,' I say. 'At one point he was most certainly one of the suspects.'

'Except Umfraville isn't dead and he is. It's a pity that you did not have the courage of your convictions.'

'In what way, Mister Thatcher?'

'If you still had Flood safely under lock and key for the attack on Umfraville, nobody would have been able to murder him.'

'I don't remember your advising me at the time to keep him locked up. Quite the reverse.'

'It would scarcely be my place, Sir John, to instruct you, as a magistrate, on your duties. I mean your proper duties rather than any you might have assumed of your own accord. Guarding prisoners, for example.'

'You will be aware, Mister Thatcher, that without a body it was difficult to detain him or anyone.'

Thatcher smiles. 'Well, we certainly have a body now, don't we? I think it might be better, Sir John, if we concentrated for a moment on the evidence before us and see where it takes us. The attacks on Umfraville and Flood are very similar. Both were struck from behind with a sharp weapon. And we are not so far from the New House where Umfraville was attacked. I assume you will agree with me when I say that the attacker was the same person in both cases?'

He puts his head on one side, still smiling and defying me to disagree with him.

'I'd rather keep an open mind on that,' I say. 'It was a single blow from a blunt axe in the case of Umfraville – that axe is now with Ben in case it is needed as evidence. The multiple wounds here suggest something with a keener edge anyway. The largest wound must be a good two inches deep.'

'Are you saying you think that the cases are not connected? You surprise me. Consider the circumstances, Sir John. Both gentlemen are from Barbados. Both had arrived very recently. One was a slave owner and the other a slave catcher. If we had an Honourable Guild of Merchant Slavers, both would qualify as masters of their trade. And then there is the slave, Nero. Mister Umfraville formerly owned him. Mister Flood was seeking to capture him for his new owner. Out of all of the men in this county, these are the two who were attacked. Perhaps, in the short time they were here, they chanced to annoy two different individuals badly enough to merit this treatment, but you have to admit, Sir John, that Nero is the only person we know who had a motive for killing both of these gentlemen. There are others in the village who might have killed one or the other, I suppose, but nobody else who would have killed both. And both were killed by a blow from behind, in a most cowardly and un-English manner. You really need to look no further than Nero as the perpetrator. Has he been sighted again?'

'We have no evidence at all as to the motive of the killer. As for Nero, we are no longer sure he was ever here.'

'But the charcoal burners saw him.'

'There was somebody else hiding out in the woods. Somebody who had recently returned from Africa after a long stay there – hence he had in many respects the appearance of a Moor, even though he had been born in this village.'

'How interesting. And why should somebody hide in the woods so close to what was, you say, his home?'

'I'm not sure. I think he found it difficult, after so long away, to talk to those who were formerly his friends.'

'Really? So, you have spoken to him already?'

'He is my brother-in-law – Marius Clifford. He is staying with me at the Big House.'

'And what had detained him so long in Africa?'

'He was captured by the Barbary pirates and held in Morocco as a slave. For twenty years he was forced to work, first as a mason and then later as a member of the Sultan's army.'

'Ah, so he was a slave himself. And the two dead men, as we have agreed, are a slave owner and a slave catcher.'

'There is no reason to suppose any connection with my brother-in-law. He was in Africa, not Barbados.'

'But he was nevertheless a slave?'

'Yes,' I say.

'And you can still see no connection? No reason why your brother-in-law might have disliked both men? Now you really do surprise me, Sir John. I suggest to you that the two murders are connected. You reserve your judgement on that. I suggest that the motive of the killer may lie in the fact that both victims were connected with slavery. You say that there is as yet no evidence as to the motive. Well, I must take your word for it since you are a magistrate and since you know Mister Clifford so intimately. Am I to assume that, like Flood and Umfraville, Marius Clifford had recently arrived here?'

'Yes. A few days ago.'

'And you don't find that yet another strange coincidence? Mister Clifford arrives. Then, shortly after, two men, whom he might consider richly deserved death ... die.'

'It would be wrong to make any assumptions until we have all of the evidence.'

'I would have thought we have a great deal of evidence already. Well, I hesitate to advise somebody who is, as you undoubtedly are, my superior by birth and by office, but are you sure that you should be investigating this matter at all, Sir John? Such a close member of your own family ... I simply ask, you understand, in the most respectful manner possible.'

He looks at me with great sympathy and understanding.

'As you say, he is my brother-in-law,' I say. 'I would also wish you to know Marius was a very good friend of mine when I was younger – I mean, as much as somebody several years older than myself could be. I greatly admired him. I mourned his loss deeply when I thought he had died at the Battle of Worcester.'

Thatcher's expression remains that of a wholly disinterested friend. 'Then you must feel you are doubly bound to stand aside?'

'No. The administration of justice in these parishes is my concern. Everything you have said is mere supposition. There is, as yet, nothing of substance to connect Mister Clifford with either murder. He knew neither of the men who were killed. Nobody has laid a formal accusation against him.'

'If you tell me, as an office holder of the King's and a gentleman, that there is nothing of substance, then there is of course nothing of substance. I shall not question your decision, Sir John. I would merely ask you to remember, if the matter ever arises again, that I drew the self-evident conflict of interest to your attention in the clearest possible manner. I would not wish anyone to think that I failed to do my duty in that respect. Your constable here is a witness to that.'

'I've never known Sir John be anything other than fair and honest,' says Ben.

I'm grateful to Ben for that, even if it's not strictly true. When you're working as a spy, being fair and honest isn't always the best idea.

'Did you not invite Mister Thatcher to dinner?' asks Aminta. 'Saffron Walden isn't far but he will be very hungry when he gets there.'

'Thatcher preferred an immediate return and a late dinner,' I say. 'Anyway, he seems to think that your brother attacked both Umfraville and Flood. It would not have been a comfortable meal, with the two of them sitting on opposite sides of the table, accuser and accused.'

'Marius is still out,' she says. 'I think that we shall have to dine without him today.'

'Did he not come back this morning?'

'No,' she says. 'Why does Thatcher suspect him?'

'Because he was formerly enslaved. He was therefore likely to feel animosity towards both victims. And he seems to have arrived in the village just as they did. Or perhaps a little before – we don't know exactly, do we? Thinking about it, there's a great deal Marius hasn't told us yet, including exactly how long he has been back.'

'But there's no more to Thatcher's suspicions than that?'

'No . . . well, not much more. Marius does seem to have been camping close to where both bodies were found. And I found this clasp knife by the road, near the shelter that Marius – or somebody – had built there. Could the knife be his?'

Aminta examines it. 'I've honestly no idea. But I've seen so little of him since he arrived.'

'The knife would seem to be English,' I say. 'At least, it's not obviously anything else – Moroccan, for example. It could belong to anyone living in the village.'

'I suppose so.'

'The Grices,' I say. 'They'd been there recently. Or Flood himself.'

'Or somebody simply travelling along the road,' says Aminta. 'What did Thatcher make of it when you showed it to him?'

'I didn't show it to him.'

'Shouldn't you have done?'

'I suppose so. But Thatcher seems determined to prove that Marius is the killer, regardless of the facts. He'd have instantly claimed it as evidence against him. I mean, if it does prove to belong to your brother. Anyway, it was twenty or thirty yards from where we found Flood.'

'Is Thatcher really so unreasonable? Wouldn't it have been better to present him with the evidence for what it's worth?'

'Maybe,' I say.

'Except that you do think the knife is Marius's, don't you? And you're worried he may have killed Flood?'

'The Marius I knew when I was young would never have attacked somebody from behind.'

'He's not the Marius we knew,' says Aminta. 'I'm not sure I know who or what he is, but he's not that.

Chapter 14

In which I take a walk round the park

The light is fading as we meet each other, halfway down the drive that leads up to the front door of the Big House. 'I saw you from the library window,' I say to Marius. 'I thought I would walk down to meet you. Perhaps we could take a turn together? Just the two of us. The sunsets at this time of year are quite magnificent and viewing them from the house does not do them justice.'

'I have already walked a long way today,' says Marius. 'If you'll excuse me, John . . .'

'I hope, Marius, you will oblige me in this small thing,' I say, taking his arm.

He shrugs, though whether to show his indifference or to make me release his arm is unclear. 'I cannot claim any urgent engagement,' he says.

For a while we walk in silence. The sky is deep red – the colour of old blood – and golden orange. The shadows are very long. It is already almost night amongst the trees. A frosty chill is spreading across the park. But there are things that need to be said and to be said in private.

'Where did you go today?' I ask.

Marius looks straight ahead. 'I went out on the Saffron Walden road. A little way in that direction.'

'Did you get your dinner there? There are several good inns in town.'

'I turned off the road before Saffron Walden. I preferred to avoid the town. Anyway, I am used to forgoing meals. Often we slaves ate only once a day. Sometimes twice, if we were fortunate.'

'I hope you will join us for supper, then. Aminta and Sir Felix would welcome it. They missed you at dinner. After so many years away, it is unkind to keep yourself from them.'

'I have consented to accompany you this evening, John. Do not press me further.'

We again walk on in silence. A group of deer crosses our path in a leisurely manner. They have no fear of us, though I have eaten many of their kin. When the danger is not obvious, it is easy to become overconfident.

'You recall that Ben and I went to see Flood's body?' I say. 'He had been murdered.'

'Oh yes . . . this morning. Who is Flood?'

'A slave catcher from Barbados.'

'What was he doing here, so far from home?'

'He was in pursuit of a slave – or to be exact, I suppose, a former slave – named Nero. For a while, some people, catching a glimpse of you in the woods, thought that you were he.'

'One slave looks much like another.'

'How long have you been in the village?' I ask. 'You've never really told us.'

'Not long. A week perhaps?'

'Why didn't you come to the Big House straight away?'

'It was difficult . . . I didn't know what sort of reception I would receive. After all that had happened. I had travelled so many weeks to get here, eager to see you all, then at the last moment . . .'

'So you waited in the woods?'

'Waited and watched you all. I saw my father walking in the park here and riding out on his horse. I naturally assumed that he still owned the house. I went to find you at the New House but it appeared to be empty. You know the rest.'

'Did you see Hubert Umfraville arrive? Did you witness the attack in the orchard?'

'I wouldn't have recognised Hubert Umfraville, not then or now. How could I? I certainly saw nobody attacked.'

'You camped in the woods near the Big House?'

'Yes. There and at another place close to where the charcoal burners are. I also sheltered for a while in the church, but it felt strange there and I was afraid I would be discovered.'

'How have you survived? You had no food other than our apples.'

'I know how to live off the land. I trapped rabbits. Skinned them with my knife. Cooked them over a low fire. I once showed you how to set a trap, remember? Sadly I have mislaid my knife – one of my few possessions. It is fortunate that I no longer need to skin anything because I have no money to buy another.'

I take out the clasp knife and show him.

'Yes – that is mine! Where on earth did you find it?'

'Close to where we found Flood's body,' I say.

'Well, that was a happy chance,' he says.

'I would not have put it that way myself,' I say.

Marius frowns. 'You are not accusing me of having anything to do with his death?'

'The coroner is.'

'Who is the coroner?'

'A gentleman named Mister Thatcher. He is holding an inquest in the village tomorrow.'

'Where? Here at the Big House?'

'At the inn.'

Marius nods. 'Well, I am happy to give evidence if he asks me to. But all I can tell him is that I have never seen Flood.'

'Marius, do you swear to me that you did not kill Flood or Umfraville?'

'I swear on my sister's life.'

I wonder how Aminta would view that oath. Touching but unnecessarily risky? Still, Marius appears to be sincere.

'Even so, I would advise you to be careful,' I say, handing him the knife.

He takes it and slides it, completely unconcerned, into his own pocket. 'Thank you, John. I shall be.'

'It would help if you acted in a friendlier way towards the villagers. I would suggest that you go and talk to them – just to say hello. Just to say how pleased you are to be back amongst them – amongst your own people. Try to be what you were before, but twenty years older. It's what they expect.'

'I'm not as I was before. That's the point, you see.'

'It's for your own sake, Marius, not theirs or even mine. You need their goodwill. Especially if the inquest produces a result that is in any way inconvenient.'

'Why would it do that?'

'Because Thatcher may try to get the jury to name you as the murderer.'

'Very well. I shall do my best.'

'It would also be helpful if you attended church on Sunday. Just for form's sake. You won't have to do much more than say the Creed and the Lord's Prayer. I assume you still remember both?'

'I've told you. I can't do that.'

'Not to save your life?'

'Not to save my life.'

'Marius, ten years after the King's return I remain a republican to my very core. If by wishing it I could have Cromwell back, then I'd do it tomorrow. But I would never admit that to anyone. Not to my former master Lord Arlington, who has the most silky and flexible conscience of any man I know. Not to Ben, who has, in the interest of his trade as an innkeeper, never openly expressed the slightest preference for King or Republic. Not even to Aminta, who claims to be able to see the very bottom of my dull, grey, puritan soul. But I am telling you. Over the past twenty years, we have all had to dissemble because there was no other way to lead a normal life. I am a committed republican who has devoted his life to, and occasionally risked it for, His Gracious Majesty King Charles the Second. As a result I have a family that I love and a very pleasant house for them to live in. Those who have insisted on a more rigid interpretation of what it means to be loyal to the old English Republic have been much less happy and in many cases their heads are now exhibited on spikes on London Bridge.'

'It's not the same thing, John. You may fool the King, but you cannot dissemble before God.'

'You insist on worshipping Mohammed?'

'We Muslims do not worship the Prophet Mohammed,

peace be upon him. I think you know that. We worship God. The one true God. We also respect the same prophets that you do. We often name our children after them – Musa, Ibrahim, Sulaiman, Isa.'

'As good Christians, we named our son after the King and our daughter after a playwright. Shall we return to the house? Aminta will be getting worried that I am about to become a Muslim as well as a republican and a puritan.'

I am again staring up at the canopy above the bed. Quite a lot has happened today.

'Marius at least ate with us tonight,' says Aminta.

'It is fortunate that cook chose to give us beef.'

'Does any religion not eat beef?'

'I was once told people didn't eat beef in India,' I say. 'But I'm not sure that it can be true. Why would they do that? Leviticus condemns only pork and shellfish.'

'Of their flesh shall ye not eat, and their carcase shall ye not touch; they are unclean to you,' says Aminta. 'I suppose that means Mohammedans read Leviticus too?'

'I suppose so. They end up with much the same rules anyway. And they seem to have the same prophets, just slightly different names. Ibrahim is Abraham and Musa is Moses. I'm not sure who Isa is. Isaiah, maybe?'

'If Christianity and Mohammedanism are so similar, I can't see why Marius can't worship with us again. Or just lead a normal life. It's not much to ask, is it? I'd forgotten how stubborn my brother could be. Perhaps if he married some girl in the village. She'd make him see sense. A wife and some children are the solution to all his problems. What about Margaret Platt?'

'She was suspected of witchcraft.'

'She's a nice girl, though, and Marius can't afford to be choosy.'

'I suppose not. He talked about what they named children in Morocco – when we were discussing prophets.'

'Well, he must have at least thought about having a family then,' says Aminta.

'The same idea occurred to me. Otherwise why wouldn't he just say that people were named in that way? Ben wouldn't approve of a boy named Isa, though.'

'No. This is England. Rupert, Charles and James are perfectly good names for boys. Jane or Mary or Catherine for girls.'

'Or Aphra,' I say.

'Or Aphra. Obviously.'

'Yes,' says Mistress Umfraville, 'we had of course heard that Flood had been killed. No loss, I think, to anyone.'

Outside the morning sun is shining. In the parlour, we are having a strangely morbid conversation for such a fine day. The Umfraville family are clustered round me, Mistress Umfraville in a cushioned chair, Drusilla and Mary on stools, George and James standing easily behind them. They might almost be sitting for a portrait.

'The body was found not far from here – a little way up the Cambridge road,' I say.

'But not killed there,' says Mistress Umfraville.

In a village this size, nothing remains a secret for longer than it takes to walk from one end of it to the other.

'No,' I say. 'He was killed somewhere else, but maybe not far away. He had apparently been attacked with an axe, as your husband was.'

'But not the same axe,' says Mistress Umfraville, 'since your constable took that one away. Fortunately your father-in-law had left us another. We do not need the rusty one back. The King may keep it if he wishes.'

'Did any of you see or hear anything the night before last?' I ask.

'No,' says Mary.

'And you, Drusilla?'

'She didn't either,' say Mary.

Drusilla gives me a shy smile. The boys shake their heads.

'We go to bed early here in the country,' says George. 'Our lives are very unexciting.'

'Had any of you spoken to Flood since he arrived in the village?' I ask.

'He'd have known better than to ask us to help him catch Nero,' says Mistress Umfraville.

'He had hopes that your husband might help him, though,' I say.

'Father would never have done that,' says Drusilla.

'I agree,' says Mistress Umfraville. 'Hubert's ingratitude extended a long way, but not that far. Whose evidence will Mister Thatcher be calling for at the inquest? Not ours, I assume?'

'Like you, nobody in the village seems to have seen anything that evening. Almost everyone possesses an axe. Other than Ben and myself, and Jim Ruggles who found the body, it will just be my brother-in-law who is called. He was camping close by where the body was found, though there is nothing else to make Thatcher suspect Marius was involved – other than his insistence that he will not change his religion. That apparently counts against him.'

'It is sometimes difficult,' says Drusilla, 'to be different from other people. If you have choice in the matter, it can take courage.'

'Foolishness, you mean,' says Mary. 'I hope that I would never do something so ill advised as to deliberately annoy people. Being different is just a form of arrogance. That's what I think.'

I look from one of the Umfraville daughters to the other. Drusilla's right. Unfortunately Mary's right too. Exactly how right is something I may be about to discover.

Chapter 15

In which an inquest is opened and closed

I think that Mister Thatcher is disappointed with the inquest we have arranged for him. He seems discontented with everything, in fact, including that the jurors that I have assembled for him are almost all my tenants, except for Jacob Grice, who is unacceptable in so many other ways.

Flood's body is laid out on the largest of Ben's tables for the jury to inspect, which they do so in the offhand manner of somebody at the market turning over goods they really have no intention of buying. Flood has been deservedly battered to death and they resent having to give up valuable time to confirm that.

Jim Ruggles, his ploughing again interrupted by Flood's death, grudgingly admits that he found Flood and informed the constable. They agreed there was no point in raising the hue and cry, the man having clearly been killed the day before. Messengers were, however, sent to the neighbouring villages on the off chance that the murderer might have gone there and mentioned in passing that they had just murdered somebody. That was, as he understood the matter, what the law required.

I confirm that I briefly examined the body to ensure that the coroner's time was not wasted. I add that in my opinion Flood's remains had most certainly been there overnight and that he had therefore been killed the previous evening. I explain why he must have been killed elsewhere. I suggest respectfully that while there are reasons for thinking the killer might be the same person who attacked Hubert Umfraville, there is no conclusive evidence. We would be wise to keep an open mind. The jury nods in complete agreement, though I think mainly because I am their landlord.

Ben gives evidence that Flood had gone out in the morning and failed to return. He had not said he was meeting anyone. He had not taken his wooden staff, though he possessed such a thing. He had not seemed anxious about anything at all. He was very cheerful in fact, perhaps because he was still hoping to catch Nero.

Finally Marius is called. He is told to swear an oath on the Bible. He declines, to the evident puzzlement of the jury.

'This is most irregular,' says Thatcher. 'Evidence cannot be given except under oath.'

'As a Muslim, I will swear on the Koran but not on the Bible,' says Marius.

'I have a copy of the Alkoran of Mohammed in my study,' says the vicar from the back of the room. 'If this court has no objection, I shall send for it. It is of course in translation, but it is well regarded by scholars at both universities.'

'Perhaps the jury would indeed have an objection,' says Thatcher, turning to address them. 'The Bible, and the Bible alone, is the true word of God. An oath on anything else cannot be even one-eighth part its value. What say you, gentlemen? Will you have a good, solid English Bible with a fine leather cover or some foreign book of mumbo jumbo?'

The jury, who have never previously heard of the Koran, in translation or otherwise, look at me for guidance. I simply nod my approval of its use in swearing oaths.

'We're happy to see Mister Marius swear on that book of the vicar's,' says the foreman.

The volume in question is sent for, while the jurors avail themselves of the non-Islamic services that the inn provides.

Marius's evidence is, however, inconsequential. He has never seen Flood before. It is true that he spent a couple of nights nearby but heard and saw little of note. He has, moreover, nothing to hide. He shows the court the knife that he dropped there and that I returned to him. That is the only weapon he possesses – he does not own an axe. The jury give their verdict – unlawful killing by person or persons unknown.

After Thatcher has stalked out of the room, one of the jurors sidles up to me.

'We didn't mind doing as you wished, Sir John. Not this once anyway. But Mister Marius should have sworn on the Bible. If it's good enough for the rest of us, it's good enough for him. It says some strange things, I grant you, but at least it was written in English. Mister Marius was brought up a Christian. No good can come of his being a worshipper of Mohammed.'

'I fear you may be right,' I say. 'But I appreciate what you have done.'

'Well, God bless him anyway,' says the juror.

But I know that he is saying it merely to humour the lord of the manor. If God prefers to strike Marius dead as a renegade, as He probably will sooner or later, then that is entirely a matter for God.

'Well, that didn't go too badly,' I say. 'I mean the verdict could have been worse.'
  'Where is Marius now?' asks Aminta.
  'He went off somewhere,' I say.
  'I wish he wouldn't do that,' says Aminta.
  'So do I,' I say.

Ben, standing before me in the library, is a one-man deputation. He fiddles with the brim of his hat and shuffles his feet.
  'What's the problem, Ben?'
  'Please don't take this the wrong way, Sir John. I mean no disrespect.'
  'I'm sure you don't, Ben. So just tell me what's on your mind.'
  'It's Mister Marius,' he says.
  The long silence after these words doesn't bode well, but I wait patiently to see what will follow.
  'There were some children playing in one of the fields. One of your fields, really, Sir John, but Taylor rents it from you. The one down by the river. He has sheep on it usually but it's empty at the moment. It floods a bit in the winter, of course, but it's good grazing – green even in the driest summer. Well, most summers anyway. You should probably charge him more for it. Or farm it yourself, maybe. If Taylor can make it pay, then so can you.'
  Ben is putting off, with less skill than he imagines, whatever it is he doesn't much want to tell me.
  'If Mister Taylor has no objection to their presence in his field, then I certainly don't.'

'Of course not, Sir John. They do no harm with their chasing games and their hoops and their balls and their kites and so forth.'

'I'm sure they don't. So what's this about? Mister Marius?'

'I was coming to that, Sir John. Anyway, after a bit the children noticed Mister Marius standing close by, in the little copse in the corner of the field.'

'And?'

'He was watching them play. He didn't say anything. He didn't shout at them. He just stood there.'

'And?'

'They said he was crying. That's what worried them. They thought maybe they'd done something to annoy him. Him being your brother-in-law and Sir Felix's son and living at the Big House and everything. They ran away, in case they were in trouble.'

'I'll speak to him,' I say. 'I'm sure he didn't mean to upset them.'

'That's what I told them, Sir John. Mister Marius meant no harm. He was ever a kind young man. Or he used to be. Before . . . you know.'

'He's suffered more than either of us ever will,' I say. 'I think he knows he's lost the best years of his life. Years he'll never get back. He's been through a lot.'

'Did you manage to speak to Marius?' Aminta asks.

'About frightening the children?'

'Yes.'

'He was very sorry. He said he hadn't intended anything of the sort. It's just, he said, that sometimes a grey cloud comes over him.'

'A metaphorical grey cloud, I take it?'

'I suppose so. I don't think he was claiming anything miraculous.'

'That's reassuring.'

'There was one other thing.'

'Yes?'

'He'd like us to address him in future as Musa, not Marius.'

'Musa?'

'It's the name he took when he became a Muslim. It was as close to his old name as he could find.'

'Musa?'

'It's no more difficult to say than Marius. In English it's Moses.'

'So you said before. Does he plan to join us for supper tonight?'

'He didn't know. I think probably not.'

She shakes her head sadly, but at what I could not say.

The fire is roaring. Aminta sits at her tapestry work, her needle flicking to and fro in the candlelight. Sir Felix has a long clay pipe in one hand and a glass of Canary in the other. I am reading *Paradise Lost* and wondering if it really is better to reign in hell than serve in heaven. I can see Satan's point, but sticking to your principles doesn't always work out the way you'd hoped.

'You would've thought that Marius would want to join us,' says Sir Felix.

'He is troubled,' I say. 'He's finding it more difficult than he expected to fit in here again.'

'Then who else should he turn to for comfort except his own family? And his own church?'

'He will not shift an inch in that direction. He wants us to call him by his Muslim name, by the way – Musa.'

'What?' says Sir Felix.

'It's the same as Moses.'

'He's not Moses. He's Marius. He was named Marius after his grandfather. I can't call him by some foreign name.'

'Marius is a Latin name,' I say. 'No more English than Musa, when you think about it. And I've had to adopt many names in my work for Arlington. Mister Black. Mister White. John Clifford on one occasion.'

'That's very different, and you know it, John. You didn't believe you actually were any of those people. Marius is the name we gave him at his baptism. It's the name that, one day, he'll be buried under. It's the name he'll answer to on Judgement Day.'

'He's been—'

'Don't keep saying that, John. I've really heard enough of it. We've all been through a lot and Marius should realise that. There's scarcely a single family in the village that wasn't touched in some way by the late wars. All over the country, mothers and fathers and brothers and sisters are still grieving. There are plenty of men who had two legs in 1642 but only one leg now. Marius did at least come home alive and with all his limbs intact. Eventually. He came home to a family that is doing its best to love him and to welcome him back, if he'd only let us.'

'Of the twenty years he was away, we know a little about the first two,' I say. 'We still know nothing at all about the rest.'

'If he told us then we would,' says Aminta, looking up from her sewing. 'What was he doing that he is now so ashamed of?'

'I've no idea. We have to try to help him regardless. He'll tell us in good time. And if he wants to be called Musa, I suppose I'll have to call him Musa.'

Aminta tugs suddenly on a bright scarlet thread and snaps it cleanly. 'Do what you like,' she says, smoothing the cloth. 'Just don't expect me to do it too.'

Chapter 16

In which Mister Jenks and I receive letters

It is two days later that a letter arrives from the Sheriff. It is brief and to the point. It has come to his attention that I am harbouring a suspect to a murder. Possibly two murders. He understands that the man to whom I am giving shelter is my brother-in-law – an apostate who has rejected the true religion and now worships Mohammed, openly and without shame in broad daylight. Word has also reached him that I have concealed evidence from the coroner's jury, to wit one clasp knife, property of the said renegade. He counsels me that Marius's guilt is clear to any reasonable Christian man and that I would be wise to commit him to the next assizes at Chelmsford, where his innocence or otherwise can be determined by a jury of men loyal to the King and the Church of England.

I reply with equal brevity that my investigations are not yet complete, that Mister Clifford knew neither victim and that there were no witnesses to one murder or the other. The knife, for what it was worth, was found some way from Flood's body and could not possibly have been used to bludgeon somebody over the head. It is not a piece of evidence, it is not a deodand and there was no reason to do anything with it other than return it to its legal owner. Mister Clifford is no more to be suspected than anyone else in the village.

But is the last of those statements true? And Marius (I cannot bring myself yet to call him Musa except to his face) has been reported to me for praying in a field, having first used a compass to ensure that he was facing, for reasons that puzzled my informant, in the direction of Saffron Walden.

Ben's next visit to the Big House proves to be more worrying.

'Jacob Grice was at the inn this morning. He says that he saw Mister Marius near the New House the evening that Mister Umfraville was attacked.'

'He's only just remembered that? He didn't think to tell you at the time?'

'He clearly didn't think to tell Flood either, for all that they were looking for somebody very much like the man he claims to have seen. Anyway, he's certain he saw somebody in the bushes. He now realises that it was your brother-in-law and thought I should be aware. He was reluctant to tell me, he said, the man being Sir Felix's son and everything, but he felt it was his duty to me as constable and to the King.'

'Marius doesn't deny having been to the New House. It adds nothing to what we know. Jacob is not claiming to have witnessed the attack?'

'Not at the moment. Who knows what he'll remember tomorrow? The Grices have lost a good source of income and they resent it. You'd think Flood was a holy martyr, the way Jacob was talking.'

'Hadn't they sworn never to work for Flood again?'

'That was when he was still alive.'

'Jacob Grice may be willing to perjure himself, but no court will believe him.'

'Depends how many of his family are on the jury.'

I nod. That's true. His brothers and cousins are numerous.

'You should have given that knife in as evidence, though,' Ben continues. 'Given it to me as the constable. That would have been right and proper.'

'I suppose so, but Umfraville and Flood weren't stabbed with anything – let alone a small pocket knife. I've told the Sheriff that too.'

'It's like not telling me about your searching the New House when I'd already done it.'

'Well, I said I was sorry about that.'

'Mistress Umfraville is now complaining to anyone who'll listen that you seem determined to have her accused of her husband's murder. She says she didn't understand why at first, but since your brother-in-law is about to be charged with the same crime, it is all much plainer to her.'

'When I searched the house, I didn't even know Marius was in the village. Anyway, when I saw her a couple of days ago, she made no complaint.'

'That's as may be. But I'd go careful if I were you, Sir John.'

I nod. I can't deny that's good advice.

I decide to make my peace with Mistress Umfraville. I may as well follow my own counsel to my brother-in-law and ensure that nobody in the village is upset without good cause.

On the way, I pass Harry Hardy's house. He is sitting on a bench outside his cottage as he so often is. He greets me cordially. I don't seem to have fallen out with him yet, but Harry is on good terms with almost everyone. We exchange pleasantries about the weather. Then he adds: 'I spoke to Mister Marius today.'

'Did you?' I say cautiously.

'I bid him good day. Do you know what he replied? Sally Laycome! When I asked what he meant by it he laughed and said next time I should reply, "Wally Laycome Sally" or something of the sort. Is Mister Marius in his right mind, Sir John? Or was he mocking me again – like calling himself "Nemo"?'

'He wouldn't mock you, Harry, any more than I would.'

'He smiled when he said it, though.'

'I am glad to hear it. He's laughed little enough since he returned. He would have meant no harm, truly.'

'Some people reckon he killed Mister Umfraville, though. And that rogue Flood. That's why he's acting so odd. Guilt has made him mad, they're saying. Children won't go near him, not for half a crown.'

'He's killed nobody, Harry. The village children will get used to him in time. I think he is genuinely fond of them. I think he regrets not having sons and daughters of his own. He's no danger to anyone, I promise you. It's just that his ways are not quite our ways.'

'That's what I tell them, Sir John. I say to people, I'm sure he's still Mister Marius beneath it all. The Mister Marius we knew of old. A few more weeks here in Essex and he'll be right as rain. Our English showers will wash the desert sand off him. We'll see him in church at Christmas, no doubt, singing the old hymns.'

'I hope so,' I say.

'There are some, though – and I hope you won't mind me saying it, Sir John – there are some who are saying that if he likes travelling so much, it would be better that he moved on. Safer for him, if he did kill Umfraville and Flood. Safer for us all, maybe. Anyway, we don't want him tarnishing the reputation of your family, Sir John. We've always respected you, and your mother, and Sir Felix, and Lady Grey. Especially your mother. Everyone in the village knows your father wasn't dead when she married your stepfather, but nobody holds that against her. She never said worse behind your back than she said to your face. People respect that round here. The point is, we don't want to see a member of your family hanged for murder. It would be in Chelmsford like as not, but that's still a bit too close for comfort.'

'Marius has killed nobody. He is not going to hang.'

Harry looks at me.

'He's not going to hang,' I repeat. 'I promise you.'

'I hope not. But I'd go careful if I were you, Sir John,' he says.

'I'll try,' I say.

Mistress Umfraville is wearing a dress I recognise as an old one of my mother's. She must have relaxed her rules on charity somewhat. It is a little old-fashioned and a little tight, even though she seems to have let out the laces as far as they will go. Still, she must be warmer in it than in the dresses she brought from Barbados.

'I must apologise again if I seemed over-zealous in searching your house a second time,' I say.

Perhaps the dress has caused her to take a more lenient view of my conduct. She certainly seems less annoyed than Ben implied. She smiles indulgently.

'Well,' she says. 'You left everything in good order. So long as you don't feel the need to do it again, I suppose what you did is forgivable.'

'I can't see why I should,' I say. 'Is everything to your liking more generally? I mean are you comfortable in the house?'

'Yes. Now that we have our chickens. I think we shall soon have an overplus of eggs to sell and increase our income a little, the rent here being so very high. It will of course be a while before Pig Hubert has fattened up enough to turn him into bacon.'

'Marius . . . Musa . . .' I say. 'It would be helpful if you avoided mocking people in the village.'

He looks puzzled. 'I've mocked nobody, John. Why would I?'

'Harry Hardy says that you spoke nonsense to him. To tease him.'

Marius's face softens for a moment. 'I merely wished him *salaam alaikum*,' he says. 'Peace be with you. I explained that the correct response, if he wished to give it, was *wa alaikum salaam*. It seems a more pleasant greeting than good morning or good afternoon. A more comforting greeting. I so wish I could hear it again whenever I met somebody on the road. Peace be with you. And with you peace.'

'I'll try to remember it, Musa,' I say.

Though we have all but abandoned the search for Umfraville, I have taken a walk out on the London road, in case I can spot anything that we missed on our earlier outings. As I am walking home, no wiser than before, I hear the creaking of a cart and the sound of horseshoes on the hard dirt road some way behind me. When I see who it is, I wait for the team to catch me up. Mister Jenks is back in the village again. He seems cross.

'Are you bound for Cambridge?' I ask.

'Yes, but I have business here first. I need to speak urgently to that rascal Flood.'

'Too late,' I say. 'Too late by some days. Flood is dead.'

'Dead? How?'

'Bludgeoned from behind. Like Umfraville but more comprehensively.'

'You've found Umfraville by now, I take it?'

'No, he's still missing. Undoubtedly dead too, but until I find a body he lives on in the eyes of the coroner. Could I ask what your urgent business with Flood was?'

He reaches into his coat and takes a letter from his inside pocket. I open it and read. Yes, that's helpful. Much more helpful than I had any reason to expect. It's not difficult to see why somebody would have wanted to kill him.

Chapter 17

In which the extent of Mister Flood's correspondence becomes clear

'So,' I say to Jenks, 'Daniel Flood accuses you of killing Hubert Umfraville, something of which he claims to have absolute proof. He says that he ought to inform the magistrate – a sentiment that I cannot possibly argue with – but he would like to discuss other options with you first. I think he is offering to become a reasonably priced accessory after the fact.'

'He is an unmitigated scoundrel.'

'I cannot argue with that either. Might I assume that you still claim not to have killed Umfraville?'

'I'd hardly show you the letter if I had anything to fear on that account. Especially since Flood is dead and only he and I know this was ever written.'

'But he sent it nevertheless.'

'Somebody in the village must have told him where I lived. I have no idea why he thought it was worth going to the effort of writing. He knew he had no proof of any kind.'

'I think that Flood had begun to doubt that he could catch Nero, even with the help of the Grice bothers, and that his visit to England might prove a costly waste of time. Then Umfraville was killed. So, why not try to blackmail you, just in case you did it? It might prove almost as profitable as slave catching.'

'I'd be one of the less likely suspects.'

'So you would. In which case, I doubt this is the only letter he decided to send.'

'When I received it, I could have murdered him for his impertinence. And who would have blamed me?'

'Precisely,' I say. 'Those were also my thoughts, Mister Jenks. To kill him on receipt of such a letter would be a perfectly natural reaction. For somebody, anyway.'

William Robinson looks at me suspiciously. 'How did you know Flood had written to me?'

I am in Robinson's comfortable drawing room. The one that Umfraville had coveted. A fire is burning brightly in the hearth, which is just as well. Since I arrived the weather has taken a turn for the worse. Heavy winter rain drums against the large window panes. The rose garden is shrouded in a watery mist.

'I know for certain that he has written to somebody else,' I say. 'He would have obtained, during his stay in the village, a reasonably good idea who had the opportunity to kill Umfraville. His correspondence may therefore be extensive. And you were very anxious to see him the other day. So it seemed probable that the letter you had received from him was not unlike Jenks's.'

'You are right, of course, Sir John. He did write to me

accusing me of murder and threatening to give evidence against me if I didn't pay him . . . As you say, he doubtless wrote many of these letters. Well, I am pleased that I shall never have to see him again. He was an evil man who thoroughly deserved his fate . . . Of course, I didn't kill Umfraville *or* Flood.'

'Didn't you?' I say. 'That Flood wrote to many doesn't mean he was wrong in every case. You were in the village the day Flood died.'

'What of it?'

'I had reserved judgement over whether the same person killed both men. But the fact that Flood wrote those letters changes things somewhat.'

'Does it?'

'I think somebody that he wrote to actually was Umfraville's killer and acted accordingly. So, just to remind you, you were in the village when Flood died. You were also in the village when Umfraville died.'

'I don't deny any of that.'

'And you can't deny that the first death – Umfraville's – was very much to your advantage. If you had killed Umfraville, Flood's death would have been equally necessary. You'd lost one blackmailer only to gain another, even less principled and trustworthy than the first.'

'I agree that it looks bad when you explain it like that. Reasonably bad, I mean. Not very bad. But are you really saying you believe I just came to the village and killed Flood without a second thought? You must know me better than that.'

'You served in the army of Parliament. Sudden and violent death is something with which you must be very familiar.'

'Yes, of course. But to attack a man in that fashion, striking from behind, is very different from confronting them face to face on the battlefield . . . or so I would imagine. I'm not saying that I've ever killed anyone away from the battlefield, obviously.'

'I was too young to have fought in the war,' I say. 'So, I don't really know either. All I can say from my own experience is that, if my life was really in danger, I'd have struck a blow from behind without thinking too much about it. I'd hardly blame you for doing the same thing.'

'But you'd still arrest me for murder?'

'Oh yes,' I say. 'If I thought you were guilty, I'd see you tried and hanged. I wouldn't have any choice. That I have known you for so long would make no difference to anything. I'd do it with reluctance but, as Mister Flood observed to me before he died, we are all slaves to the law. Well, I must return to Clavershall West, while there is still daylight to do so. I need to ask one or two other people whether they have had any letters lately.'

The candles have been burning for an hour or more in the parlour of the New House. Outside, the winter evening has settled upon the village, but here there is a cosy red glow from the fire.

'Knowing Flood as I do,' says Mistress Umfraville, 'I ought not be surprised that he has acted in such a base manner . . . to accuse poor Mister Robinson so.'

'But you yourself also received such a communication?'

Mistress Umfraville considers this for a moment. Perhaps she receives a lot of post of that sort.

'I regret to say I did,' she says, very slowly and carefully. 'It was a little vague. It merely suggested that a member of my family was responsible for my husband's murder. Of course, it offered not a shred of proof. How could it when, as we know, my husband is not even dead?'

'Can I see the letter?'

'I used it for kindling the fire, I'm afraid. Such a nasty thing. And good dry kindling is in short supply. Had I known the letter would have been useful to you in some way, I would have carefully preserved it. Of course I would. But I didn't know and sadly it is now ashes.'

'Thank you,' I say. 'It's still helpful to know you received one. No other member of your family could have also been sent one? Independently of you, I mean?'

'As mistress of the house, all post is placed into my hands and my hands alone. This was, now I think about it, pushed under the door early in the morning, but since I am usually the first to rise, I would have seen if there was another letter with it. In any case, to send two such letters to the same household would be a waste of ink and paper.'

'Well, let me know if you do hear of such a thing,' I say. 'There may well be more about the village.'

'It gives us a motive for Flood's murder,' I say.

'You seem relieved,' says Aminta.

'A lot of people were beginning to suspect your brother. Now we know that Flood almost certainly died because he was a blackmailer, not because he was a slave catcher.'

'On the other hand,' says Aminta, 'it's much less likely now that Flood killed Umfraville, unless he really thought he could blackmail people for something he'd done himself. You have lost your most likely suspect for Umfraville's murder.'

'True, but I still don't think it was Musa.'

'Who?'

'Your brother.'

'Don't call him Musa, John. He's Marius. That's his name. Isn't it bad enough that he spends his days walking the footpaths and eating with us only when we beg him to do so? Then refusing perfectly good food because of the religion he insists on following? Then, when he will actually eat with us, refusing to say Amen when my father says grace before and after the meal. Everything he does is a slap in the face for me and for you and for our father. But I don't complain because he is my brother Marius. If he is telling us that he's not even that any more, what's the point in his coming home? What exactly does he want from us? And what does he plan to give us in return?'

'I don't know what he plans to do about anything,' I say. 'But at least we don't have to worry now that he'll be dragged off to Chelmsford Jail before he's had a chance to think things through. Not on the basis of the evidence we have now anyway.'

'I stayed at the inn last night,' says Jenks. 'I got talking to Bowman about the sorry state of things in England today and, when we were done, it was too late to go on to the next town. I apologise for disturbing your breakfast, sir, but Bowman said something that jogged my memory.'

'Thank you for coming over to tell me, Mister Jenks. What exactly do you now recall?'

'It was nothing almost – I thought I must have imagined it. That's why I didn't mention it to you before. But when we were all going to the New House, the night Umfraville was attacked, I fancied I saw something moving in the woods nearby. I thought I saw a Moor – running away from the direction of the house. Then I blinked and there was nothing. Well, it would have been an odd thing to see in Essex, so I told myself I was wrong. Just a poacher, maybe, which was none of my concern. Or nothing at all. When you're alone on the road, you can think you've seen some very odd things. Anyway, even if I had seen him, he was going in the wrong direction to have killed Umfraville – by the time Umfraville was attacked he could have been anywhere. Then Bowman told me confidentially that a Moor had come to the village and had been suspected of the crime. So, I thought I'd better tell you.'

'How was he dressed, this so-called Moor?'

'A black suit of clothes. Periwig. Broad-brimmed hat.'

'Are you sure about all that? Was he definitely in a periwig? Could the clothes have been blue? Like a sailor? A blue canvas suit and no periwig?'

'It was dark in those woods. Yes, it could have been blue, I suppose. And maybe I am misremembering his hair. It's difficult to tell sometimes what's real hair and what's false.'

'And the hat?'

Jenks closes his eyes for a moment, then shakes his head. 'It's over a week ago, of course,' he says. 'I thought he was wearing a hat. I mean, what man goes out without a hat at this time of year? But now you ask . . .'

'Did you tell Ben Bowman what you saw?'

'Yes. Is there any reason why I should not have done?'

'You did the right thing. I wish you a safe road to Cambridge, Mister Jenks.'

'It makes very little difference,' I say to Aminta. 'Musa told us he went to the house, found a strange family there and came away. The only thing that's changed is that somebody more reliable than the Grice brothers saw him leaving. And Jenks was so uncertain about the details that there has to be doubt about who or what he really saw. Musa has never owned a periwig, for example. And the only hat he had was a woollen sailor's cap.'

Aminta grimaces, more at the name I have just used twice for her brother than at the fact of a new witness. She shakes her head and sighs.

'Jenks's evidence will be a lot more convincing than Jacob Grice's.' she says. 'He's going to say he saw Marius there almost precisely when Umfraville was attacked. And he'll say Marius was running away through the woods – not walking openly and honestly down the road. Marius has never told you he was running away, has he? That's a bit of information he's decided to omit.'

'I agree,' I say. 'But Jenks clearly saw him before Umfraville was attacked. Being near the house at midnight – or even running from the house – isn't the same as being seen running away from the orchard at one o'clock in the morning. That would be damning, but it's not what Jenks is telling us.'

'I suppose so,' she says. She is less comforted by these undoubted facts than I am. She knows that logical argument does not always sway a jury, or a judge for that matter. And Marius's policy of alienating the whole village, by changing his name and religion, won't help matters if others are called to give evidence.

'Also bear in mind that Jenks claims the man he saw was dressed in black and wearing a periwig,' I say. 'It's true it was dark and it would have been difficult to see whether the clothes were black or blue. I doubt that a jury would care very much about the discrepancy. Still, it's something if it did come to trial.'

'Do you think it will?'

'I don't know. But it's more important than ever that Marius does nothing that would make people suspicious of him. Where is he at the moment? Still in his bed?'

'He went out at first light. I don't know where. One day it's going to get him into trouble.'

'But hopefully not today,' I say.

A footman shows Ben into the sitting room. He is turning his hat in his hands, as he does when he doesn't much want to be somewhere but nevertheless is.

'I've had a message from the constable at Farndon,' he says. 'They've arrested a Moor. For acting suspicious. They want you to go and charge him, so they can get on with the hanging.'

'Charge him with acting suspiciously?' I ask. 'It's not a crime, let alone a capital offence.'

'Seems it is in Farndon. I think you'd better go quickly, Sir John, just in case it's Mister Marius. You may have a bit of talking to do.'

'I'll go over in the carriage,' I say. 'There's nothing like four horses and a postillion to impress a mob with the majesty of the law. And I'll need a way to get Musa back home afterwards.'

'Who's that?'

'Marius,' I say.

'Sorry,' says Ben. 'I must be getting deaf. I thought you said "Musa". I hope they don't make the same mistake at Farndon, eh? Suspicious behaviour and a funny name – that's all the evidence you'd need for a conviction there. And they like a good hanging in Farndon.'

Chapter 18

In which I investigate a case of suspicious behaviour

The King's Arms at Farndon is a poor, broken thing. It crouches just off the main road to Royston, as if hoping that the traveller will politely overlook it. The whitewash is flaking from the walls and the thatch is untidy and almost black after many winters of snow and summers of rain. It's the inn that Farndon deserves. It's actually the second most substantial house in the village.

I allow my postillion to jump down from his seat and open the carriage door for me. Then I descend in my new periwig and glossy beaver hat. I adjust the broad, fringed sash from which my sword hangs. It glows scarlet in the autumn sunshine. Finally, I brush a speck of dust from my velvet breeches. If I can't extract Marius Clifford (as I must remember to address him here) from his current predicament, then it won't be for the lack of good London tailoring.

There is a press of faces at the grubby, leaded windows to observe the miracle of modern coach building before them.

One or two also glance at me, taking in not only the profusion of lace at my neck and my cuffs but also the prominent scar on my cheek – both good reasons, each in its own way, for addressing me in a respectful manner. I push the door open with a spotless glove and stride into the inn.

At first, it is difficult to identify any individuals in the gloom, but a man approaches me and I recognise him as Smithers, the Farndon constable and owner of a small farm nearby. He makes his living in part by acting as paid substitute for anyone elected as constable who doesn't want to do the job. That's most people, really. Smithers is at least a reasonable man with an almost superstitious regard for the law. He removes his hat and clutches it to his chest as if he fears it might escape.

'Good day, Sir John,' he says. 'We are much obliged that you have found the time to come over. The prisoner is in the stables, under guard. If you will follow me, you can tell us what we should do with him. Will you try him now or do you want to commit him to the Chelmsford Assizes? I'm assuming, for a capital offence, it will have to be Chelmsford?'

The crowd, which is probably hoping for a hanging this afternoon, parts reluctantly but respectfully to let me through, and I am led out of the back door and towards the stables.

'What exactly has he done?' I ask as we walk across the straw- and shit-covered yard to a building even lower and more decrepit than the inn.

'He was just sneaking around,' says Smithers. 'Came up to the window and peered in, then decided not to stay.'

'And his crime is . . . ?'

'Well, sir, you have the book learning and I don't, but I'd have said he was obviously planning to steal something, then changed his mind when he realised there were stout Englishmen there to stop his Moorish tricks. I'd say you could still charge him with theft, though, if you thought that was best.'

'So, did he run off when he saw you were on to him?'

'These Moors aren't that clever, are they? He just stayed there, smiling at us, and we came out and we took him.'

'Did he resist at all?'

'He doubtless saw that resistance was pointless.'

'Perhaps he felt he had done nothing wrong and had nothing to fear,' I say.

Smithers laughs politely at what he assumes is my joke. 'He'll feel a rope round his neck pretty soon,' he says. 'Once you've tried him, of course.'

'You can hang him only if he's guilty of a capital crime,' I say.

Smithers laughs again. He hadn't realised that magistrates made so many jokes.

We have reached the stables. It isn't a big yard. Flanking the double doors are a couple of young men, one armed with a scythe and one with a cudgel. They are both dressed in leather jerkins that probably belonged in former times to a father or an older brother. They wear the simple woollen Monmouth caps that became popular during the late wars, though neither would have been born when the war ended.

'This is the magistrate from Clavershall West, lads,' says Smithers. 'He's here to deal with that thief you've been guarding.'

'Shall I fetch the rope now?' asks the one with the cudgel.

'No, he'll need to be judged properly according to the law. Plenty of time to fetch the rope after that.'

'Perhaps I might talk to the prisoner?' I say. 'If it's not too much trouble, Mister Smithers?'

'Open the door, lads. Give the magistrate elbow room to do his job.'

The boy entrusted with the scythe props his weapon against the wall and pulls the door open with two calloused hands. The hinges squeal rustily. I enter. There are four stalls, all empty. In one corner there is a bale of hay. That would seem to be everything.

Smithers senses my puzzlement and comes to stand at my side. 'Where's the prisoner, boy?'

Both of the guards look into the stables. 'He was there ten minutes ago,' says one of them. 'But seemingly he's gone.'

I examine the rear of the building. There is no great mystery to be solved. Three rotten planks have been kicked or pushed out of the back wall. It is even less secure than our village lock-up. Perhaps the Moor was cleverer than they were, after all. It looks as if I'll be travelling home alone anyway.

It is evening before Marius returns.

'Musa,' I say, 'could I have a word with you?'

'Yes, of course, John.'

'You seem to have walked some way today.'

'Far enough. I find walking . . . just helps.'

'You got as far as Farndon?'

'Ah . . . so you've heard about that?'

'If you were going to the inn you should just have walked up to the door and entered – not peered in through the window like a thief. They called me over in the hope I would say they could hang you.'

'I needed refreshment. I saw what I thought was a ruinous old cottage, where I could at least ask for some water from the well. Then I realised it might be an ale house. I glanced through the window to check. I meant no harm at all. I merely wished to avoid going into a place that sold things that are *haram* – forbidden to me.'

'They thought you were a foreigner.'

'Well, I am, aren't I? I've lived in Morocco more than I've lived in England. This no longer feels like my country. These people no longer feel like my people.'

'You should at least have told them who you are.'

'I don't know the answer to that question myself. Life would be easier if I did.'

'That is the sort of self-indulgent sophistry that will get you killed. It would have been easy enough to tell them that you are Sir Felix Clifford's son.'

'Legally that makes no difference, as you know well. It's not as if it gives me the right to claim the benefit of clergy. The sons of knights and baronets are obliged to observe the same laws as anyone else.'

'You don't seem to understand the danger you are putting yourself into by almost everything you do.'

He eyes me warily. 'I'm not changing my religion.'

'It isn't just your religion. What I don't understand is this strange restlessness – this need to walk the roads all the time.'

'I ought to be somewhere else. Not here. When I'm moving, it doesn't feel as bad. It feels as if I'm doing something about it.'

'I have no idea what you mean.'

He sighs. 'I'll try to explain tonight,' he says. 'Over supper. But it won't be easy – either for me or for the rest of you.

Worse for the rest of you, because you'll be hearing it for the first time.'

'Is it that bad?' I ask.

'Yes, it's that bad,' he says.

Chapter 19

In which Musa continues the story that Marius began

We have eaten well. Our cook has grown used to not serving pork or ham. Marius has some residual reservations about other meat, which I do not entirely understand, but is prepared to set them aside. Sir Felix has perhaps drunk more wine than he should have done. I have drunk almost no wine at all. I suspect some of us may need clearer heads than others.

Marius has been silent for a lot of the evening, as if running things through his mind, trying to arrange facts and events in some order that will make sense to us and perhaps even to himself. He waits unit the servants have cleared away the last of the plates and doors have been respectfully closed in their wake. Their footsteps fade towards the kitchens. For the rest of the evening, they are at liberty.

'I told you,' says Marius, 'that after two years of working as a mason, I decided that I would convert, of my own free will, to Islam. As a result, though I remained a slave, I became a soldier in the Sultan's service – indeed, I became one of his captains. Of course, I had as little choice as ever where I served. For a while I remained in Marrakesh, helping to oversee building work. Then for almost ten years I was in the mountains. The sultans have been fighting a long war against some of their more unruly subjects. There were periods of peace during which life was pleasant enough and I had the leisure to hunt and to study the Holy Koran. There were also short, sharp campaigns with heavy casualties on both sides. In one of those, my commanding officer was killed and I was appointed to replace him. But I was still no more free than I had been during my first journey through the desert to the slave market.

'I was surrounded by comrades but it was, for all that, as lonely a life as you could imagine – especially after I became their commander. Then, out of the blue, the Sultan chose to visit the *Kasbah* that we were then guarding. He questioned me and asked if I lacked anything. I said as before: serving such a ruler as he was, I had all I could possibly ask for. He pressed me – insisted on a better answer. All of the Sultan's subjects had that. What did I need personally? I knew that my life might depend on the answer I gave. The merest hint at disrespect or ingratitude would be enough to condemn me. So, I jokingly said, that I merely lacked a wife and children. He looked around the courtyard we were in. It chanced that we had, that day, taken some hostages from the Berbers, including the daughter of one of the local sheikhs. She was a beautiful girl of sixteen or seventeen, dark-haired, dark-eyed. The Sultan's eyes fell upon her. I had no way of stopping what happened next.

'"There is your new wife, Musa," he said. "Have you ever seen a girl so beautiful? How wise you were to confide in me. The two of you will be married tomorrow."

'At that stage she spoke almost no Arabic and so she simply smiled, assuming that the Sultan had paid her some innocent compliment. It wasn't until the following day when we were all assembled and she and I were dressed in our finery ... Of course, she too realised, every bit as much as I did, that it would be death for both of us if either of us protested. The will of the Sultan was absolute and to refuse his slightest wish was treason.

'Later – very much later – she told me of the young man in her village that she had hoped to marry and who was, in all likelihood, still waiting for her to be returned to her father's house. Two days after our wedding, my regiment was transferred to another part of the country. I have no idea whether her family even knew what had become of her. Twice I tried to send a message to her village on her behalf, but I've no idea if either of my messengers reached her home or if any member of her family was still alive when he did. No reply ever came back to us.

'For ten years we lived together as man and wife. We had three sons who survived – Ibrahim, Sulaiman and Isa – and two daughters who did not. If my wife regretted the choice that the Sultan had made for her, she never complained. I think we were happy. I think she loved me. The wages I received from the Sultan were enough for my family to lead a comfortable life. But I remained a slave, unable to return to my native country. Then, about a year ago, we were posted to the coast. The Sultan's relations with the kings of England and France were ever changing. Sometimes I was instructed not to let an English crew land on our shores under any circumstances. Sometimes, if a treaty was being negotiated, I was told to assist them to find water and supplies. But I knew better than to ask a ship's captain to help me escape. I would have been seen travelling out to the ship and, when I failed to return to the shore, we would have been chased by the Sultan's frigates and captured. Not only I but also my rescuers would have been sent directly to the slave market. I would have been set to labour again as a mason or, worse, as a galley slave. Then one day a large English man-of-war anchored off the coast – a first-rate ship big enough to see off almost any opposition. I was assisting the landing party on my own – directing them to a nearby well and helping them purchase fresh meat – when the first mate complimented me on speaking English as well as he did himself. I don't know why, but I told him my story and of my hopes, in spite of having become a Muslim, of one day returning to England. He said that his ship was sailing within the hour and offered to smuggle me on board with the supplies. It would be hours before I was missed and they had in any case no fear of pursuit once they had raised the anchor and were under way. I asked if I could go back to my quarters and return to the beach with my wife and children. He said that such a delay would be utterly impossible and would risk everyone's safety, but he would take me if I went with him at that very moment. To my everlasting shame, my desire for freedom was such that I accepted. Two weeks later, I was in London.'

There is a long silence. Eventually Aminta says: 'So, you left your family behind?'

'Yes,' he says.

'And how, Marius, do you think they will fare on their own? With your wife a stranger in that part of the country? With three children and no breadwinner?'

'The life of a soldier is forever an uncertain one. We had agreed long before, if news of my death in battle reached her, she would attempt to return to her village and her family. Unlike me, she was free. When I did not come home this time, she would have assumed I was dead – killed in a skirmish with the treacherous Christians. She would have put into effect the plan we had discussed. At least, I think she would. I now know it is difficult to return to a place where you were once a different person. She may have found the same.'

'Well, Marius,' says Aminta, 'that is an interesting story, to be sure. Full of incident. I do indeed understand things better. But I think I am tired now. If you will all excuse me, I shall retire to my chamber.'

She stands, kisses her father goodnight and walks out of the room.

The three of us who remain by the fire say nothing at first, then Marius also excuses himself and departs. The door closes, sending a draught across the room that causes the candles to flutter. His footsteps echo down the hallway.

Sir Felix gives a long sigh. 'So, I have three grandsons of whom I knew nothing,' he says.

'Ibrahim, Sulaiman and Isa,' I say. 'The same three names he quoted to me in another context.'

'Did he? Then I suppose he hasn't forgotten them entirely,' says Sir Felix. 'My three grandsons, I mean. He still recalls their names at least.'

'Of course he does. How could he not?' I say.

'This is a strange business, John. I'm pleased to see Marius back – of course I am. But even so . . . this . . .'

'It must have been a difficult decision for him,' I say.

'I disagree. My duty would have been clear enough to me.'

'You would have stayed?' I ask.

'Of course.'

'My father, though under slightly different circumstances, chose to leave his family and go to the Spanish Netherlands.'

'So he did. And my wife went with him. It changes nothing, however. Nothing at all. We all know that sometimes the price of freedom is high, but it's not a price you should expect others to pay on your behalf.'

I am again in bed and unable to sleep. It has nothing to do with the mattress or the pillows.

'Your brother knows he made the wrong decision,' I say.

'But, even so, how could he?' says Aminta. 'How could he walk out on his wife and children? She had no choice but to marry him. And he deserts her, far from her home, with nothing but a vague plan that she might somehow try to find her family again, assuming they even want her back.'

'But surely you understand his need to see you and your father again?'

'He seems to take little pleasure in my company or my father's.'

'Perhaps because of the guilt he feels,' I say. 'It explains his constantly walking the roads, anyway. He feels he is in the wrong place.'

'No, John, you have to stop making excuses for Marius. His problems are of his own making. He embarked on a slave ship. He abandoned his religion. He decided to leave his family behind. Each time, he had a choice. From now on, he can do as he pleases. He can walk the roads all day. He can stay away from church. He can stay away from us. And I certainly won't lie for him if he's accused of murder.'

'To be fair, he hasn't asked us to lie. Nor do I think he ever would. Not the man I knew twenty years ago, anyway.'

'He isn't the man we knew twenty years ago. That's the point, isn't it? I thought, now he was back in England, it was all very simple. He was free again. He could forget everything that had happened to him and live a normal life. In which case, why would he want to kill Flood and Umfraville? But none of that is true, is it? In his heart he's still in Africa and he's still a slave. So, yes, I can see why he'd kill Umfraville and why he'd kill Flood. I know you don't want to believe Marius is the killer and nor do I, but we have to face the facts, John. He was camped close to where both were attacked. Even ignoring the Grices' dubious testimony, the carter saw somebody very much like him just before Umfraville was struck over the head. His knife was found close to where Flood was killed. Marius has no alibi whatsoever on either occasion. Only when both Umfraville and Flood were dead did my brother finally feel able to come to us here. Until then he found it necessary to skulk in the woods, for reasons that he now finds very difficult to explain to us. Forget Robinson, who you know wouldn't harm a fly. Forget the carter, who met Umfraville only a day or two before the man died and had no need whatsoever to kill Flood. Forget James Umfraville, who is neither better nor worse off than he was before. Forget Mistress Umfraville, who had far less reason to kill her husband here than she had over the previous twenty years, and whose death has now left her in a very precarious position in a strange country without friends or money, albeit rather better off than Marius's wife. Forget Nero, whom nobody has even seen here. You have not been able to come up with one person in this village with a better reason or more opportunity to commit murder than Marius has – a reason that I finally do understand. And the only defence that you can mount for him is that, twenty years ago, he was not, in your own personal opinion, the sort of person to ask us to lie? The Sheriff thinks that my brother is a murderer. Mister Thatcher thinks my brother is a murderer. The village thinks my brother is a murderer who threatens to destroy the reputation of the whole family. Maybe they're not all wrong.'

Chapter 20

In which I receive a visitor and Aminta pays a visit

I am working in my library when I notice a cloud of dust on the Saffron Walden road. It approaches rapidly and sweeps off the highway and through the gates, revealing itself as a coach and six. With a great crunching of gravel it drops expertly into place in front of the steps. Two footmen in my own grey and red livery run and assist the passenger to disembark. They usher him into the house. It is Sir Gilbert Mildmay, the Sheriff. I wonder what he wants? Perhaps he found my reply to his letter unsatisfactory. The sound of feet in the passage outside suggests that I shall soon find out.

'This is a very pleasant residence,' says Sir Gilbert, taking in, through the library window, a fine view of the park and of his own carriage on the gravel drive. 'Has your family owned it long?'

'It belonged to my mother's people for many years. Then they were obliged to sell to the Cliffords, my wife's family.

Then my mother regained it through an arguably bigamous marriage to a roundhead colonel, who had bought it after my wife's father was ruined by fines during Cromwell's time. You might say that both families are now happily restored to it. I manage the estate, when I am not undertaking my duties as a magistrate, and my father-in-law has free run of the cellars. It is close enough to London for my wife to continue her career as a playwright.'

Sir Gilbert nods. All's well that ends well. He can see no problem with discreet and undetected bigamy. If only other dispossessed royalist families had had equally good opportunities, they would have seized them without hesitation.

'I hope that you will be free to live here for many years to come,' he says.

He says this in a suspiciously offhand way.

'I hope so too,' I say.

'Have you considered further what I said to you in my letter?'

'About my brother-in-law?'

'I assume he still declines to worship as the rest of the village does?'

'He has been a Muslim for much of his life. Some years ago, while travelling to the Americas, he was captured and held by corsairs. He converted while in Morocco.'

'Held as a slave?'

'Yes.'

'English sailors held as slaves in Africa are, of course, a great source of sadness and concern to His Majesty. He receives a constant stream of petitions from their families, including many here in Essex, asking him to free them by purchase or military action. I have myself suggested to the King that we send a couple of warships and a regiment of foot to Morocco to see if we can force the issue. But, as you know, we can scarcely hold on to our port of Tangier in the face of attacks from the Moors – let alone venture inland or further along the coast to where the slaves are held. The Spanish are having difficulty in defending their own forts, of course – it isn't just us. North Africa is an awkward place to be. And, as soon as we buy a few of our people back, the corsairs capture another half dozen of our ships to replenish their slave pens. Arlington suggests that we should just bribe the Sultan to restrict himself to French and Spanish boats in future. You can see his point.'

I nod. Selling out both the French and the Spanish to the Sultan; Arlington is maintaining a carefully balanced approach to foreign policy.

'I suppose eventually we shall have to send another envoy to Rabat and hope that he can return with a couple of dozen ancient, broken-down sailors, purchased at some ridiculous price. There are hundreds there of course – thousands probably. Hundreds of thousands, if you want to count the French and Spanish and Dutch and Genoese and Venetians. Nobody really knows. And the Sultan certainly isn't going to tell us. Also a lot of those we know were taken are probably already dead. A slave's life is pretty short. And those who turn Turk don't count, because they've given up any right to return here.'

'I am fortunate that I have only to worry about this small part of Essex,' I say.

'Two murders are, of course, quite a lot to worry about. And your brother-in-law remains the most likely suspect in both cases, does he not?'

'As I've told you, there is no good evidence, Sir Gilbert, as to who killed either man.'

'Nevertheless, it must be difficult for you. I'd like to offer you the opportunity to stand down and allow somebody else – somebody with no conflict of interest – to complete the investigation.'

'Mister Thatcher?'

'He tells me he has generously offered to be of service to you. I think you should accept.'

'He would be able to discover no more than I have.'

'Perhaps I should warn you that, if Marius Clifford did prove to be the killer, and you had sheltered him and concealed evidence, a penknife for example, you might find yourself on trial as an accomplice – not sitting in judgement on him?'

'Marius is the King's loyal subject,' I say.

'He doesn't attend church though. As he is required to do by law.'

'Marius has been back in the village only one Sunday,' I say. 'No magistrate in the country fines his neighbours for missing one service. The King is not in so much need of a few shillings.'

'These are not Cromwell's days,' says Sir Gilbert with an indulgent smile, 'when every little omission was the cause for a vindictive penalty. The law is nevertheless the law, as you will doubtless agree. And a conflict of interest is a conflict of interest. There's no getting away from it. You'd be better accepting Mister Thatcher's offer. What good could it possibly do your family if you and your brother-in-law hanged together? If you hand over to Thatcher now and let him gather the evidence he needs against Marius Clifford, I can promise you that no blame would attach to you for your past obstruction. I give you my word on it.'

'Several of my ancestors were beheaded for treason,' I say.

'At least according to my mother. Sometimes there is a price to be paid for doing the right thing.'

'Oh, beheading for treason is perfectly respectable. Hanging for common murder is another matter entirely. I wouldn't recommend it at all.'

'Give me just a little more time and I shall present you with the murderer of both Umfraville and Flood.'

'Very well. I hope that you do not live to regret that request. I shall return in ten days to see what progress you have made. I really can't allow you more than that. For your own sake as much as mine. There's a limit to what I can overlook, even for a county family as old as your mother's.'

'Whose coach was that I saw, heading out of our gates and towards Saffron Walden?'

'The Sheriff. He decided to pay us a visit,' I say.

'But not to wait for my return from the New House?' asks Aminta.

'Well, perhaps his main purpose was to warn me that, unless I do something about your brother, he will take the matter of the death of Umfraville and Flood out of my hands. He may also have me tried as an accessory. I have promised to present him with a murderer, but I have no idea who that will be. It is exactly as you have already said. The cases against Jenks and Robinson are weak. The Grices might have killed Flood in revenge for the humiliations he heaped upon them, I suppose, but they had no conceivable argument with the Umfravilles – they even supplied them with livestock. As for the Umfravilles themselves, none of them wanted very much to come to Essex, but that is, for the most part, as far as their discontent with Hubert went. I know of no fresh act or insult that would have made any of them want to kill the head of the household. I am still unsure how Hubert's death affected James's prospects and his marriage to Lucy – but there is no evidence even against him.'

'The evidence for James's innocence is actually stronger than for any of the other family members,' says Aminta.

'Is it? Well, that doesn't make much difference to Marius's case.'

'Strangely it may, as I shall explain. I have discovered a little more about what happened on the night of the attack on Hubert, and the good news for Marius is that there was most certainly somebody else in the village at the time – Nero.'

'So, somebody saw him?'

'Saw him and had a conversation with him.'

'Who?'

'Drusilla. I've just visited the New House. While I was waiting for Drusilla in the parlour, Mary sneaked in to see me. She'd been talking to Drusilla and Drusilla had accidentally let slip that she had spoken to Nero since the family arrived in England, though Mary was not certain how that could be. She added that she thought Drusilla had allowed Nero to become regrettably familiar with her in Barbados – more familiar than an adopted member of the family should have been with somebody who was, when all was said and done, a mere slave. There may have been a hint of jealousy there – even that Nero had quite openly rejected her own advances. But she was certain that Nero and Drusilla had been in contact.'

'Did you ask Drusilla about it?'

'Of course I did – just as soon as I was alone with her. She immediately confessed that Nero had travelled to Essex to convey the message to James that Lucy had not utterly abandoned him. Indeed, she is plotting to get a passage on a ship to England just as soon as she can escape her father's watch. That's why James has not abandoned all hope.'

'That is good to know. Did Drusilla tell you any more than that?'

'Don't worry – my questioning was, in the nicest possible way, as thorough as even you could have wished. On the day they arrived here, the female members of the family had an early supper and, not wishing to waste more tallow candles than was absolutely necessary, went directly to bed. Just before ten o'clock, Drusilla heard small stones being thrown at the window. They had not awoken her sister, and she crept cautiously out of bed and saw Nero in the front garden below. She put on her mantle and her shoes and ventured out into the cold damp night. Nero revealed that he had ridden up from London, where he had gained employment with a sugar merchant. He had concealed his horse in the woods so as not to draw attention to himself passing through the village, and then made his way cautiously along the road on foot – she didn't know how far, but some way, she thought. Nero had noted, before the candles went out, which bedroom Drusilla was in and knew where to throw his stones. While the two of them were outside talking, it started to rain, but, damp though she now was, Drusilla crept back to her own bed without disturbing anyone else. Later she was able to tell James the good news.'

'You mean she was able to tell James before Hubert was attacked?'

'She was telling James at the very moment Hubert was being attacked. After the cart was unloaded and the family, other than Hubert, went to bed, Drusilla lay awake, waiting for a chance to sneak out of her chamber and across the landing to the boys' room. Just as she thought it might be safe, she again heard her father's voice down in the garden. Then there was silence, then her father once more, but more distant, as if he was walking away. That, to her, seemed very odd indeed.'

'Did she go back down to discover who it was?'

'No. She went to get James, guessing he might still be awake. That was the point at which she quickly passed on her message. Anyway, the two of them then went outside into the garden together. But by that time there was nobody to be seen. They both went back to bed.'

'James never mentioned any of that,' I say.

'Well, in the end, they didn't see anything, so there wasn't much to tell you. And they were probably worried about incriminating themselves or each other by admitting they were up and about then. We'd always assumed Hubert had gone with somebody from the house to the orchard – it sounds as if that is what Drusilla heard. We don't know who it was. But it certainly wasn't James.'

'Then Drusilla seems to have cleared James's name. But perhaps at the expense of Nero's. Nero had more reason to bear a grudge against Hubert Umfraville than Marius did. And Drusilla has confirmed what we previously suspected – that Nero had a horse that he could, once he had retrieved it from wherever it was hidden, have used to transport the body the following day. Jenks wasn't at all mistaken about the way in which the man he saw was dressed, as I had first assumed, because it wasn't your brother after all. It was Nero. Jenks saw him running away just before midnight, but he must have returned quite quickly. When Umfraville was finally alone in the garden, Nero somehow lured him into the orchard – that was the conversation that Drusilla half-overheard – and killed him. Then, Nero spent the remainder of the night back in the woods in the shelter that Marius had built and then abandoned. The following day, he returned to the house at first light to retrieve the body, but there were already too many people around. Finally, George went to his dinner, leaving the body unattended. Nero collected and disposed of the body somewhere.'

'Why didn't Nero go back to the New House straight away, under cover of darkness?' asks Aminta.

'Because the noise of the horse's hooves on the road would have been heard as they passed through the village in the still of the early morning. The following day, with more traffic on the road, it would have been less remarkable.'

'Nobody saw him though, did they? They'd have reported it.'

'Maybe he was just lucky.'

'And where did he hide the body?' asks Aminta.

'He must have taken the Cambridge road to avoid going back through the village. The body is probably in a ditch somewhere between here and Cambridge.'

'Very well,' says Aminta. 'You've explained how he hid the body. Do you understand why he hid it, knowing it had already been found?'

'No,' I say. 'He'd have been better off just leaving the village as fast as he could.'

'But, according to this version of events, we have to assume Nero did not return to London even then? He stayed for Flood?'

'He could have discovered that Flood was in the village looking for him. But at first, whenever he went out, Flood had the Grices with him in their capacity as assistant slave catchers. Then Flood foolishly alienated the two brothers and so was obliged to search alone. That was Nero's opportunity. He followed and killed Flood, used his horse again to take the body to where it was later found, then finally rode away, back to London.'

We look at each other. It's all perfectly possible, of course, but there is something inelegant about the story. Too much depending on chance. Too much depending on an insatiable desire for revenge that fits with nothing we know about Nero.

'Did you suggest to Drusilla that the killer might have been Nero?' I ask.

'Yes, of course.'

'And?'

'She was shocked that I should even think that. She said that she would not have mentioned it to me if she'd thought there was any chance at all that Nero was to blame. She added that Nero was devoted to Hubert Umfraville and that anyone you asked would tell you the same. There was no animosity at all. None.'

'Mistress Umfraville told me much the same. She thought Nero was utterly loyal to her husband. But you only had to listen to your brother's story to realise that a slave is obliged to tell his master whatever it is that the master wants to hear. That the Umfravilles thought Hubert was loved by Nero, or by any of his slaves for that matter, doesn't mean that he actually was. Nero was given considerable trust and responsibility, just as your brother was. It didn't make Nero free.'

'I would still trust Drusilla's judgement.'

'You've known her only a few days.'

'Sometimes you can tell.'

'You could hardly blame Nero for killing Umfraville and Flood, though,' I say. 'Especially Flood, who was actively trying to capture him. The problem for Marius is that, if Nero is guilty, I should be as reluctant to bring him to justice as I am to tell Lord Arlington where Robinson's regicide brother is to be found.'

'I disagree. However much you sympathised with Nero, however reluctant you might be, you know you'd have to bring him to justice if you thought he was guilty. It's not like Robinson's brother, who is miles away and nothing to do with you. This is in our village and very much your affair. But, knowing what we know still helps Marius. Nero is clearly a witness at the very least. A witness worth seeking out both for Marius's sake and indeed for yours if the Sheriff is determined to hang you as an accessory.'

'Did Drusilla say exactly where Nero was to be found?' I ask.

'My suggestion that her close friend Nero might be a murderer made her somewhat cautious. She claimed not to know his address, though she had, as I say, already mentioned his employment in the sugar trade. If James's life or freedom was in danger, and she herself needed Nero as a witness, I think she might suddenly remember which sugar merchant he was working for. Otherwise, I think not.'

'Never mind,' I say. 'We may not be sure which sugar merchant Nero is with, or even how many sugar merchants there are in London, but I do know somebody who can find out for me.'

Chapter 21

In which things get more difficult than they already were

I have just finished writing a letter when the vicar is ushered into the library.

'I don't want to trouble you, Sir John, when I know you have so many other problems – the two deaths and so on – but I am getting a lot of complaints about Mister Marius.'

My visitor's regretful smile says both that he sympathises with me and that he warned me this would happen.

'What complaints?' I ask.

'He prays a lot,' says the vicar. 'That's not good. Not in the fields as he does. It's not good at all. Even if they were Christian prayers, the Church of England prefers to keep that sort of thing safely inside a consecrated building. The Church also likes people to use the proper words – the ones in the Prayer Book. Nothing extempore and nothing too fervent – it reminds people of the worst excesses of Cromwell's time. And absolutely nothing at all in a foreign language, which is the very hallmark of Popery. To pray, as your brother-in-law does, in the open air and in a heathen tongue ... people simply won't have it.'

'Musa ... Marius ... says the Koran enjoins him to pray anywhere except in one or two places where it would be disrespectful to do so. I think he hopes that, if the village sees him pray, they will also see there is nothing to be feared in his religion. He has nothing to hide from them.'

'I can assure you that is not the effect it is having. Quite the reverse. The more they see, the less they like it.'

'Very well. I assume nobody will object if he prays in this house? Or in the deer park?'

'Thank you. The deer park, discreetly hidden behind the brick wall, would be very acceptable. But it would be far better if he also came to divine service next Sunday.'

'He wishes to continue to worship as a Muslim.'

'Well, I can't see any problem with that, if he just does it in the deer park. The whole point of the Act of Uniformity, Sir John, is that you are seen to conform on Sundays. On other days of the week, you can be a Catholic – or a Mohammedan, I suppose – as long as you do it privately and don't plot against the King. The main thing from my point of view ...'

'... is that the Bishop doesn't find out. Yes, I think you mentioned that before.'

'It really is in his best interests. Marius's, I mean, not the Bishop's. The Grice brothers are spreading all sorts of stories about him.'

'I know they are saying they saw him near the New House when Umfraville was attacked, but so are other people. Anyway, he doesn't deny it. The Grice brothers can say that all they want. It makes no difference.'

'They are saying that they saw him bowing down to a statue of Mohammed on a camel.'

'Where is Marius supposed to have found a statue of Mohammed in Essex, on a camel or otherwise?'

'I agree that it sounds unlikely, Sir John, even if Muslims actually worshipped idols of any sort. Which they don't. But there are other stories too. The Grices are telling the children that Mohammedans kidnap small children and carry them off to Africa.'

'That's not true either.'

'Well, there's a small grain of truth in it. Boys of eleven or twelve have been taken from English ships by the corsairs. Not often, but it has happened.'

'Marius isn't going to carry anyone off anywhere. Africa is the very last place he'd want to go, though there are some children in Africa that I think he misses very much.'

'Just tell him to act normally. Like everyone else. It's not always easy, but it saves a lot of trouble.'

'He won't do it,' says Aminta. 'You know he won't.'

'I'm not sure which is the more intractable problem,' I say. 'Finding Umfraville's killer or persuading your brother to act in his own interests. Where is he at the moment?'

'Out wandering the roads and the fields again. I worry every time he leaves. Sooner or later he's going to get into real trouble, like Farndon but with more solid walls. How is your other problem, by the way?'

'I've written to London. Hopefully I shall have Nero's address before too long. But I am no closer to finding Umfraville's body than I was before. We've checked every inch of woodland and every field in Clavershall West. All of the hedgerows and barns and haystacks and outhouses. I can't see how such a solid body has vanished so completely.'

'When does the Sheriff arrive with Thatcher in tow?'

'Eight and a half days.'

'Something will turn up.'

'Yes, something will happen.'

'Sorry to disturb your dinner, Sir John – it's not really magistrate work. But I thought you ought to know anyway. One of the village children has gone missing. Probably nothing.'

'You were right to let me know, Ben. Which one?'

'Abigail Reeve.'

'Matthew and Kate Reeve's daughter?'

'That's the one. She's only five. The youngest of the family.'

'Where was she last seen?'

'In the meadow – the one you rent to Taylor. The one where Mister Marius sometimes goes. She was playing with her brothers and seems to have wandered off on her own.'

'How long has she been gone?'

'About three hours. Her family started to worry when the boys came home to dinner and she didn't. We've got men out checking the woods and the streams. Just in case.'

'I'll come and help you. I'll get a couple of footmen to come as well.'

'No need for you to worry, Sir John. I've them all organised, searching different areas.'

'The more of us there are searching, the sooner she'll be found.'

Ben looks at me. 'Still, maybe it would be better if you didn't come. Under the circumstances.'

'What do you mean, Ben?'

'I mean they're saying maybe Mister Marius took her.'

'That's nonsense. I'm sure the girl's disappearance has nothing to do with Marius in any way. And even if it did, if a crime has been committed it's my concern. Just give me ten minutes to get ready.'

'I'll see you down by the stepping stones, then,' says Ben. 'That's where I'm meeting the others. Maybe they'll have found her by now. Let's hope so, eh?'

When I arrive at the stream, a small gaggle of men and women are there. They seem to be reporting back to Ben on what they have discovered during their respective searches. Judging by their faces, the answer appears to be that they have so far met with no success. Matthew and Kate Reeve are there, as are two of their boys, both a little older than Abigail. William Taylor is standing on the bank, leaning on his staff. He is flanked, in a very respectful manner, by a couple of his shepherds. Ben's stable boy is sitting on a tree stump, wringing out his stockings. He's obviously had the unenviable job of wading along the stream. One of the young women, Margaret Platt, is talking in a kindly way to one of the Reeve boys. Aminta's right. She would make somebody a good wife, in spite of the witchcraft charges. They all turn when they hear our footsteps. Taylor raises his hat to me, but Matthew Reeve simply looks on sourly.

'I'm sorry to hear Abigail has gone missing,' I say. 'I take it you've all had no luck yet? I'm sure that Ben is organising the search very well, but I thought you might need a few more pairs of eyes. So, the three of us will join you wherever we can best be used.'

'Thank you, Sir John,' says Reeve, 'but we have all we need for the moment. I'm sorry you have been troubled.'

'She may have wandered off anywhere,' I say. 'There's a lot of ground to cover. The more of us there are the better.'

'Not wandered, Sir John. Taken,' says Kate Reeve.

'You can't be sure of that,' I say.

'Taken by your brother-in-law,' says her husband. 'The boys have just told us. At first they said she'd gone off on her own, but now they tell us Mister Marius took her.'

The boys look at the ground and nod almost imperceptibly. They're in trouble. They're just not sure how much. Margaret Platt gives one of them a reassuring squeeze on the shoulder, then reaches over and takes the hand of the other. She doesn't seem to blame either of them. I'm not sure the others do either.

'The boys say the three of them were playing together in the meadow,' says Ben. 'They thought they saw Mister Marius hiding in the bushes but thought nothing of it, because he often does. The next thing they knew, Abigail had gone and there was no sign of Mister Marius either. They were frightened to say so at first, but they've finally told us.'

The boys nod again. One of them gives a sob.

'If she did go with my brother-in-law,' I say, 'then I am sure she will be completely safe – wherever they've gone and for whatever reason. But unless any of you are suggesting that I was in some way complicit with Marius's actions, then I think it would be best if I and my men join you. You need everyone you can get.'

'True,' says Taylor.

That single word from one of the village's largest landowners seems sufficient to admit me to the search party. But the Reeves are not entirely happy. Kate Reeve purses her lips and looks away. Matthew Reeve shrugs. For once they should have heeded the Grices. They've been telling everyone who will listen that Marius is not to be trusted.

For the next couple of hours I oversee the checking of hedges and ditches along the London road, up to my own steward's cottage and beyond. Ben has respectfully but firmly allocated me one of the less likely areas to search, but somebody would have had to do it anyway. It's not a complete waste of time. Eventually my small search party turns back, no wiser than we were before, and I make my way to the village inn to see if others have been more successful. As I reach Harry Hardy's cottage, I see Marius emerge, followed by Harry.

'Good afternoon, Sir John,' says Harry. 'Mister Marius and I have been having an interesting talk. He's been telling me all sorts of stories about Africa. You wouldn't believe most of it.'

'I fear I may have talked too much and tried his patience,' says Marius. 'I've been boring him with my tales since mid-morning.'

'Not at all, sir,' says Harry. 'I was most interested to hear about the Moors – how they dress, what they eat and how they pray. And Mister Marius has been teaching me some of their language, Sir John. If I ever go to Africa, I'll be able to greet people properly and count up to twenty and buy vegetables in the market, though they seem to have different vegetables there from ours in Essex.'

'You've been here most of the day?' I ask.

'Yes, I've said I'm sorry—' says Marius.

'You haven't been to that meadow of Taylor's?'

'Where the children play by the river? No, not today.'

'Had you heard Abigail Reeve was missing?'

'Is she the girl who comes there with her brothers? She usually goes off to the little bower she's constructed for herself, while the brothers are making each other wet and muddy in the stream. I assume they've checked there?'

'Maybe not,' I say.

'So,' I say to Aminta, 'what happened was that Abigail's brothers were supposed to watch her but didn't. It was a couple of hours before they even realised they didn't know where she was. When they couldn't find her, they panicked and ran home, telling their parents she had wandered off. Then, when they realised they were going to get blamed for their inattention, they made up a story that Marius had taken her, knowing it would be believed. She was actually playing only twenty yards or so away, but her bower was her own private place, and she'd never told her brothers where it was located. When we went back and searched there, we found her fairly quickly. She was bored with her hiding game by then and getting hungry, so she answered straight away when we called, unlike earlier in the day.'

'I hope the Reeves were embarrassed at inconveniencing half the village?'

'Very. They also apologised to me for having tried to reject my offer of help. They were most contrite.'

'And Abigail's brothers?'

'They burst into tears, which they kept up loudly until it was clear that everyone was so relieved to see Abigail safe that nobody was going to get beaten for it.'

'And Marius?'

'He didn't come to the inn with me. I doubt if people would have welcomed him, however thoroughly his name had been cleared. He went off somewhere. I suppose he'll be home before it gets dark.'

'It's going to be like this all the time, isn't it?'

'Like what?'

'Whenever anything odd happens in the village, Marius is going to get blamed for it. If something goes missing, they'll say Marius took it. If somebody falls sick they'll say Marius cursed them in a strange language. If Marius walks down the street, mothers will call their children into the house.'

'Harry Hardy seems to have enjoyed talking to Marius. He put up with hours of it.'

'Harry is the exception to many things. He's always been an island of reasonableness in a sea of ignorance and suspicion. The village is beginning to fear Marius. This isn't going to end well.'

'I'll try talking to him again. I doubt that it will do much good.'

'I'm worried about him, John. I'm still angry with him – how can I not be? – but I'm also really worried.'

'He's been a soldier for twenty years. He at least knows how to take care of himself.'

The sun is already down when Marius returns. We are just finishing supper when he staggers into the dining room, holding his head. At first, I think he is drunk, then I notice the blood seeping between his fingers.

'What on earth has happened to you?' I ask.

'It's nothing,' he says. 'A couple of men attacked me as I was coming back through the village.'

'Who?'

'They had scarves tied round their faces. And it was too dark to see anything. I just need to wash the blood away. Then I'll be fine.'

'Did you hear their voices? Did they say anything?'

'They warned me to go back to Africa. I didn't recognise their voices, but local men, I would have said.'

Aminta has called for water and is examining her brother's wound.

'It's not deep,' she says. 'In fact, it's more or less stopped bleeding already, but I should clean it up and bandage it. Usually it's my husband who fails to see the ambush in time. I'd expected better of you, Marius.'

'We'll have your assailants tracked down and charged,' I say. 'Somebody in the village will know who they were. Ben may hear something. I'll talk to him tomorrow.'

Marius shakes his head. 'It will only make things worse,' he says. 'Do you think they will love me better in the village if two of them are sent for trial at the county court? Just let Aminta clean the wound and forget the whole thing ever happened. It's better that way.'

'Attack on Mister Marius? That's bad,' says Ben. 'Very bad. When was it?'

'Early yesterday evening.'

'And he didn't see who it was?'

'They had their faces covered.'

'Just the one blow? They didn't try to kill him or take anything?'

'No.'

'Grice brothers,' says Ben. 'Bound to be. They've been stirring up trouble for days. Only the Grice brothers would cover their faces then be stupid enough to speak and give their identity away.'

'Marius didn't recognise the voices.'

'Does he know the Grice brothers well?'

'I'm not sure he's ever spoken to them.'

'Exactly. It'll be Nathan and Jacob then. Shall I arrest them? I'll bring them to the Big House and you can question them. It doesn't need to go to the county court. You can just fine them for disturbing the peace.'

'We've no evidence,' I say. 'No witnesses. And Marius won't bring a complaint anyway. Unless they choose to confess, I'll have to release them. But if you hear anything from any of your other customers – if they saw something or somebody has boasted to them of having taught Marius a lesson – then please let me know.'

'I suppose we can always roast it,' I say.

'It was free anyway,' says Aminta. 'Somebody left it on a pole in the garden last night.'

'Why?'

'Marius says that it is a calculated insult to him as a Muslim. He says that it at least shows that they have learned something from him about his religion.'

'In that case they might have left a side of pork rather than a pig's head. It would have been equally un-Islamic and much more useful.'

'I'll have this cooked for supper tonight,' says Aminta. 'It should roast for at least six hours. There's cold beef from yesterday that Marius can eat.'

'We should enquire who in the village has recently killed a pig.'

'The Grices keep a lot of pigs. But plenty of families will be salting down pork at the moment or smoking ham. Let's just make the most of the gift.'

*

'Perhaps it would be better if I left the village,' says Marius. 'I'm doing no good here.'

'You have caused someone to supply a good supper,' says Aminta. 'For most of us anyway.'

'I need employment of some sort. I wondered if I could take up soldiering again – for the King, I mean.'

'It isn't as easy to get a commission as it was in Cromwell's time, but I'm sure it could be arranged at a reasonable price, if you're not fussy which regiment you join. You'd need to swear an oath of allegiance, though. And I doubt if you could be choosy over what food you ate. Or what prayers you said.'

'The problem is that I've done little else except being a soldier.'

'You speak Arabic well. That must be useful to somebody.'

'I suppose so. I can't stay here for ever anyway. That's clear enough.'

'No, but you can stay a little longer,' I say. 'The village will just have to put up with it. What's the worst they can do?'

Chapter 22

In which I go to Saffron Walden

'Have you heard from London yet?' asks Aminta.
'No, not yet,' I say. 'Perhaps I was expecting too much, even of my friends there.'

It is five days until the Sheriff returns. If Umfraville's body is still out there, it will now be almost unrecognisable – bloated, decayed and dined on by the local wildlife. One final attempt to locate it this morning has resulted in two footmen, two gardeners, one steward and myself returning to the house muddy and bad-tempered. I do not think we shall go out again this afternoon. Dark grey clouds have been gathering since dawn and the rain is now starting to fall again in large drops on the parterre outside. The neat balls of lavender shudder in a sudden gust of wind and the tall sash windows rattle in their frame. The world has become very grey.

I shake my head. 'I might as well have not asked the Sheriff for additional time. I shall have nothing more for him than

I had before, other than the evidence for James's innocence, which you so kindly uncovered.'

'Then it is fortunate that I have found out something else for you,' says Aminta. 'At a slight cost to ourselves admittedly, but I think it was worthwhile.'

'What was the cost?' I ask. 'Have you bribed the Grices to tell the truth?'

'If you don't take this seriously, I won't tell you anything until after the Sheriff has visited.'

'I apologise unreservedly for my levity.'

'Your apology is accepted. So, I loaned our coach to the Umfravilles for the morning. They were going into Saffron Walden for a dress fitting, and it was clear this was a day neither for walking nor riding. Mistress Umfraville and Mary were the customers for dresses but, a seat being available, Drusilla went with them for a change of scenery. She had not yet been to Saffron Walden or anywhere much outside the village since they arrived, poor thing.'

'And there was a revelation at the dressmaker's?'

'I have no idea. Drusilla, who is my informant, decided to wander round the town and admire the shops rather than watch her family try on country-made clothes. To pass the time she stopped at the silversmith's in the High Street, to admire his work and to purchase a packet of steel pins, which he also sells.'

'It's a useful shop. She did well to find it.'

'I suppose her mother or her sister must have heard of it and mentioned it to her. Anyway, one of the things she picked up to admire was a silver watch. Then she noticed something odd about it.'

'What?' I am obliged to ask, because Aminta has paused

significantly and will not continue until I acknowledge that this is a turning point in the story.

'It was her father's,' says Aminta.

'She was certain?'

'Well, it looked like his and it had his initials on the case. "H" is not an uncommon first initial but relatively few surnames begin with "U". She enquired, in a conversational manner, how the silversmith had come upon it. He said that a gentleman had recently sold it to him. She then asked if he could tell her more about the gentleman – his appearance and where he was from. Also exactly when the purchase had taken place. At this point the silversmith became less talkative and claimed to have forgotten all further details about the transaction, which perhaps, on second thoughts, had not taken place at all. He took the watch from her and put it out of sight behind the counter. She paid for a small quantity of steel pins and departed.'

'From which you conclude?' I ask.

'The same thing that must have occurred to its current owner – that the unfortunate silversmith was in possession of stolen goods. More specifically, that Hubert Umfraville's killer sold the only item of value he had found on the body at the first town he came to.'

'Nobody who lived round here would take that risk,' I say. 'The silversmith might have recognised them.'

'I agree,' says Aminta. 'And that certainly rules out Robinson as the seller of the watch.'

'It also makes it relatively unlikely it was anyone heading back to London,' I say. 'I mean, Jenks or Nero. Neither would have wanted to make a wholly unnecessary detour into Saffron Walden. And both would have been better off selling it in the relative anonymity of the capital. They'd have got a better price too.'

'We don't know how desperately Nero might have needed money.'

'Yes, that's true. I suppose his role at the sugar merchant's would be relatively junior. He might be paid very little.'

'It's a shame that Drusilla wasn't able to find out more. But she couldn't oblige the silversmith to tell her.'

'I can though,' I say. 'I'll get the coach back out again after dinner. I doubt that our man will have had a chance to dispose of the watch yet. Let's see what story he decides to tell me, eh?'

The rain eases off as my coach rumbles along the cobbled streets of our nearest town. With the great spire of St Mary's church to guide us, we make our way down the High Street between rows of ancient half-timbered houses with glistening tiled roofs.

The silversmith's shop is modest enough and there are no other customers in the low-beamed interior. The owner, rubbing his hands at the prospect of a customer who arrives in his own carriage, greets me with a wide smile. A smile that sadly does not last long.

'A silver watch?' he asks. He clearly wishes that he sold only pins and candlesticks.

'Yes, with the initials "H. U." on it. Formerly the property of Hubert Umfraville, late plantation owner in His Majesty's colony of Barbados.'

'I recognise you now. You're the magistrate from Clavershall, aren't you?'

'Yes,' I say.

'So, it's stolen then, the watch? I knew it. A bit too cheap, really, though I didn't complain at the time.'

'Who sold it to you?'

'Not somebody I'd ever seen before,' he says. 'I'm not even sure I'd recognise him again. A man – medium height or a bit above. Dressed in a dark blue suit of clothes, but with a cloak wrapped round him up to his nose and his hat pulled well down. I scarcely saw more than his eyes. Well, no honest citizen hides their face when selling you their watch, do they? I've been a fool.'

'When was this?'

'I don't know. Almost two weeks ago. The Wednesday before last, I think.'

'Did he say where he was from?'

The silversmith laughs bitterly, as well he might. 'What do you think?'

'Was there anything else about him that it might be useful for me to know?'

The silversmith thinks for a bit, then says: 'Yes, there is. It's difficult to describe exactly. But, even bundled up as he was, I thought: you've been ill, my friend.'

'Ill?'

'Yes, there was just something about him. Something not quite right with him.'

'Could he have recently had a bad knock on the head?'

'Well, as I say, I didn't see much of his head, front or back. But, thinking about it now, maybe that was it. His gloved hand shook as he took the money from me. I do recall that.'

'You've no idea where he went afterwards?'

'Out of that door, my good sir, and into the wide world. I suppose I'm not likely to see that watch again, am I?'

'I'll let you know,' I say.

*

Aminta looks at the silver timepiece on the table in front of her. 'So, you think the seller could be Hubert Umfraville himself? You've finally decided he might not be dead?'

'We at least have to consider it as a possibility. Let's say, just for a moment, that I was wrong and that he came to and fled the scene of his attack some time between my first viewing of the body and midday when Thatcher arrived. He'd have needed money to go wherever he was going and selling his watch would have been a good way to get some. Umfraville was wearing a dark blue suit when I saw him on the ground in the orchard, just like the seller of the watch. The customer went out of his way not to let the silversmith see his face. And if he was still suffering the effects of the blow to the head – as would be almost certain – then he would have seemed . . . well, ill, as the silversmith described it. His hand might well have shaken in the way he described.'

'Good news for the silversmith – that's not stolen property in that case, and he is entitled to have it returned. He really did get a bargain from somebody who needed cash quickly in his shaky gloved hand.'

'I failed to inspect Hubert Umfraville properly when I had the chance to do so. I thought I saw his hand and chest move but dismissed it as a trick of the light. I can't find a body. And now somebody very much like Umfraville has turned up in Saffron Walden, looking sick but bundled up so that his face and his wounds were conveniently hidden. It certainly explains why the body vanished when it did. He just walked away.'

'Much though I am enjoying your admission you might be wrong, that still fails to explain Flood's murder,' says Aminta. 'If Umfraville's alive, nobody Flood threatened to expose could have actually been a murderer. They might have attacked Umfraville and thought they had killed him, but when the body vanished they'd have known different. They might have worried that Umfraville would report them for assault – that was a very real danger – but they'd no need to kill Flood at all. Flood was an irrelevance.'

'Maybe they had no more idea what had happened to the body than I did and still believed they'd killed him. Flood therefore still needed to be silenced. Or maybe Flood was killed for some other reason that doesn't relate to Umfraville's death in any way. Let's not worry about Flood for the moment. If Umfraville is alive, where would he go?'

'He always relied on Nero,' says Aminta. 'If I were Umfraville, injured and with good reasons for getting out of Essex, I'd have gone to London.'

'Do you think he would know where Nero was?'

There is a respectful knock at the door.

'I have a letter for you from London, Sir John,' says our steward.

'At last,' I say. 'If this is what I think it is, then I'll set out first thing in the morning.'

Chapter 23

In which I learn how many sugar merchants there are in London, but visit only one .

The sun is setting deep red over the many sooty roofs of London as my carriage passes through Bishopsgate and inches along the still-crowded and malodorous streets. My coach horses have had plenty of exercise lately, and will need to travel back to Essex, God willing, the day after tomorrow. They and I can rest tonight. I do, however, send a message to somebody this evening, courtesy of one of the serving men at the inn, to let him know I'll see him in the morning.

'It is a great pleasure to welcome you to London again, Sir John,' says Williamson. 'I hope my letter was helpful?'

'Thank you, Sir Joseph,' I say. 'It was certainly very helpful as far as it went. I'm intrigued to know more. But, first, may I congratulate you on your knighthood?'

Williamson shrugs off my felicitations, but I think he is still very pleased. He has been Lord Arlington's right-hand man for many years, and this is finally some acknowledgement that the department could not function without him – perhaps even that he will succeed Arlington in due course. Williamson is as stiff and correct as my Lord is smooth and malleable. I cannot imagine the two not working together, Williamson's bony hand in Arlington's soft Spanish leather glove. But, as sure as night follows night, it will happen. At some point in the future, other people will oversee the King's many secrets. Eventually too, it will be a different king. But the work of this department, or one very much like it, will go on for ever.

Of course, I could never have asked Arlington for the favour that I have requested from Williamson, even though Arlington owes me a great deal and Williamson almost nothing.

'I have had this list of sugar merchants copied out for you,' he says. 'That was easy enough. There are directories available. The one who imports most from Barbados, however, is Martinson in Cheapside. I think you might profitably try him first. At the very least he should have heard if a mulatto from that island has found employment in London.'

'Thank you, Sir Joseph,' I say.

'Do you have any reason for taking an interest in sugar?'

'Somebody from that island has disappeared. Nero may be able to enlighten me as to where he has gone and why he went there. I am very grateful to you for your help.'

Of course, Williamson could have simply sent me the list with the letter. But he's called me into the office to collect it. There will be a reason for that. With Williamson there is a reason for everything.

'It may be that you could do something for us in return,' he says, as if I have done nothing for him and Arlington over the past dozen years and this small piece of paper now puts me, on balance, in their debt.

'It is always a pleasure to be of service to you, Sir Joseph,' I say.

He proposes something to me. I decline politely. We talk about the current negotiations for the freeing of English slaves in North Africa. I sympathise with him and pass on such information as I have obtained from Marius. Williamson shows some interest in this – gratitude, almost. He makes another suggestion. I propose slight changes to his plan that might make it workable. He nods. We understand each other. We part on good terms. Williamson never parts with anyone on bad terms unless Arlington has specifically instructed him to do so. That, and his systematic knowledge of everything under the sun, is why he is so valuable to my Lord, who has more enemies than I can count.

As I leave Williamson's office, I notice that the weather has become less favourable. Earlier this morning, it had been clear with only the smoke from fifty thousand sooty chimneys veiling the blueness of the sky. Now everything is closing in. Low, ochre-coloured clouds obscure the sun. I regret not bringing my cloak with me.

It is not a long walk to Cheapside over the rubbish-strewn cobbles, though anyone who knew nothing but a small Essex village would find the streets disconcertingly loud and inexplicably crowded. Voices, carriage wheels, horses' hooves and blacksmiths' hammers all compete to see who can assail my ears more painfully. Everyone is in a hurry to get somewhere else and everybody thinks that their own business is more urgent than mine. It is not considered impolite to barge somebody in the back and send them sprawling amongst cabbage leaves and dead rats. There was a time when this seemed normal and necessary to me too, but I've been in the country too long. I won't stay here longer than I have to.

Above Martinson's door is a large wooden representation of a sugar cone, painted in a creamy white, just in case anyone isn't sure what he sells. The smell of spices emanating from the shop suggests that he also stocks other produce from the West Indies.

'I'm looking for somebody named Nero,' I say to the apron-clad boy who greets me on entering the premises.

He looks puzzled and then says: 'Oh, you mean Mister Umfraville? The gent from Barbados?'

'I suppose so,' I say.

'I'll see if he's free to talk to you,' he says.

He knocks on a door at the back of the shop and has a hurried conversation with somebody. He beckons me forward. 'Mister Umfraville will see you now,' he says. 'But he says he can spare you only a few minutes.'

The man at the desk is making an entry in a leather-covered ledger. He is wearing a new-looking suit of black velvet and a large black periwig. He looks up as I enter the small walnut-panelled office. His brown face looks at me quizzically.

'Yes?' he says, putting his head on one side. 'What can I do for you, Mister . . . ?'

'Grey,' I say. 'John Grey.'

'How can I help you, Mister Grey? Jem says that you wished to speak to me rather than one of the other partners?'

'You are Nero Umfraville?' I ask.

'That is correct,' he says.

'I have come from Clavershall West,' I say. 'I am the magistrate there.'

He shows no particular sign of surprise.

'But of course. Clavershall West. I do of course now recognise your name, Sir John. You are very welcome here.'

'I assume then you are aware that Mister Umfraville ... Mister Hubert Umfraville ... has been attacked and has subsequently vanished?'

'My father, you mean?'

But of course. I knew already that Nero was of mixed race, was trusted completely by Hubert Umfraville and had been free to travel to England, albeit not with the rest of the family. It should have occurred to me long ago that Nero was Hubert's son. He seems quite proud to be an Umfraville. I suppose, in spite of his exotic appearance, Nero has rather more Norman blood in his veins than I do.

'Yes,' I say. 'I mean your father.'

He nods. 'My sister Drusilla has written to me. She is puzzled as to what has happened to him, but I fear he must sadly be dead. He has not contacted me – and he most certainly would have done if he had been alive and in need of help.'

And Drusilla is his sister. Not adopted sister. Not half-sister. His sister. Well, that should have been obvious too. I know now anyway.

'When you came to Essex, it was just to deliver a message to James?' I ask.

'Yes. To my brother. My half-brother, I suppose I should say. I had told Lucy I would deliver the message in person and so I did.'

'You didn't wait to see your father?'

'I had no idea when he would arrive and I needed to get back to London. A large consignment of spice was due to arrive presently from Sumatra – Martinson's is a large concern and we have dealings with the East Indies too. Had I known my father was only hours away, I should of course have stayed to see if there was a chance of speaking to him as well. It had never occurred to me that I should not see him again. We had thought in Essex he was finally safe.'

'Drusilla has clearly told you exactly what happened? The circumstances around the attack?'

'She gave a very clear account in her letter.'

'Could he have had some new threat against his life since arriving in England?'

'None that Drusilla divulged to me, Sir John. I had no chance to speak to him myself. There was danger in Barbados certainly. In London perhaps there was a small residual risk, but he was satisfied that in the depths of the country, far from ... I'm sorry, I do not wish to be rude about your little village, but you must agree that it *is* far from civilisation ... he felt that there, amongst simple country people, he would be in no danger at all.' Nero smiles. 'But I can see that a great deal of this is strange to you. Should I start at the beginning?'

'Please do,' I say.

'My father was not the first planter – nor I fear the last – to have children by one of his slaves – in this case the woman that Drusilla still believes, I think, to be her aunt. I am trying to arrange for the lady concerned – that is to say our mother – and possibly her husband also, to travel to England to join me. I cannot in all conscience leave them where they are, and the price of their freedom will not be excessive at their advanced age. I have instructed an agent in Barbados to obtain them at the lowest fee he can negotiate. Of course, some planters can find it difficult explaining to their wives the perfectly reasonable arrangements of the sort my father had. He always thought it would be ... well, better, shall we say? ... to maintain the fiction that I was an orphaned child whom he had educated out of charity and eventually taken on as his trusted clerk, and that he had similarly identified and adopted Drusilla as a suitable companion for their only daughter, Mary.'

'And your mother never suspected anything?'

Nero pauses and considers. 'I could not say for certain, Sir John. Perhaps. Perhaps not. My father was quite capable of dissembling. Indeed, in Barbados, he was one of the most noted liars on the island. I wish that were not true, but it is. For a long time Drusilla actually believed this fiction herself – I mean our mother being her aunt, for example. I have never told her otherwise. She's a bright girl, however – if she worked it all out, I don't think she ever gave anything away, even when Mary was at her most objectionable and telling her might have shut her up for a few minutes. I did my best for my father in Barbados – I truly did. But there was his drinking and his lack of any business sense whatsoever – I must have inherited my head for figures from the other side of my family. My mother was nothing if not an efficient housekeeper and her father had been a very prosperous trader in Benin – gold, ivory, slaves and so on. James and George worked hard as well, of course. But in the end we had to sober father up with a bucket of water and explain to him in simple terms that we were more deeply in debt than we could ever manage. I did my best to raise what money I could by legitimate means, but the multiple sales of the same land to different people were entirely my father's work. I stayed in Barbados long enough to see the family safely on their boat and to ensure, through friends I have there, that my mother would be properly looked after by the plantation's new owners. Then I slipped away to the harbour myself. It was easy enough to obtain the position of supercargo on one of the ships bound for England – indeed, I was able to negotiate a very satisfactory share of the profits for arranging the sale of the sugar in London after we had arrived. I knew Martinson from his occasional visits to Barbados. He'd already offered me a place here, if I was ever able to get to London, and now I was in a position to accept.

'Before I left Barbados I had also managed, at some risk to my own safety, to contact Lucy and offer to take a message to James. Accordingly, as soon as I was able to obtain a temporary leave of absence from work here, I rode up to Clavershall West. In the end, I wasn't able to speak to James directly but I did manage to rouse Drusilla. I perhaps should add that it had seemed to me that it was better, for all sorts of reasons, that Mistress Umfraville should not know that I had been there – hence my decision not to knock at the door. My father told me, even before we left Barbados, that I should at all cost avoid arousing her suspicions about what our true relationship was and that it would be inconvenient for him if she found out. For the time being, it seemed best she should preferably not even know I had followed them to London.'

'And she didn't see you?'

Nero considers this point carefully.

'Not the first time,' he says.

'There was a second time?'

'Unfortunately, yes. I realised that I had conveyed only part of the message to Drusilla. I returned hoping to awake her again, but regrettably I met with Mistress Umfraville herself. I explained, of course, that I had already spoken to my sister and asked Mistress Umfraville to convey the last part of the message to James.'

'Did you actually refer to Drusilla as your sister?'

'I had been travelling all day. I was more than a little fatigued. I was somewhat unprepared for my encounter with Mistress Umfraville. So, yes, I may have inadvertently done something of the sort.'

'And did you by any chance refer to Mister Umfraville as your father?'

'It had been a very long day.'

'And then?'

'I went back to the woods and slept in my shelter until dawn. Then I rode back to London. Later, as I say, Drusilla wrote explaining that our father had disappeared and that she feared that he was in fact dead. She said that the local magistrate – whom I now know to be you – was investigating. And that your wife was being very kind to her, for which I hope you will thank her on my behalf. I was sorry to hear of my father's death, of course, but it was difficult to argue that he had not brought it upon himself. And it was very obvious to me what had happened, as I'm sure it must be to you. I hope that explains everything in a satisfactory manner?'

We look at each other.

'You really shouldn't blame Mistress Umfraville for killing him. She had put up with a lot for a very long time.'

We look at each other.

'I've honestly no idea how she disposed of the body, of course.'

Chapter 24

In which I am mistaken for somebody else

The rain has started to fall heavily. Large cold drops that sting the face. I have accepted Nero's offer of the loan of a cloak, which I shall send back to him by my coachman later today. The wind, swirling down the cobbled streets, tries to whip it away and I pull it tightly round me. The roads are emptier now, as everyone who can scurries back to their homes and work-shops. That is why I am surprised, as I take a shortcut down a narrow, more-than-usually-piss-scented lane to hear footsteps approaching rapidly behind me. Before I can turn I am grasped by two strong arms that attempt to pin me where I am.

'I've got him!' yells my attacker. 'Give me a hand and we'll get him tied up.'

Sadly he does not have a tight enough grasp to stop me jabbing my elbow sharply into his gut. His grip becomes less enthusiastic, allowing me to bring my heel down with some force onto his foot. He yelps with pain and releases me. I turn, take two steps back and free my sword from the folds of my cloak. The man's accomplice, still running to his assistance, stops suddenly, skids on the wet cobbles and crashes into him. In a moment they are in a tangled heap before me.

'Good morning, Nathan,' I say. 'Good morning, Jacob. What brings you both to London?'

Both Grice brothers look up at me with their mouths open. Even though they outnumber me, I'm not sure they could still carry out their proposed plan. In any case, they no longer seem to want to.

'Sir John . . .' says Jacob.

'Can we get up?' says Nathan, eying the point of my sword an inch or two above his face.

'No,' I say. 'You can stay where you are and explain yourselves.'

'We meant no harm,' says Nathan. 'We thought you were him. Nero.'

'You see,' says Jacob, 'you came out of the place where he's hiding and you were wearing a cloak just like his, so we assumed . . . After all, with Flood dead and everything, there was no reason why we shouldn't go after the slave ourselves and see if we could get the money Flood had been promised. We'd worked for it back home. It's not as if we didn't deserve it. Can we get up now?'

'No,' I say. 'How long have you been in London?'

'A few days,' says Jacob. 'We posted notices asking for information leading to Nero's capture – with the reward of a guinea.'

'Do you have a guinea?' I ask.

'No,' says Nathan. 'But, if anyone came, we were going to say we'd pay after he'd been returned to his master and we were given our money. Anyway, we found out where he was ourselves, so we don't need the guinea. All the more profit for us, eh? Can we get up now?'

'No,' I say. 'Where were you going to keep Nero until you could find a way of shipping him to Barbados?'

'We hadn't thought,' says Jacob. 'We reckoned we could deal with that when the time came. Obviously we knew we'd have to take him to the Barbadoes, wherever that is, to get paid our proper reward. In the meantime, we thought we'd maybe keep him tied up in our room at the inn. He wouldn't need a bed or anything.'

'Where are you staying?'

'The Golden Eagle.'

'Then I suggest you go back there, pack your bags and return to Essex.'

'But it will only take another day or two to capture him. Look, we can share the money with you if you like. In exchange for telling us where the Barbadoes are and how we get there.'

'If you don't want to be charged with assaulting a magistrate, I would suggest that you return home today.'

'All right,' says Nathan suddenly. 'We'll do just that. Thank you, Sir John, for your advice.'

Jacob frowns at him for a moment and then smiles at their combined cleverness. 'That's right, Sir John,' he says, 'we'll go back to Essex today. At once. We won't try to catch the slave. You don't need to worry about us. Can we get up now? We're getting wet down here.'

'Do what you like,' I say. 'Just don't have second thoughts about going back to Essex. You'll regret it if you do.'

'So,' I say to Nero, 'the Grice brothers want to get Greengrass's reward for your capture and they know where you work. They are medium height, dark-haired and one wears a faded red suit of clothes and one green. They have promised faithfully to return to Essex, but their ability to tell a lie in a convincing manner is negligible. They are for the moment staying at the Golden Eagle Inn. Fortunately, they won't be able to afford to stay there much longer but I'd suggest for the next week or so you might like to be careful.'

Nero nods thoughtfully. 'I have seen them standing outside the shop with their mouths open, though I didn't know their names. Don't worry, Sir John. I can deal with them. They pose no threat.'

'I'd still be careful.'

'I shall certainly be thorough. Do you know a Mister Pepys at the Navy Board?'

'Yes,' I say.

'I have recently signed a contract with him to supply the Navy with sugar and rum. The terms were satisfactory for this house and very satisfactory indeed for him personally. Perhaps not quite so good for the King. I think he may owe me a favour in return for his commission.'

'And he can help you with the Grices?'

'We may be able to come to some mutually beneficial arrangement,' says Nero. 'You will now return to Essex yourself?'

'Tomorrow,' I say. 'I think that my work in London is done.'

'So,' says Aminta, 'on the night Hubert Umfraville vanished, his wife had just discovered that he had two illegitimate children, whom he had tricked her into bringing up as her own?'

'I'm not sure that Nero's status as an adopted son was ever quite as well defined as Drusilla's status as an adopted daughter. But in all other respects you are completely right.'

'Umfraville arrived, argued with the carter, thus extending his life by a good half hour or so. Once the carter had gone, and then Robinson had been seen off, Mistress Umfraville said that she would like a quiet word with Hubert in the orchard. They discussed, in a general way, what had been happening in their lives for the previous twenty years or so.'

'Nero is, I would say, in his early twenties so, yes, roughly that period of time,' I say. 'At some point Hubert turned to go back to the house, having explained his position as fully as he felt he needed to. Mistress Umfraville didn't agree that the conversation was yet over. Your father's gardener had left a rusty axe nearby. Hubert did not get very far before his wife smashed the back of his head in.'

'She couldn't shift the body on her own,' says Aminta, 'so she went to bed to think about it. Obviously, she had killed him – or she thought she had – but she would have recalled that Hubert was not without enemies. Anyone might've done it. They'd have to prove it was her. It was just a question of how she was going to handle things. Perhaps the body should be left. Perhaps it should be made to disappear, with the help of one or other of her sons.'

'In the morning, she had no choice but to mention in passing to the girls that their father had vanished,' I say. 'To do otherwise would have looked odd. But James, having heard suspicious noises the night before, had already gone out at first light to see what he could see. He announced to everyone that he had found his father's body. Mistress Umfraville realised that she could not keep the knowledge of his death a secret to just one or two members of the family. So, at some point during the day, she confessed everything to them and begged for help.'

'Not to Drusilla, I think,' says Aminta. 'She has been genu-inely puzzled all the way through. I suspect Mistress Umfraville knew that Drusilla was the only genuinely principled mem-ber of the family and that it might be as well to keep some minor details of the murder from her. I was surprised that she was sent to visit us for the day, but that explains it. Since James had already blurted out in front of Drusilla that Hubert was lying in the orchard, the option of hiding the body and pretending that he had just run off was now out of the ques-tion. The Umfravilles therefore decided collectively that they would simply brazen it out. Hubert had been attacked by an unknown person – perhaps he had heard a suspicious noise in the orchard and had gone to investigate. They reported the death to you because they had no other choice.'

'I agree,' I say. 'Except that you suggest she merely thought she'd killed her husband. I know the man who sold the watch may have been Hubert, but equally it may have been somebody else. My guess remains that Hubert was definitely dead.'

'We can't say that for certain. Not yet. He could well have lived to sell his silver watch. Let's assume he was merely injured in the attack. He came round and overheard his nearest and dearest discussing how they were going to get away with his murder. He bided his time. George went off to have dinner. Hubert ran for it. But he had very little money with him. So, passing through Saffron Walden, he sold the only thing of value he possessed. After that, the world was his oyster – the great metropolises of Thaxted, Colchester and Sudbury were all available to him. Who knows which he chose? But that's possible. Don't you agree?'

'I agree it's possible,' I say. 'But there's something about that that doesn't quite work.'

'What?'

'First, Nero said that if Hubert was still alive he would have contacted him. We thought that too. With almost no funds and nowhere to go, he'd have returned to London so that Nero could do what he'd done before – help him manage his life and put things right again.'

'You're still cross that you made that mistake, aren't you? You thought Hubert was dead and so didn't check the body properly. That's why, even now, you don't want to admit he's still alive somewhere.'

'I agree I'm still cross with myself, but it's not just that. There is something about the whole Saffron Walden business that doesn't work,' I say.

I close my eyes and try to see Umfraville on his journey from the orchard, via some obscure back lane to the Saffron Walden road and thence to the High Street of that same town and the silversmith's shop. Heavily muffled in his hat and cloak, face concealed, he hands the watch over. He takes the pittance the silversmith has offered, because he has no choice. He needs money fast. He clutches the coins in his gloved hand and leaves the shop. The high road to Colchester opens wide.

Why can't I believe that? What little detail in this story still strikes the wrong note?

'He's dead,' I say. 'And by the time the Sheriff gets here, I'll have proved it. Mistress Umfraville has my sympathies but—'

'You are the slave of the law?'

'Exactly,' I say.

Chapter 25

In which I pay another visit to my old home

'**D**o you think I'm a fool, Sir John?' Mistress Umfraville smiles at me indulgently. 'Do you imagine a wife does not know what her husband does? You would be well advised to consider that Lady Grey knows everything worth knowing about you, and a little more perhaps. Of course Nero was Hubert's son. I'd never doubted it. If I chose not to let my husband know that I knew, what of that? Yes, I met Nero when he returned a second time. He gave me his message. I congratulated him on how prosperous he looked. I believe I even offered him a bed for the night, though he said he needed to return to where his horse was tethered. That I should have taken it into my head to murder my husband over so little – when I had endured so much for so long – is ridiculous. In any case, you have just said, he was sufficiently alive the following day that he went into Saffron Walden and sold his watch.'

'Perhaps,' I say.

'Perhaps? A man in my husband's clothing, with my

husband's watch, clearly injured about the head. It seems very clear to me, Sir John. And if Hubert was alive then, I could not have killed him.'

'The silversmith said "ill", not "injured". He would not have been able to see his face properly, let alone the back of his head.'

'I fail to see that that makes any difference. If that wasn't my husband, where is he?'

'I don't think his body ever left here,' I say.

'You and your constable have both searched the house and garden very thoroughly.'

'Ben didn't know the house at all well. When I searched, you raised your voice to alert the rest of the family that I was looking for your husband and that they should take action accordingly – though whether to move a body or divert me from the burial place, I don't know.'

'So, do you intend to search it again?'

'No,' I say. 'Wherever the body was then, you've had plenty of time to dispose of it. But I shall work out what has happened, and, I warn you, I shall be back when I do.'

'And very welcome you will be, Sir John. In the meantime, you might ask your father-in-law if he would reduce our rent a little. Now that my husband has gone – and I am utterly alone and defenceless – our possible sources of income are fewer than they were. I am sorely in need of protection and assistance. For which I would of course show much gratitude. But perhaps it might be better if I explained things to your father-in-law in person?'

'I shall pass on your message to him,' I say.

'I can see that they might have difficulty paying the rent,' says Sir Felix. 'Now that, for all practical purposes, she no longer has a husband. I can certainly go and discuss the matter with her.'

This last remark might have appeared more generous and disinterested had he not given the ends of his moustaches a tweak as he said it.

'I could convey a message to her if you wish,' I say. 'There is no need for you to have to walk over to the property. It's quite a long way. At your age.'

'No, these things are always better done in person, in my experience.'

'Hubert thought he would be safe,' I say. 'Hidden in the country. Sadly he wasn't.'

'An easy mistake to make,' says Sir Felix. 'Prince Rupert always imagined that safety lay in charging at great speed into the centre of the enemy lines. With hindsight, I'm not sure he was right either. I see that the sun is out. I always think one should take every advantage one can of favourable conditions. I might take a stroll over in the direction of the New House.'

'Oh dear,' says Aminta. 'Well, I suppose that Mistress Umfraville is capable of looking after herself. As is my father. Having spoken to her again, do you still think she killed her husband?'

'Of course she did. If Nero's visit was the irrelevance that she implies, she would have mentioned it long ago. But the absence of a body offers her an escape route and she knows it. Like Nero, I don't know how she disposed of the body, but I am sure that it has gone.'

'And her husband's appearance in Saffron Walden shortly after he was killed?'

'It was James or George impersonating him.'

'Do you have any evidence for that?'

'No. But the need to avoid the silversmith seeing his face is telling.'

'It's a pity that William Robinson didn't see who was running away from the orchard that evening,' says Aminta. 'He would have needed to remain only a short time.'

'He said he thought there was more than one person because they made a lot of noise running through the grass. A woman's skirts would also have made a lot of noise, brushing through the long grass. There would have been blood on the dress too. Difficult to wash away. And Mistress Umfraville has been quick to order some new clothes from Saffron Walden. Not to mention accepting that old dress of my mother's from you in the meantime.'

'The otherwise unaccountable acceptance of our charity would seem fairly conclusive,' says Aminta. 'So, do you intend to tell the Sheriff that my father's tenant is a murderess?'

'If he'll listen,' I say.

'He and Thatcher will insist that Marius killed him?'

I nod. 'It is, you might say, an article of faith for them.'

Chapter 26

In which a conclusion is reached concerning the case I have been investigating

The following day, Saturday week as agreed, a coach swings across the gravel in front of the house and comes to a firm and definitive halt. Two gentlemen emerge. First, a portly Sheriff descends and takes a pace or two towards my front door. He stretches his arms and legs, perhaps to emphasise that he has just made a tiring journey for my benefit. Then he smiles in anticipation of an enjoyable day to come. Behind him, a thin face appears and sniffs the air of Clavershall West. The expression on the face is suggestive of distaste and disdain in equal measure. For a moment I think that Josiah Thatcher will remain in the coach, but he condescends to join the Sheriff on my raked gravel. They confer for a moment in whispers, though they must have had leisure to say whatever they wished to each other in the journey from Saffron Walden. Are they telling me that they represent a united front, against which I will struggle in vain?

I hear the front door being opened for them. In a moment they will be shown into the library.

'So,' says the Sheriff, 'have you found Hubert Umfraville's body, Sir John?'

'No,' I say.

'Have you conversely found him alive?'

'No,' I say. 'I have found a new witness – a silversmith in Saffron Walden who purchased Umfraville's watch the day after he was attacked. But I think the man may have been mistaken that the seller was Umfraville himself. It was almost certainly somebody else. Probably one of his sons. The person hid his face with a cloak – even his hands were covered with gloves.'

'To what end would one of the sons do that?' asks the Sheriff.

'So that we would think Umfraville was alive,' I say. 'In case one of the family was accused of killing him.'

'But surely nobody is suggesting that it was a member of Umfraville's own family?' asks the Sheriff.

'If you give me a chance,' I say, 'I shall explain.'

'Excuse me for a moment,' says Thatcher. He takes the Sheriff into a corner of the room and they confer in whispers. After a short time they turn to me again.

'The idea that it might be one of the sons seems to us improbable,' says Thatcher. 'The man must have been Umfraville himself, who had survived Marius Clifford's attack on him and fled. Sir Gilbert has, however, just pointed out to me – and I do of course respect his view – that the impersonation could as easily have been carried out by Marius Clifford, who had obtained a blue suit from somewhere and gloves to disguise his sunburnt hands. But, as I have most respectfully suggested to Sir Gilbert, in cases like this, we must look for the simple explanation, not the labyrinthine.'

Sir Gilbert nods, but I can see that he is not happy to have his point about gloves dismissed so easily. He was rather pleased with that.

'Clifford attacked Umfraville,' Thatcher continues, 'and later killed Flood. Umfraville, unlike Flood, survived the attack – as we would have been able to confirm if Sir John had only done his job properly. The silversmith's evidence merely confirms what we already knew. Umfraville got away and is alive. Or was alive a day or so after the attack.'

'Umfraville,' I say, 'was and remains most certainly dead. And he was not attacked by Marius Clifford.'

'Then who do you think attacked him?' asks the Sheriff. 'If it wasn't your brother-in-law?'

'I believe it was his wife,' I say.

Thatcher raises his eyebrows at this, but he is at least willing to listen.

'Has she admitted to it, then?' he asks.

'No.'

'Are there any witnesses?' asks the Sheriff.

'No. But there is good evidence – circumstantial, I admit – of a strong motive. She had just discovered that her husband had fathered two children on another woman – one of his own slaves.'

'How had she discovered this?'

'Nero, the slave Flood was seeking, was one of the children. He had visited the household on another matter and let slip that Umfraville was his father. She knew that she had in effect been tricked into bringing up these two children in her own household.'

The Sheriff considers this point carefully. 'Just two?' he asks.

Of course, he has a point. This is a fleabite compared with what our beloved monarch has inflicted on the Queen. At least Umfraville didn't make his mistress a duchess and a lady-in-waiting to his wife.

'Yes,' I say, 'just two.'

'Does she complain of his behaviour?'

'No,' I say. 'Not in any way. She claims to have known about it for some time and not cared greatly.'

'Then I don't think that will take us very far, Sir John. In which case, in the absence of better evidence, we must ask ourselves if she is generally of good character. Who could vouch for her? I realise that she has arrived here recently, but who, for example, is her landlord?'

'My father-in-law,' I say, with a sinking heart. 'Sir Felix Clifford.'

The Sheriff looks from me to Thatcher and back again. 'Sir Felix Clifford? Why didn't you say so before, Sir John?' He turns to Thatcher. 'Why didn't you tell me, Josiah, that Sir Felix Clifford was Marius Clifford's father?'

'It scarcely seemed relevant,' Thatcher replies.

'Not relevant? He is a member of one of the most distinguished families in the county – staunch royalists throughout the whole war. And nobody saw fit to tell me this important fact?'

Did I also fail to tell the Sheriff? Perhaps I just referred to Sir Felix as my father-in-law. After all, he is neither a suspect nor a witness nor somebody with any knowledge of the facts of the case. He is merely the person who is about to be asked definitively whether Mistress Umfraville is a murderer.

'I'll send for him,' I say.

A few minutes later the door to the library is flung open. My father-in-law strides into the room.

'Sir Felix?' asks the Sheriff. 'Well, this is a pleasant surprise! It must be over twenty years since we last met – twenty-five, almost, I'd say. So, the man Mister Thatcher wishes to accuse of murder is your son? But I'd heard your son was killed at the Battle of Worcester?'

'That's what we all thought. What had actually happened was that, en route to the royalist stronghold of Barbados, he'd been taken prisoner by the Sallee Rovers and held as a slave in Africa for twenty years.'

'Sir Felix and I served side by side under Prince Rupert,' says Sir Gilbert to the room in general. 'And his son, as you will gather, fought for the King at Worcester. I rejoice at the news that he survived. You must be proud of him, Sir Felix. Not that you can expect the King to show gratitude, of course. He's forgotten us old cavaliers. Half of the present crop of royal ministers served Cromwell, one way or another. This wasn't at all what we'd hoped for at the Restoration. The King's former foes rewarded and his friends forgotten.'

Thatcher coughs pointedly. 'Nevertheless,' he says, 'I would urge you to consider the evidence against him. When we have disposed of that against Mistress Umfraville anyway.'

'Thinking about it, the evidence against Marius should not detain us long,' says the Sheriff. 'We may as well get it out of the way first. I wonder if, after all, it isn't rather circumstantial. Did anyone witness Marius Clifford attacking either Umfraville or Flood?'

'No,' says Thatcher, 'but—'

'Did Marius Clifford actually know either gentleman?'

'No,' says Thatcher, 'but—'

'Do we have an informant who claims that Marius Clifford expressed any intention of killing them?'

'No.'

'Has Marius Clifford attempted to flee?'

'Clearly not,' says Thatcher.

'And we need not question his good character. He fought bravely for the King. Then, attempting to reach Barbados to carry on the fight, he was taken prisoner and suffered twenty years in Africa for His Majesty's sake. Twenty years, gentlemen! Though Josiah here put forward some superficially plausible reasons for his guilt, the case against him is beginning to look very shaky indeed in my view.'

I wonder if the Sheriff is still smarting over the dismissal of his glove theory. Thatcher will have difficulty persuading him of Marius's guilt anyway. Nevertheless, he tries.

'Could I remind you, Sir Gilbert,' says Thatcher, 'that Marius Clifford has turned Turk? He is a renegade who has abandoned the church of his birth for a false faith.'

'He's not a Catholic, though?'

'No, he's not a Catholic.'

'Or a republican?'

'Obviously not.'

'Then I can't see that he poses any danger to the state.'

'Surely the case against him requires more detailed consideration than we are giving it?' asks Thatcher.

The coroner looks at me. Suddenly I realise that we are on the same side. We have always been on the same side. We both wish to seek out the truth. We both wish to condemn the right person for the right reasons. Though we may have initially reached different conclusions, eventually we would have found common ground. But deep down we must both know it is too late. Thatcher is still going to try, but he is doomed to failure.

'Very well, I agree that we should put the accusations against Marius Clifford to one side for the moment,' he says. 'Sir John did, however, present valid arguments for the killer being Mistress Umfraville. We need to consider those.'

The Sheriff nods. 'Well, that is a good point. We still need to do that. We were considering her good character, which is why we summoned Sir Felix to help us.' He turns to my father-in-law. 'As her landlord, Felix, you know her better than any of us. Would you think her capable of murdering her husband?'

'Most certainly not,' says Sir Felix. 'She is a fine, upstanding woman. Honest. Industrious. She would make any man a perfect wife. I would be happy to vouch for her character unreservedly.'

'Then that is the end of the matter,' says Sir Gilbert. 'I would trust your judgement on that, every bit as much as I trusted your judgement when we were comrades in arms.'

'Thank you, Major Mildmay,' says Sir Felix.

'Not at all, Captain Clifford,' says Sir Gilbert.

Thatcher gives a long sigh. 'So, who are we willing to consider?' he enquires. 'I merely ask, as the officer responsible for ascertaining the cause of death of these people. We have one man badly injured, at the very least, and now missing, and we have one most certainly dead. Somebody undoubtedly attacked them. We've come all the way here from Saffron Walden. If we are now ruling out, as a matter of course, anyone who fought for the King and those known personally to ourselves, who is left?'

He looks at me again, as if appealing to the only other sane person in the room. But I can give him no help. It really is far too late.

'Well,' says Sir Gilbert, 'let us not forget this slave Nero. He was in the village according to Sir John. And he would have had a grudge against both Umfraville and Flood.'

'Umfraville was apparently his own father,' says Thatcher.

'A father who had kept him in slavery!' says Sir Gilbert. 'I'd say Nero killed Umfraville, later disposed of the body while the Umfravilles were at dinner, and took the watch to sell in town. The money he obtained might not be much for any of us here, but it would be a small fortune for a man like him. Necessarily he needed to keep his face as much hidden as he could – which the silversmith is adamant that he did. And, gentlemen, do you remember my theory about the gloves?' He looks at us all pointedly. 'Nero, even more than Marius Clifford, would have needed to disguise his hands. That is perhaps the most telling argument of all. In my view anyway. This Nero person returned via the village, money in his purse, only to discover that Flood was lodged here and seeking to capture him. He killed Flood, in exactly the same way he had killed Umfraville, and rode back to London.'

I do not doubt that, if we put Nero before a jury, they would find him guilty. There would be Jenks's sighting of him running away, together with whatever evidence the Grice brothers decided to invent following their failure to capture him. It might even come out that Hubert Umfraville was in the habit of giving Nero his cast-off suits of clothes and that Nero could, in Saffron Walden, easily have been wearing one not unlike that in which Umfraville was killed. Above all, there is the fact that he is a slave. Actually that one fact in itself would be decisive. Nothing, even the gloves, would convince a jury more thoroughly.

I catch Thatcher's eye. We both want justice, but what sort of justice? I think we also share the conviction that Umfraville's death was well deserved. Perhaps, after all, it is better that the investigation is swiftly and ludicrously terminated than that the wrong person is hanged. I could simply tell the Sheriff where to find Nero, but I shall not, any more than I shall tell the King's ministers where Robinson's brother is hiding.

'The problem,' I hear myself saying, 'is that Nero has long since fled. It will be almost impossible to track him down. At least, not without a great deal of hard work.'

Sir Gilbert shakes his head sadly. 'I agree. He will have vanished utterly into the underworld of London. He would be capable of no more than menial employment – lifting, carrying. And he will doubtless have changed his name. Unlike ourselves, he will have no particular pride in his ancestry. Don't you agree, Sir John?'

'I think there would be nothing to be gained in trying to find him,' I say.

The Sheriff frowns thoughtfully. 'Then that concludes our deliberations. Forgive me, gentlemen, if you think I am overstepping the mark judicially, but I am not inclined to think that either Umfraville or Flood were a loss. The slave catcher Flood seems to have been a republican of the very lowest sort. A danger to the peace of the Kingdom. And I remember stories about Umfraville at the Battle of Newbury. His precipitous retreat cost the lives of some good men. We should waste no more of the King's time on him. In spite of the lack of one body, I am content to regard both Umfraville and Flood as being dead, killed by the slave, Nero. And a man can after all be murdered only once, gentlemen. It's not as if we need to protect Umfraville or Flood from some further attack. We've done for them as much as they need or deserve. You are to be congratulated, Sir John, on having discovered as much as you have. I shall ensure that the King is aware of your efficiency and your zeal. Now, I think we have time for a walk in your park before dinner? You will join us, Sir Felix? It would be good to recall some of our old campaigns. The young people have little interest in them – the King included.'

'So,' says Aminta, 'your colleagues have agreed, over what I hope was a good dinner, that there is no point in charging Marius with murder.'

'Or Mistress Umfraville,' I say. 'And since they have departed for Saffron Walden, I think that is the end of the matter. Officially at least.'

'My father is over at the New House again this afternoon. I think he is providing advice on the garden.'

'If he wishes us to think his visits are innocent, he must stop twirling his moustaches like that.'

'He used to do the same thing when he set off to visit your mother.'

'Yes, I remember that very well.'

'If he plans to marry the lady, I do think he should consider what happened to her last husband. Unless the Sheriff has somehow talked you into believing Hubert is still alive?'

'As I have said repeatedly, Umfraville is dead. And I do think I now know exactly what happened. I've just realised what it was about his supposed visit to Saffron Walden that was so improbable and that proves that he was impersonated by somebody who knew him well – though not by Nero. I have also worked out why the body was first left for me to examine but then had to be disposed of, very urgently indeed.'

'And what prompted this sudden revelation?'

'It was what the Sheriff said – a man can be murdered only once. Except that Hubert Umfraville was murdered twice. And that explains everything.'

'Twice? You're sure about that?'

'I shall be when I've spoken to Mistress Umfraville again.'

'However many times she did it, you still won't convict her. It isn't just that my father has vouched for her character. However many times Umfraville died, there is still no body.'

'No body, no murder,' I say. 'Still, she may as well know that we know.'

'It's always useful for your new mother-in-law to understand you could convict her of murder,' says Aminta. 'In principle, if not in practice. If you're going over to tell her, I may as well come with you.'

'Yes, do. It is an entirely social visit. My official role in this is already over.'

Chapter 27

In which my wife and I have a helpful conversation with my future mother-in-law

'You have just missed your father,' says Mistress Umfraville to Aminta. 'It has been a great pleasure getting to know him better. A most gallant gentleman. You would have thought that he was ten years younger – at least – than he claims to be. Can he really be old enough to have fought as a captain of horse under Prince Rupert? He is also the owner of a fine house, of course. And he is of a most distinguished family of ancient lineage.'

'I'm pleased that you get on so well,' I say. 'But would your husband not object to such frequent visits in his absence? Since you tell me is alive.'

'I do begin to wonder if Hubert is not dead after all. The man he sold the watch to said he looked very ill. And he has not been seen since. I fear he may have very sadly died of his wounds.'

She looks at me to gauge my reaction, then at Aminta. There are various directions in which she could take this conversation and she is not yet sure which way to go.

'It was George or James who sold the watch, as you know well,' I say.

'Lawks! What strange ideas come into your head, Sir John!'

'Nevertheless, it is true, is it not?'

'To what end? We are not so poor as to need the few shillings the silversmith paid.'

'To convince us that Hubert was still living and that you had therefore not killed him. You knew – or hoped – that word would get back to us of a man looking like your husband, still alive and well the day after his apparent murder. When it didn't immediately, you ensured that Drusilla, who I think knows nothing of all this, was sent to the shop, where she would probably chance upon the most interesting thing that the silversmith had recently purchased. Being an intelligent girl, she would immediately see the watch for what it was and report back. If, by any chance, she hadn't done so, I assume the next stage was to tell me directly that there was a rumour the watch had been seen at a shop in town?'

'You seem very confident that you know what happened,' says Mistress Umfraville. 'Bearing in mind that neither of you were there when my poor husband was attacked. Why don't you tell me exactly what you believe transpired?'

'Very well,' I say. 'I shall. Though you may have suspected that Nero and Drusilla were your husband's children, I think that you did not discover that for certain until Nero's visit. As a result of what you learned from Nero, you and your husband went to the orchard where you could discuss matters without disturbing other members of the family. The house, as you have pointed out to me, is not a large one. There, in the orchard, you killed Hubert Umfraville.'

'We are going over old ground,' says Mistress Umfraville impatiently. 'Hubert and I in the orchard. The silly axe. I've said plainly that he was alive the following morning, even if he is probably dead now. Your father-in-law, if he were still the magistrate here, would not doubt the word of a lady in this unchivalrous manner.'

'Very well. I will concede that your husband may have still been alive, albeit grievously injured, the following morning. Unlikely but possible. You nevertheless thought he was dead, for all that, and that you had killed him. George watched over Hubert's apparently dead body while I questioned suspects. But a number of things have troubled me about your account of that morning. You said that George left the body in the orchard and went to have dinner. Surely, as a family, you would not have left Hubert's body alone, the prey to passing dogs and foxes? It simply isn't believable that one of you wouldn't have taken over the duty of guarding him in a decent and Christian manner. I think that person was you, Mistress Umfraville – you took over George's duties, didn't you? So there was never a time when the body was unattended and Hubert could just wander off to Saffron Walden. He didn't go anywhere. Why then did his body have to disappear? What I think happened was this. You watched him for a while then, to your horror, you thought you saw him move.'

I pause and look at her. There is real fear in her eyes as if she was reliving such a moment.

'Of course,' I say, 'I'm not saying he really did move. But I noticed something similar the first time I was in the orchard – the running shadows made it appear that Hubert's hand quivered. For a moment, I thought he was alive, and for a moment you did too. Alone in the orchard you panicked. If Hubert wasn't quite dead, he was very shortly going to give evidence against you for assault, at the very least – murder if he inconveniently died later. Quite wrongly, you believed you had only one option. The axe was still in the orchard. You decided you would have to kill him a second time. Unfortunately, you then had a body with many more wounds than it had had before. I couldn't be allowed to see it. You called George. He fetched James from the inn. You agreed on a new plan of action. You probably discussed who else would be let in on the secret. Drusilla could not be.'

'It was very clever of you,' says Aminta, 'to encourage her to remain at the Big House for as long as she wished, so that she saw as little as possible of what followed. I did enjoy her company, of course. I congratulate you on a very accomplished daughter.'

'Thank you,' says Mistress Umfraville. 'I have tried to bring her up to appreciate learning and refinement. I do think that is so important for a young girl.'

'Your husband's bloody remains,' I continue, 'were placed somewhere temporarily. You encouraged Ben to search the house, even though you knew I would do it better, because you wanted to hide the body later in the safest possible place – that is to say, one that had already been searched and ruled out. It was no great problem to move Hubert from room to room while Ben blundered about a house he didn't know well. When I searched it later, it was I hope more of a problem for you. As I said before, you needed to rally all your troops and therefore raised your voice in protest so that the others would hear and know what was happening.

Whatever needed doing, you did. But you were even more aware you had to dispose of Hubert permanently. You'd ordered some livestock, including a pig from the Grices. Pigs will eat almost anything, won't they? When you started to feed your husband to the pig, and whether you did so whole or diced, I do not know. Certainly, when I visited, you were careful to warn me that the pig was dangerous, so maybe there were already bits of your husband lying around in the orchard. If I searched now, of course, there would be nothing left to find. Hubert Umfraville has genuinely vanished.

'But just having the body disappear wasn't enough. That's why George or James was sent off to Saffron Walden, the afternoon following the murder, in your husband's blue suit – a trifle too big for either of them – to sell the watch in a hopefully memorable manner. For some time, I couldn't work out why this transaction seemed so odd. Then I realised what it was. Hubert, lying in the orchard, was dressed in his coat and breeches – no hat, no cloak, no gloves. But the seller of the watch was muffled up, necessarily, in all of those things to avoid identification. Even the gloves were necessary, since the boys' relatively slim hands would not pass for your husband's fat and calloused paws. Where had the purported Hubert obtained these additional garments during his precipitous flight? He certainly hadn't been seen returning to the house to collect them. The silversmith said that the watch seller looked ill. He would have seen little of his face. But he would have seen how loosely your husband's capacious clothes hung on George or James and he might have concluded that the man in front of him had lost a great deal of weight recently.'

Mistress Umfraville smiles. She was worried for a moment, but now she knows what my case is against her. And things could be worse. After all, I still don't have a body. The Pig Hubert has that.

'Complete nonsense,' she says. 'Pure speculation. You have no proof at all. Next you'll be accusing me of killing Flood. Well, say whatever you have to say on that. It makes no difference to me.'

'I agree it makes no difference at all, but here is what happened next anyway. Flood wrote to you, as he wrote to many others, saying that he had discovered that you had killed Hubert Umfraville. Unlike the others, you knew that you actually had. You invited him to the New House to talk to him. You'd known him in Barbados. You knew how unpleasant he was. You knew you could not afford to fall into his clutches and be bled dry by him. So, you killed him, just as you killed Hubert, in the orchard with one of the other axes that my father-in-law had helpfully provided with the house – one that hadn't been left out in the rain. George and James then helped you carry his body – not far, but at least out of the grounds of the house.'

'You'll never prove any of it,' says Mistress Umfraville. 'Your father-in-law tells me that the Sheriff is convinced of my innocence.'

'But the magistrate in front of you is clearly not,' says Aminta. 'And nor am I. You may think you have destroyed the evidence, but Hubert's blue suit of clothes clearly did not go to the pig and will almost certainly have his blood on it. So will the dress you were wearing. The one you needed me to replace for you.'

'Perhaps, my Lady, I should add that we had a little bonfire the other day of things that we brought from Barbados but do not in fact need. I think that an old dress of mine went onto it. And possibly a suit or two of Hubert's. I tell you just to save Sir John the trouble of going through my clothes or my husband's. Should I get married in the near future, I imagine that my future husband will buy me some new clothes, so the loss of the dress is unimportant.'

'If you are still claiming Hubert is alive, you will not be able to marry anyone,' says Aminta.

'As I said, I now have doubts on that score. I feel sure that in the next day or two I shall receive a letter from somewhere telling me that my husband has died of his wounds. That should be adequate. No clergyman, asked to conduct a joyful wedding service, would think of cross-examining a grieving widow in the impertinent way you are both questioning me now.'

'Then you will be pleased to know that I have finished,' I say.

'Not before time.'

'Make no mistake, Mistress Umfraville, we know exactly what happened.'

'But can't prove it without a body.'

'Or a confession from one of your accomplices.'

'Which you will not get.'

'You will have to remain on very good terms with your children,' says Aminta, 'and your new husband, if you get one, for the rest of your life.'

'Why should it be otherwise?'

'Indeed,' I say. 'Why should it? Then, in conclusion, let me thank you for the frank and open way you have assisted with my investigation.'

'I am always pleased to help the officers of His Majesty in the administration of justice. Of course, Sir John, if you'd examined Hubert's body properly when you first found it, it would have saved us all so much trouble . . .'

'That is a mistake that I shall not make again,' I say. 'I plan to revert to the close and detailed examination of all corpses. And who could possibly object to that? I am, after all, the son-in-law of a very old friend of the Sheriff's. I think I may now outrank the coroner in every possible way.'

Aminta puts her head on one side. 'You do realise that nothing you said rules out Hubert Umfraville having been alive the following morning, when you examined him – that he might have moved in reality rather than in Mistress Umfraville's imagination?'

'Very unlikely,' I say.

'It really matters to you, doesn't it, whether Hubert actually came to or whether Mistress Umfraville imagined it? Because in the former case you were wrong. In the latter case you were right all along.'

'She's still guilty either way.'

'But one way you score off Thatcher and the other way you don't.'

'I think I misjudged Thatcher,' I say. 'I expect every cooperation from him in future.'

'Well, if it helps, I think you were right. Hubert was dead when you saw him in the orchard.'

'Exactly,' I say.

'She never needed to kill him a second time.'

'Quite.'
'Or dispose of the body as she did.'
'Very true.'
'When she kills that pig, I'm definitely not eating any of it.'
'Nor am I,' I say.

Chapter 28

In which four people receive letters from London, resolving certain issues

The first snows of the winter are dusted over the deep brown furrows, and frost coats the roofs of the cottages and grander houses alike. Aminta, dressed in a furred cloak, and I are walking in the park. The frozen grass crunches beneath our shoes.

'Has your father said anything about his forthcoming marriage?' I ask.

'No. I think it may be less of a forgone conclusion than Mistress Umfraville hoped. There are two other ladies in the area – both widows of independent means – who had also hoped to be asked for their respective hands. For a while they have been observing each other warily and keeping their powder dry. But the appearance of a rival in the village has spurred them both into action. My father has just ridden over the icy road to Elmdon, where he has been invited to dinner. He sups with the other lady the day after tomorrow in her cosy parlour. I regret to say there is quite a spring in his step.'

'Then, sadly, my long wait for a mother-in-law continues,' I say. 'One impediment at least has been removed, however. The vicar told me that Mistress Umfraville has informed him of the unfortunate death of her husband. The letter about which she had that remarkable premonition has now been received. Hubert Umfraville has already been buried in a graveyard in London – she was unsure which one.'

'He travelled a surprising distance with a fatal wound,' says Aminta.

'There has been so much about this case,' I say, 'that is truly remarkable.'

'Mistress Grice has finally heard from Jacob and Nathan,' says Ben.

'That must be a great relief for her after all this time,' I say. 'Where are they?'

'In the Barbadoes, apparently. It seems that they were taken by a press gang while they were in London. They have been forced to serve in the Navy and are at present on a ship stationed in the West Indies. I'd heard the press gangs were out, there being a war and all, but Nathan and Jacob know nothing of the sea. I fear there was some mistake when they were taken.'

'It almost sounds as if some unkind person directed the press gang to them.'

'That Mister Pepys you know in London – he's something to do with the Navy, isn't he? Could he get them freed?'

'He's Clerk of the Acts to the Navy Board. But if the Grice brothers have already been impressed, I suspect there's little he can do to help them at this stage.'

'They've been made slaves of the Navy, almost. Who would do such a thing?'

'I couldn't possibly tell you,' I say.

'I've just had a letter from Betterton at the Duke's Company,' says Aminta.

'Does he wish to commission another play?' I ask.

'He certainly enquires what I am working on at the moment. But it is mainly in reply to a letter that I sent a couple of days ago. I said that there was a young lady in the village, diligent, of considerable intelligence and able to quote whole scenes of Shakespeare.'

'Drusilla can do that?'

'Well, a large number of lines. There's no point in under-selling your assets. Anyway, I told him that she was wasted here in the country and asked if he knew of suitable employment for her. He said that he badly needed an assistant stage manager, and that if she cared to report to him next week, she could have the job on a three-month trial.'

'She'll enjoy that.'

'I thought so too. I'll go over and let her know.'

'She will be conveniently near her brother. And the rest of the family if Nero has been able to bring them over from Barbados. She won't be without friends in London.'

'Exactly.'

'I doubt that she'll miss her sister. Her adoptive sister,' I say.

'Or her father's killer. On the whole, I think that's worked out rather well,' says Aminta.

'I have received a strange letter,' says Marius. 'From somebody called Sir Joseph Williamson.'

'Really?' I say.

'He says that Lord Arlington needs a gentleman with a good command of Arabic, an understanding of the Islamic religion and the ability to handle a sword to undertake a diplomatic mission to Morocco. His lordship needs to know how many English slaves are being held in the country and how best he and Williamson might proceed to liberate them. Williamson suggests that I might like to take up the appointment myself. I've no idea how he's even heard of me.'

'Williamson is nothing if not well informed,' I say.

'He says that I could safely return to Morocco as the King's ambassador. The Sultan is trying to establish better relations with this country at the moment and would not dare to arrest a British envoy.'

'I should warn you that what Williamson means by "safely" and what other people mean by "safely" are not always the same thing. Still, you could return to Morocco more securely as the representative of the British government than as almost anything else. If that's what you wanted to do.'

'He says that I may be kept waiting some time by the Sultan for an answer to certain questions they wish me to ask, but that would give me the leisure to travel the country if I wished.'

'Your diplomatic credentials should ensure that you could do that without any official hindrance.'

'Yes, it seems Williamson would provide the necessary documents for me to enter Morocco and for me and possibly others to leave. Why others? Does he mean freed slaves?'

'Williamson never makes himself clear if he doesn't have to. But it certainly means you would have the opportunity to seek out your family there. And perhaps bring them back with you.'

'How does Williamson know I have a family there?'

'Williamson's knowledge of the world never ceases to surprise me.'

'Very well. I shall travel to London and speak to him.'

'That is wise of you. It would be even wiser to ensure that you are paid all of your expenses promptly and that you stress that, once you have undertaken this mission for Arlington, you intend to return to Essex, or some other peaceful place, and never leave it again.'

'*Insha'Allah*,' says Marius.

Acknowledgements

Writing, as I may have observed somewhere before, is a bit of a team effort. Though only one name appears on the cover (mine, in case you hadn't noticed), you would not be reading this without a great deal of work by other people. Krystyna Green, Amanda Keats and Howard Watson at Constable have been magnificent in their support for me at the various stages of production. I couldn't wish for a better team. Sean Garrehy deserves a special mention for his patience, ingenuity and consummate skill during our discussions on the cover design – I'm delighted with the final result.

I am grateful as ever to my agent, David Headley, and everyone at the DHH agency, which is, as I write, celebrating its tenth anniversary. (Many congratulations, DHH!)

My thanks are also due once again to my family, and in particular to my wife, Ann, who was the first to read the manuscript, and also to our daughter, Catrin, who made some invaluable and insightful comments on the language used. Finally, my life was also made a great deal more fun during the year by our grandchildren – Ella, Ieuan, Reggie, Raya and

Trystan, the last two of whom were born while I was writing the book, which is dedicated to Raya. (That means of course that I now have to start work on another one to be dedicated to Trystan.)

A Note on Historical Accuracy

The reader of historical fiction (that's you, unless you've skipped the whole book and gone straight to these notes) can expect two things for their money – an entertaining story and a reasonable degree of accuracy. Occasionally the two things conflict and history has to be twisted or simplified a little for the sake of the plot. But I have always stuck to the principle that, where this has been done, the reader should be duly warned. A historical note has therefore usually been added to each book in the John Grey series to reveal where I have stretched the facts or, contrary to what the reader may believe, actually stuck very closely to the improbable-sounding truth.

The problem comes when the historical facts, honestly set down, may offend some people. Though this book is about the detection of a murder, and only that, it is undeniable that the murdered men are a plantation owner and slave catcher, and that two of the suspects have in the past been slaves. To write the book I therefore had to do some research on slavery in the early modern period, just as I researched the respective roles of magistrate and coroner, meal times and the fashions of the 1670s. Though I thought I knew about slavery, I was surprised by a great deal of what I found.

First, there is a popular misconception – then and now – that slavery in England in early modern times was illegal and simply didn't exist, whatever might be happening in the Americas. This view is often based around the Cartwright case of 1569, which ruled that English law could not recognise slavery ('England is too pure an air for a slave to breathe in'), and the Somerset case of 1772, when Lord Mansfield also ruled that slavery was not recognised by English law, and that James Somerset, a slave who had been brought to England and then escaped, had to be set free and not forced to return to Jamaica. So far so good, and much as I remembered. But the fact that separate judgements two hundred years apart had to rule on much the same thing suggests a great deal of confusion in between. Thus in 1677, in *Butts vs Penny*, it was held, apparently contradicting the Cartwright judgement, that 'Negroes being usually bought and sold among merchants, so merchandise, and also being infidels, there might be property in them'. Moreover, in 1729, the Attorney General ruled that baptism did not bestow freedom or make any alteration in the temporal condition of a slave and, additionally, a slave did not become free simply by being brought to England. It is also worth noting that ten years after the Somerset judgement, the same Mansfield was called to rule on the strange case of the slave ship, the *Zong*. In 1783 the *Zong* ran short of water in the middle of the voyage across the Atlantic. The solution was to throw part of the cargo – 132 slaves – overboard to drown. The ship's owners ended up in court, not facing murder charges but because they were suing their insurers for failing to compensate them properly for their losses. A sympathetic jury awarded the owners £30 for each slave lost, on the grounds that 'the case of slaves was the same as if horses had been thrown overboard'. This was admittedly overturned by Mansfield on appeal, but it shows that, even ten years after the Somerset case, public sentiment in Britain was far from hostile to slavery.

That slavery was tacitly accepted in seventeenth-century England is also apparent from the evidence for enslaved people living there with their unfree status unchallenged. Samuel Pepys is known to have owned at least three – a cook-maid named Doll and two males. He sold one of the male slaves in 1680. The other, named Sambo, proved so troublesome that Pepys, never one to get his own hands dirty if he could avoid it, arranged to have some Admiralty watermen kidnap him (in much the same way that my fictional Pepys has the Grice brothers kidnapped) and transported across the Atlantic to be sold to a planter, the profits from the sale being invested in whatever goods the captain of the ship thought best. The existence of slavery is similarly shown by the number of notices that were issued asking for information concerning runaways. Often the escapees could be identified by the information on the metal collars (usually brass or silver) that they wore round their necks. The reward for information leading to recapture was almost invariably set at one guinea – another nice little irony, guineas being minted from African gold – suggesting that small sum was enough to persuade people to turn the runaways in. Had Flood lived, he might well have been able to track Nero down and return him to Barbados.

Again, so far, so good. The second surprise from my research, however, was the extent of white slavery at the hands of African enslavers. It is undisputed that approximately 12 million Africans were transported across the Atlantic to work as slaves in the Americas. What is less well known is that, at the same time, around 1.2 million Europeans were enslaved in North Africa and elsewhere in the Ottoman Empire. The main centres for this trade included Morocco, Tunis, Tripoli and Algiers. It is difficult to know why this is now relatively forgotten when it was, for so many years, a persistent concern of successive English governments, who were (as Williamson observes) constantly petitioned by the captives' families for action to free them. There is also the evidence of the so-called 'captivity narratives' that were published, often quite profitably, by returned prisoners and are still available to read in various editions. Though they may have exaggerated some aspects of their captivity to help sell their books, there is no doubt that they and many others were enslaved as they describe. English sailors were regularly seized by North African privateers, as Marius is, while sailing close to the African coast. Those who have read Defoe will know that the same thing happened to Robinson Crusoe. Raiders also ventured north and carried off people from their homes. In 1631 Murat Reis took an Algerian fleet to Baltimore, County Cork, and captured almost the entire village. In 1640 a raid on Penzance resulted in sixty men, women and children being enslaved.

Whether it was worse to be an African slave in the Americas or a European slave in Africa is perhaps an invidious question to ask, though the answer is a very simple one: you really wouldn't want to be either. Some of the very worst conditions – for example, the unremitting misery of being a galley slave, chained night and day to his seat – fell to European captives; but a few Europeans were, conversely, able to rise to positions of significant power and eminence, as Marius later does, in the armed forces or at the courts of their masters. The biggest advantage that the European captives had, however, was that they were closer to their original homes and would, for the most part, have known exactly where they were. They would never have completely given up on the hope of being freed, either by ransom or by escape. And, if they could escape, then it was feasible to attempt to get home again in a way in which a slave in the West Indies could never have contemplated.

Since the action in the book is seen almost entirely from a small village in Essex, it is worth asking how much the average English man or woman would have known of all this. You may have noted that my characters have a carefully graded knowledge of the outside world and of the North African Islamic world specifically. Many, like Ben, would have been keenly aware of 'Turks' and 'Moors' as Britain's hereditary enemies, 'who from a native barbarousnesse doe hate all Christians and Christianitie, especially if they grow into the violent rages of Piracie, or fall into that exorbitant course of selling of slaves, or inforcing men to be Mahumetanes.' This type of information would often have come from mummers' plays that Ben refers to and from the popular, so-called 'black-letter', broadside ballads. Those, like the Grey family, who could afford to buy books would, however, have been able to consult accounts such as Richard Knolles's 1603 *The Generall Historie of the Turkes*, and might have been aware, to some degree, of the beliefs and customs of the Muslim world – they would not have given any credence, for example, to the suggestion that Muslims worshipped statues of Mohammed on a camel. Some, like the fictional vicar of Clavershall West, could have actually read the Koran in translation. Additionally there were theatrical productions such as William Davenant's Interregnum opera, *The Siege of Rhodes*, which dared to suggest that Christians might have something to learn from Islam. But for the majority of people, Islam was alien and threatening, and returning 'renegades' who had converted were regarded with suspicion and made to endure humiliating rituals to be readmitted to the Church. Anyone, like Marius, who made the decision to remain a Muslim would have been deliberately placing themselves outside the community in which they lived. It would have been a brave and very unusual decision.

Though the enslavement of Europeans in Africa and Africans in the New World existed side by side, I have found very little to suggest that one might have had any direct influence on the other. It has to be conceded, however, that it would have been difficult (though not of course impossible) to argue for a unilateral abandonment of slavery on purely moral grounds by either side so long as the other side persisted in their actions. In fact, people of the seventeenth century scarcely seem to have regarded slavery as a moral issue at all – merely as one of commercial advantage. For them it was the natural continuation of a state of affairs that had existed in the Bible, in ancient Greece and Rome and in all parts of Africa. To complicate matters, for those who like moral issues to be simple, European renegades assisted in the enslavement of Europeans, and Europeans purchased African slaves, out of necessity, from African traders, who had enslaved them and transported them to the coast – something that Nero mentions in passing.

But, as I began by saying, this is not a book about slavery – let alone one that attempts to make moral judgements. If the book is about anything, other than revenge and sudden death, it is about freedom and what an individual might be justified in doing in order to make themselves free. But, as you will be muttering to yourself, Sartre already has that sort of stuff covered and did it better than I have. Anyway, it is not something on which I am likely to be criticised for a lack of historical accuracy. Fortunately, therefore, it requires no further comment here.

Further Reading

The following may be of interest to those who wish to follow up some of the topics in this book:

Jeremy Black, *A Brief History of Slavery, A New Global History* (London: Robinson, 2007).

Richard Ligon, *A True and Exact History of the Island of Barbados* (Indianapolis: Hackett, 2011).

Giles Milton, *White Gold, The Extraordinary Story of Thomas Pellow and North Africa's One Million European Slaves* (London: John Murray, 2005).

Simon P. Newman, *Freedom Seekers: Escaping from Slavery in Restoration London* (London: Institute of Historical Research, 2022).

Katie Sue Sisneros, "'The Abhorred Name of Turk": Muslims and the Politics of Identity in Seventeenth Century English Broadside Ballads', doctoral dissertation, University of Minnesota, 2016.

Daniel J. Vitkus (ed.), *Piracy, Slavery, and Redemption: Barbary Captivity Narratives from Early Modern England* (New York: Columbia University Press, 2001).

James Walvin, *A Short History of Slavery* (Harmondsworth: Penguin, 2007).

Simon Webb, *The Forgotten Slave Trade, The White European Slaves of Islam* (Barnsley: Pen & Sword, 2021).

Eric Williams, *Capitalism and Slavery* (Chapel Hill: University of North Carolina Press, 1944).